BUSTER

BUSTER

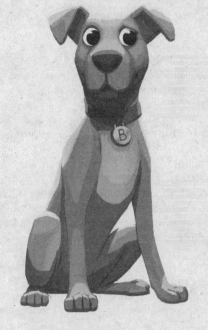

Caleb Zane Huett

Scholastic Inc.

Copyright © 2021 by Caleb Zane Huett

This book was originally published in hardcover by
Scholastic Press in 2021.

ISBN 978-1-338-54189-2

10 9 8 7 6 5 4 3 2 1   22 23 24 25 26

Printed in the U.S.A. 40
This edition first printing 2022

Book design by Maeve Norton

For Bogart

⋙ Prodogue ⋘

You never know how many bones you've buried until somebody digs them up. Buster tried to shake the old saying from his head, but it was stuck like peanut butter on the tip of his nose. *You have to focus,* he reminded himself.

"Everything is going to be fine!" Lasagna Morris, a golden-brown corgi with a clip-on tie attached to his collar, nudged the latch on his briefcase to gently click it into place. He patted the top with his paw in an attempt to look confident, but Buster could tell he was nervous. "I'm the best Dog Court lawyer in South Carolina!"

Buster checked himself in the mirror. It made him look like a furry red balloon, puffed up and huge, so he tried the next mirror. That one made him look like a pile of sticks, and not even the sturdy kind. *Why did we have to get ready in the fun house?* he thought. Out loud, he observed, "They said you were the *only* lawyer in South Carolina."

"That's, well . . . true. So I'm right for sure." Lasagna gave a short yip, a gentle one, to get Buster's full attention. His eyes were serious, and his ears were swiveled in a position that meant he was being sincere. "The most important thing is that I'm on your side. You're a Good Dog, Buster, no matter what the Court says."

1

"Thank you." Buster bowed his head. "That means a l—"

A grinning clown face built into the wall laughed through a crackly speaker, causing Lasagna to leap stiff-legged into the air and bark wildly. After he landed, he tucked his tail in embarrassment. "Remember: *Don't lie.* Judges can always tell, so there's no use. They're specially trained." Lasagna lifted a paw and checked his watch. "The trial starts soon. Are you ready?"

Lasagna's words had helped. The little voice in Buster's head—the one that was still saying, *You messed up, you broke Dog Law and deserve to be punished—* quieted down. He hadn't buried any bones. And Tonio needed him.

Dog Court could dig all they wanted.

"I'm ready."

Juicy Fun Theme Park and Strawberry Orchard had been abandoned for years, *really* abandoned, like whoever-owned-it-disappeared-from-the-country-without-telling-anyone-so-nobody-could-do-anything-to-it abandoned. No humans other than teenagers had bothered to go inside for years.

"All rise for the honorable Judge Sweetie!" the Dog Court bailiffs, four pugs wearing pointy blue hats, howled in unison. "Now sit. *Sit.* Come on. *Sit.* Good."

Some dog had reconnected the power, but most of the rides in Juicy Fun were too broken-down to use. Dog

Court was held in the bumper car arena: Busted old cars teetered atop one another in a pile the judge was climbing with graceful leaps. Colorful lights flashed and spun in patterns over everything.

The judge slammed her squeaky rubber gavel down three times, and all barking, yipping, and yelping settled. Terriers and retrievers, boxers and schnauzers, greyhounds and huskies all squeezed into the seats of discarded bumper cars—so many that larger dogs were graciously lying down to allow smaller ones to sit on their backs. Dead silence fell on the courtroom, and everyone was staring at Buster, who shared the only spotlight that wasn't spinning.

The light made Buster feel small, but somehow made the judge—a serious-looking borzoi with a coat as black and white as her sense of justice—seem impossibly huge and intimidating. He remembered a trick someone had told Tonio for dealing with nerves: *Imagine everyone in their underwear.*

He tried thinking of the judge in big human boxers. That *might* be funny, but she was so confident and poised he was certain she could pull it off with style.

Maybe the trick didn't really work with dogs.

"Do you understand, Buster?" *Oh no.* The judge had been talking the whole time he'd been totally distracted thinking about underwear.

"Buster? Are we boring you? Too famous for us?"

"No, I—" He froze. He definitely could not tell her what he was thinking about. The judge's ears rotated and folded, just slightly, to show she was irritated.

"Your Honor." Another spotlight clicked on, over a husky with perfectly groomed fur and a twist to his tail that meant he was expressing humor. "Buster clearly doesn't grasp how serious this situation is, considering this is his *second* time on trial for the baddest crime a dog can commit: revealing his true intelligence to a human." The husky shrugged and looked directly at Buster with a sneer. "Perhaps, for him, this is just another day at the park."

A cry rang out from the crowd. "THROW HIM IN THE BONE PIT!"

"The bone pit is for celebrations, Sadie," someone else whispered.

"THROW HIM IN THE REGULAR PIT!"

The judge banged her gavel, and its squeaks quieted the crowd again.

"Your Honor," Lasagna said, "the speaker for Dog Law hasn't even introduced himself, and he's already trying to build a case against Buster."

The judge turned her head toward the husky. He rolled his shoulders and stood, tail wagging rhythmically like a clock pendulum.

"My name is Pronto, Your Honor, and as the little lawyer says, I'm here on behalf of the Law." He bowed toward the tower of bumper cars. "While you, of course, have final ruling over this dog's fate, I believe the law here is clear: Buster Pulaski showed a human the truth, putting all of us in danger. I am officially requesting that you send him to The Farm."

A gasp rippled through the crowd, and a chill raised Buster's fur. "Your Honor." He awkwardly mimicked Pronto's bow, just in case. "I never meant to put Dogkind in danger. I made a hard choice—but I'd do it again if it meant helping my human."

Lasagna winced. Buster was not supposed to be talking.

Pronto clicked his claws against the hood of his bumper car in a sarcastic clap. "Such a hero! Buster the Miracle Dog!"

Buster's eyes fell to the ground. *I guess there was no chance they'd forget.*

Pronto leaned back on the side of his car and spoke to the crowd behind them. "We have no idea how humans will react when they realize the truth—and they are, historically, a very dangerous species. Our silence, our continued secrecy, is the *only* thing that keeps us safe. You have threatened this safety, Buster, all for the sake of this . . ." He checked his notes. *"Antonio."*

The sound of his boy's name made Buster bristle. "Tonio is a good boy. My job was to protect him."

"Your *job* was to lay low!" Pronto barked a laugh. "To

live the rest of your dog years in Bellville, *quietly*, without making any more trouble."

"Tonio was my responsibility. I couldn't just do *nothing*!"

"Well, I sincerely hope this human was worth the rest of your life."

Lasagna finally worked up the courage to squeak out an argument. "Your Honor, this is all out of order. Buster hasn't even had the chance to tell his side of the story."

"He doesn't need to!" Pronto turned back to the judge. "The line between Good and Bad Dog behavior is very clear. Furthermore, thanks to Buster, the humans could be planning something as we speak. We don't have time to waste on this trial."

This is it, Buster thought. *I'm not even going to get a chance.*

Lasagna shook his head. "I understand the urgency of this situation, but Dog Law is very clear that anyone accused of Bad Dog behavior must be allowed to tell their side of the story. You of all dogs should know that, Pronto."

The judge turned her snout from Lasagna to Buster to Pronto. *We must all look so small to her, up there*, Buster thought. When she spoke, all ears perked up to listen. "He is correct. The accused will speak."

Pronto bowed again. "Of course, Your Honor." He turned his sneer on the corgi. "This won't change anything, Lasagna. You're begging for scraps."

The judge returned her gaze to Buster. "Begin."

Life at The Farm would mean no more days at the dog park. No more scratches behind his big, floppy ears. No more humans. And no more Tonio.

A deep breath. A strong stance. Buster kept his eyes up and looked straight at the judge. "For everything to make sense, I have to start with the last time I ended up in Dog Court . . ." He glanced at Lasagna, who bobbed supportively.

". . . back when I was Buster the Miracle Dog."

Buster's Testimony

I've never been very good at the sit-and-stay. When I decided to become a fire dog, I was told over and over by humans and dogs to follow my orders and only my orders. Do the tricks. Never make my own choices. That's what makes a Good Dog.

And I believed it! I took it to heart and followed every rule as closely as possible to make sure I was the Goodest, most helpful, most fire-doggiest fire dog I could be. As a puppy, I imagined myself with one of those big red hats on my head, tugging a hose around in my mouth and carrying babies out of burning buildings.

Turns out that's not what fire dogs do anymore, if they ever did. "Sit for the picture, Buster!" they'd say. "Stay here and watch the station until we get back, okay, buddy?"

"Isn't he so cute in that little hat?" and "He's so lucky, getting to lie around all day."

"*Such* a cutie." Or the worst: "What a mascot!"

Mascot. I was a Good Dog who might as well have been a stuffed animal.

So I started chasing fires. I would listen in to where my humans were being sent, then sneak out on my own and try to help without getting caught. My team covered only a small area of the big city, so I could make it to the majority of emergency calls on foot.

Most of the time I could only help in small ways— every once in a while I'd sniff out a piece of important evidence and lead someone there, or I'd run along the perimeter and push people out of the danger zone. Usually, I would find humans after they'd been saved and comfort them the best I could.

The time I became Buster the Miracle Dog I was playing low-contact no-human Fetch (street rules) with some other dogs in the park, when I smelled smoke.

One sniff: Hungarian food. No, not that. Two sniffs: smoke. Definitely smoke from an active fire. Started with grease, maybe? Probably from a kitchen, mixed with—three sniffs—*Hungarian food*. The restaurant was on fire!

I didn't hesitate, didn't think about being a Good Dog. I dove in. By the time the rest of my team from the station had arrived, I'd evacuated the restaurant with some vigorous barking.

I was too lost in the action to remember most of it, and I thought the humans didn't see me do anything un-dog-ly, 'cause the smoke was thick and they were all panicked. But afterward, a couple insisted that I had saved their baby from his high chair and carried him outside myself. I don't actually remember doing that, maybe I did, but either way, someone from the news listened to their story and came up with the name.

The concentrated smoke messed up my nose (it's a little farsmelled now), but I didn't mind being known as a Miracle Dog. My station was overjoyed, the treats flowed like rain, and it felt like the whole city wanted to shake my hand. But you know how it ended. Dog Court thought I was getting too much attention, hit me with several counts of Reckless Lassie Behavior, and quietly shipped me to Bellville, where nobody knew who I was.

I still think about my team, sometimes. Do they miss me? I guess they probably think I ran away. Just like Tonio will always wonder what happened, if I don't—

Never mind.

I was supposed to get adopted as a house pet. I was warned to stay out of sight, out of trouble, and make sure no one recognized me . . . but it sounded so *boring*. I looked for another chance to do a job, any job, and realized that humans selected service dogs from a shelter in town. Being a psychiatric service dog isn't exactly big news, so the judge let me try, as long as I promised I wouldn't make the same mistake again.

I was sure that I wouldn't. I really tried.

And then I met Tonio.

"What kind of dog is he?" An adult human with a dripping-wet black jacket, long curly wet hair, and tough-looking boots knelt down and inspected me. (This was Tonio's mom.) I stood stiff and straight to look capable and serious.

My trainer, Jocelyn, shrugged. "He's not any one thing. He's got the ears and color of a vizsla, but there's something smaller in him, too. Maybe a couple somethings."

A man who was wearing a green uniform with a spaceship logo on it nodded while he folded his umbrella. "Some boxer, I bet." (This was Tonio's dad.)

"Sure, maybe." Jocelyn shrugged again.

"Maybe poodle?"

"Mm, I don't know about that." Tonio's mom tapped the toe of her boot absently on the mat to knock some mud off. "I could see some kind of terrier in there, but poodle?"

"I think definitely there's some poodle."

Booooooooriiiiiiiing! Humans *love* to talk about us like we're not there. Not that I had much to add—I never knew my parents.

"What do you think, Tonio?"

I tilted my head to watch the boy. He was about eleven

human years old, with curly brown hair that normally hangs just above his eyes, but since it was wet and sagging from the rain, he was constantly pushing it out of the way. He said, "Can my parents get their money back if this doesn't work out?"

"Oh, Tonio." Mrs. Pulaski gave my trainer an apologetic look. "Don't worry about that."

"What if he doesn't like me?" The boy stared at me with wide eyes, like I was absolutely terrifying. "Or what if I can't take care of him the way you're supposed to?"

Before the trainer could answer, Tonio's mom spoke again. "That's not anything you need to worry about, Tonio. We'll figure that out if it happens."

"But I—"

Mr. Pulaski cut in and started talking to my trainer. I watched Tonio tug at one of his dripping curls, and had an idea: an old trick I learned as a fire dog. Whenever a kid was scared of dogs, or nervous around me, I'd do something totally goofy and cute to help them calm down. I was sure the same thing would work here, so I jingled my collar for his attention.

He looked up right away. I did a big, exaggerated shake of my whole body, like I was the one who was wet.

Tonio didn't get it. *It's easy*, I thought. *Just shake off the water.* I took a deep breath and shook even harder, like a ghost had just passed through me and I had a chill all the way down in my bones. *It's the fastest way to get dry, see?*

I saw it dawn on his face. His head tilted like a puppy's, and after a second, he shook his head, just slightly, and flung little droplets around. I wagged my tail and wiggled my body again. He shook his hair out harder and laughed.

"Did you hear that, Tonio?" His mom grabbed his attention, and my trainer began to explain the different ways I had been trained to help with his anxiety. I performed the ones she asked me to demonstrate and tried to look as professional as possible, but I spent the rest of the training session thinking about the rain-shaking moment we'd shared.

Most humans don't know how to talk. They can speak, sure, but any puppy with a few treats in front of them can *speak*. I could already tell that Tonio knew the most important part of really talking: paying attention. Every time he looked at anyone—the trainer, his parents, even me—he was watching them with so much focus. He didn't make as much noise as the other humans, but he listened, and he watched. I felt lucky to get paired with him.

"So try this," my trainer said to Tonio, who was paying close attention. "Let's say you're about to have a panic attack and you want to get out of a room full of people. Just tap on your leg like this." She tapped on her leg and I broke my stance, whining and pawing at her ankle. "Buster will start pretending he needs to use the restroom. Then it's easy for you to say, 'Oh, just a minute, I need to go take my dog out.' Now you try."

My trainer handed Tonio the leash. He put his hand on his leg and repeated the tapping. "Like th—*achoo!*" He sneezed, but since he'd done the hand signal right, I whined again and pawed at his leg. He sniffled and didn't even seem to notice I'd done anything—he was totally frozen.

"That's great!" Jocelyn continued. "You can give him one of those treats as a reward."

I perked up. As you know, it's essential that, in front of humans, we pretend that food is the most important thing in the world, so I had to look excited at the word *treat*. Tonio nodded but didn't move for the bag. Instead, he rubbed at his nose and stared off into the distance. He was starting to sweat, just a little, and I could hear that his breath was changing.

"Tonio?" His mom's wet boots squeaked on the floor. "Are you all right?"

"I, uh, I don't—I'll be right back." He made a straight line to the door with a very fast and serious walk.

Both of Tonio's parents followed him into the hallway and shut the door for privacy. I, of course, could hear everything.

"I think I'm allergic to him. I must be allergic to dogs,"

the boy said. *So that's what this is about*, I thought. *The sneeze.*

"I don't think so, honey," his mom said. "We just took that allergy test, remember?"

Tonio was breathing fast, with just the top part of his lungs. He was almost panting, like I do after a long run. His voice was different—it was moving up higher, and quicker. Not slow and quiet like he'd sounded before.

"My nose feels weird," he said, then paused to gasp a few times. "I think it's . . . because of the dog. I can't breathe."

"Try to slowly take a deep breath." I could tell Mr. Pulaski was reciting advice he'd heard before, something he'd said a bunch of times. "We've been here for a while—if you had a severe allergy, it would have acted up sooner."

"Maybe not! Maybe—maybe—maybe it's because I held the leash for the first time. I touched him, and I'm allergic, and you already paid for him, and now—" His voice broke. He was crying.

That's when I realized he was having a panic attack. Jocelyn had pretended to have them so I'd know what they looked like, but I'd never witnessed a real one before. Because of his anxiety, Tonio was worrying more about his sneeze than most people would. He thought something was wrong with him, and that was making him scared. The fear made him panic—and when someone panics, it's harder to breathe. Then when it got harder to breathe, he thought it was because of the sneeze. That convinced him the allergy must be really bad, which scared him more, which made his breathing even worse. A bad circle.

I tried to decide what a Good Dog would do. My training was to help when he was having a panic attack, but I was only supposed to respond to what I *saw,* not what I heard from another room.

But he was hurting. And if I could just go out there and distract him, maybe I could help. I could pretend I really *did* have to go out: The trainer would open the door, I could distract Tonio, and that would break the bad circle.

Then I thought about the fire. I thought about the trouble I'd already gotten into.

I couldn't risk it.

I'll help you next time, I thought. I laid down on the ground and tried not to hear him crying. *I promise.*

His parents seemed too flustered to help much. They kept asking if he was okay every few seconds, and if he needed to leave. He didn't, or couldn't, answer. I felt terrible. Jocelyn and I waited another five minutes, and I listened to his crying stop, his breath slow.

"I'm sorry," Tonio mumbled. "We can go back inside."

"You don't have to apologize, sweetheart. If this is

already bothering you, then it's probably a bad idea. We should stop."

Tonio gave in. "If you think so. Yeah. We can just go home."

I looked up at Jocelyn. She couldn't hear anything. She was just sitting there tapping on her phone while my new family walked away! I couldn't stand it anymore! I pawed at my trainer's ankle and whined. I tucked my tail down low. *I'm not pretending! Well, I am pretending, but I'm pretending to not be pretending! Listen to me!*

The trainer finally understood. "I guess it's time to check on them, anyway. Let's go." She grabbed my leash and opened the door. *Perfect.*

Tonio and his parents were getting ready to go.

"Heading out already?" Jocelyn asked.

Tonio's mom sighed. "I don't think this is going to work out."

"Are you sure?" Jocelyn gave them a concerned look. "What happened?"

I tugged my way over to Tonio and bumped up against his hand. I licked the back of his palm, and after a moment, he scratched the top of my head. I rubbed my face all over his hand while the adults talked and tried to hold his attention. I was betting that he wasn't *really* allergic, and hoped with all my heart I was right.

I stepped back just a little and shook my body again,

like I was wet. He shook his hair, and some of the last few drops sprinkled down. *Good! Yes! Now pay attention. Watch me.* I lifted my paw up and rubbed it along my nose.

He must have thought I was rubbing at the water drops or something, because he didn't do anything. I rubbed my nose, bumped the hand he had petted me with, then rubbed my nose again.

Tonio watched me, then looked at his hand. He tilted his head like a puppy again, took a deep breath, lifted his hand up to his face, and rubbed it all the way down, from his forehead to his chin.

I wagged my tail. *Good. Yes.* I touched my nose to his knee and took a loooooooong sniff. He held his hand in front of his nose and took a deeeeeeep breath.

"I didn't sneeze," Tonio mumbled. "I'm not allergic."

"What's that, honey?" Tonio's mom looked down at him. He was grinning.

"I didn't sneeze! I touched him all over with my hand, and then I touched my face, and I'm not even itching. I don't think I'm allergic, Mom!"

"Maybe not, but I still think we pushed you into this too quick. We should go home, talk about it."

Tonio shook his head. "I want to try. I want to take Buster home."

I wagged my tail. *Yeah, you do!*

"Ready if you are," Jocelyn said. She held the leash out.

Mr. Pulaski asked Tonio, "Are you sure?"

The boy watched me closely. I wagged my tail and sniffed around like I wasn't listening. Like I was just a Good Dog.

Tonio reached out and took the leash.

A Classic Lassie

Pronto was rolling his eyes before Buster finished the sentence. "Your Honor, the accused has already broken Dog Law *twice*, and he's barely even started his story! This wet-hair-allergy pantomime is direct communication. They were talking. Case closed."

The judge tilted her head to Buster. "He makes a good point. Your argument so far is built on the necessity of your crime. This boy's *need*. But here, you show yourself ready to break our Law immediately."

Lasagna pulled a paper from his briefcase. "At this point, Buster has done nothing outside of what humans expect from a Good Dog. Especially a service dog. Even the Lassie Regulations say that service dogs may communicate as long as they are responding to a solid, visible, and known piece of information. Good Dogs understand wetness, so long as they see water."

"So if I see rain outside," Pronto argued, "I'm allowed to check the weather app on my owner's phone?"

"Either way, Your Honor, we know Buster pushed the boundaries—that's why we're here. But he does not deserve a life on The Farm just because he cared about a human!"

"He does if he's putting that human before the rest of Dogkind!" Pronto sat back and leaned against the side of the car.

The judge's face remained still and gave away nothing about her opinion. "Please continue, Buster. I'll reserve my judgment until the end."

Buster's Testimony

Imagine the most fun place you possibly can. First, obviously, mud *everywhere*. Then good toys, the ones you can chew on and they don't break. There's so many of them that even if you bury one in the mud, you've got a hundred more within mouth's reach. There's . . . a giant *Apatosaurus* skeleton! It's from a museum, except no one cares if you chew on it. The walls are lined with tennis balls and your tail chases itself. Imagine *paradise*.

Now imagine all that paradise was behind a glass wall. *That* is what Tonio's house was like. The Pulaski family had collected dozens of action figures, records, books, and collectibles that were scrunched up on high shelves, leaving lower shelves bare because they didn't want me to get to them.

We'd spent two days training together, and then another few days learning all the things you have to learn when you get new roommates: when they go to the bathroom, what times they eat, and which of your personal objects you can't leave out because they'll chew on them. It was almost a whole week before I started to feel settled and Tonio's parents felt comfortable leaving us alone.

The house looked out over Bellville Square and was actually made up of the two stories above his dad's store, Tomorrow Grocery. On the third floor, behind a door covered in marker doodles, was Tonio's room. His space was considerably tidier than the rest of the house, but one of the walls was covered in tall piles of shoeboxes, neatly stacked on top of one another in rows.

"I draw a lot." He mumbled like it was an apology, and gestured to the wall of drawings I was sniffing around. "Most of the stuff on that wall is stuff I can see from the window. I don't draw new stuff, really. Just whatever I can see."

He made it sound like it was a bad thing, but I am here to tell you that his drawings were *amazing*. I'm not an artist myself, so I'm no expert—but the squirrels he'd drawn were so realistic that I almost believed I could scare them away with a bark. He'd drawn the famous bell in the center of Bellville Square, and almost every storefront on all four sides. "I love drawing stuff I can see, because when I start, I always think I know what it looks like. And then when I start drawing, there's so much more than I thought. There's always a bunch of stuff I didn't notice. It's like the same thing I've looked at over and over is really different from what I thought."

This Tonio was totally different from the Tonio I'd

met at the training center. Suddenly, alone in his room, he looked comfortable.

"You can sit on my bed, if you want. I bet the floor is cold."

That sounded nice. I turned toward the bed and then caught myself. *I'm a dog,* I thought. *I don't know what he's saying.* I pretended I was distracted by something on the floor and sniffed at the ground.

And it was good that I did. Tonio was staring at me *very* closely. After a moment, he stood and walked over to the bed. "Up!" he called, and patted the mattress. I jumped up and settled down on the edge. He sat beside me and scratched behind my ears.

And then he said—and I'm saying this because I'm going to tell the whole truth—"I guess you are just a normal dog. At the center, I thought . . ." I tried very hard not to move at all. He didn't finish. "Never mind. That's stupid."

Careful, Buster! I closed my eyes and pretended to rest, but my heart was pounding like I really had chased the sketch squirrels. *You just started a new job and you almost messed up already. Be a Good Dog.*

Apparently convinced I'd gone to sleep, Tonio got up and moved over to his desk by the window. I cracked open my eyes to keep watching while he pulled the highest shoebox off the stack and opened it. The shoebox was stuffed full of small rectangles of thick paper—he pulled out the one closest to him and set it on his desk, twisting the neck of his bendy lamp to get a better look.

He clicked on a computer monitor and typed something into the keyboard—a few seconds later, he was looking at a picture of a trading card on a website for something called Beamblade. He picked a pencil out of the cup on his desk and started drawing on the little rectangle, checking the image on the computer in between lines.

More curious than tired, I slid off the bed and went over to look at the box. Each of the little rectangles in the box was a hand-drawn version of a Beamblade card, with all the information printed on the bottom in Tonio's neat handwriting, and pictures of mechanical dragons and cyborg wizards at the top.

"I always wanted a pet." I nearly jumped—I didn't know he'd even noticed me come over. Tonio's pencil scratched against the paper. "I wanted a cat, really. But I also said I'd be okay with a dog. Just not as much. Sorry." I resisted a shiver.

Apology accepted, I thought. *But let's not talk about cats.*

"And my parents always said no." He pushed his curls away from his eyes—and they immediately fell back into place. "Oh, *yikes*. I need to start over." He crumpled up the card he was working on—Klakzon the Noisemage, DJ of the future—and threw it into a trash can. His pencil quickly started flying across a new blank card he pulled from the box. I moved to the window so he wouldn't think I was paying *too* close attention for a Good Dog.

"I think Mom and Dad only said yes to having a pet because I had a panic attack at the science fair. And again while I was helping at Dad's store. And then I threw up during yearbook signing." Tonio's eyes popped up to watch me for a second, then went back to drawing. "And now I have you, because they think you'll make me better. This one's bad, too." He ripped the card in half and threw it out, but didn't start again right away. He stared at the page and told me, "Everyone at school saw me throw up, which means everyone in Bellville saw me. I couldn't think of what to write in Devon Wilcrest's yearbook, which isn't even a big deal, and I should have just written *Have a great summer* or something, but I was thinking about how the only thing I knew about him was that Miles and Parker always made fun of him when he wasn't in the room because he was the new kid." He picked up his pencil and started drawing again. "I had never even actually talked to Devon before, but now, when I had the chance to write something I knew he would read, I thought that if I *didn't* say something nice to him, or at least tell him what they were doing, then I was just as bad as Miles and Parker. And I couldn't stop thinking about it, and I couldn't write anything, and my stomach was flipping, and I couldn't breathe, and I threw up on his yearbook. And on him."

Tonio looked exhausted—once he started remembering, his mind must have been looping through the feelings all over again. It fell out of him like he wasn't telling it on purpose—it was more like he had to get it out of his body.

"I said I didn't want to go back to school after this summer, and Dr. Jake said to try getting you first, and that over time I might change my mind." He paused again to look at me, then erased a line of his sketch. "I can always tell that Mom and Dad are embarrassed when I start feeling bad in front of people, and Dr. Jake pretends like I'm doing fine, but I know he wishes I was better." Tonio's scribbling slowed down.

"I don't want to disappoint you, too. I need to take care of you." He held up the picture and showed the beginning sketch of Klakzon to me. (His Time-Traveling Turntables looked great.) I sniffed at the drawing to get a close look, and Tonio laughed. "You like it? Good boy."

"TO-NI-OOOO!" his father's voice boomed from downstairs. He didn't just yell Tonio's name, he sang it like an opera singer would. Tonio gave me a look.

"My dad's a dork."

"IT IS TIIIIME FOR YOUR APP-OOOOINT-A-MENT!"

Tonio set down his pencil and jumped up. "I forgot it

28

was Wednesday!" He grabbed my blue harness, labeled *Service Dog*, and I stepped into it. "You get to meet Dr. Jake!"

I loved Dr. Jake. Dr. Jake was the *best* . . . and I'm not just saying that because he had a jar full of treats ready when we showed up for Tonio's therapy appointment.

Okay, all right, *you caught me*, I am saying that *exactly* because he had a jar of treats ready when we showed up for Tonio's therapy appointment. First impressions are important!

Dr. Jake was tall and thin, like he was made out of good throwing sticks. He shot us a big, kind smile and asked permission as soon as we walked through the door to give me some very good scratches. We sat in two beanbag chairs—a big blue one for Tonio and a small red one for me—and he folded onto a short stool. While he spoke to Tonio, he tossed me a chewy ball to gnaw on. I liked having something to do while I listened.

"Tonio! Ring, ring! I see everything worked out at the center—how are you and Buster getting along?"

"Ring, ring, Dr. Jake. Really good!" Tonio glanced over at me. I chewed on the ball. "He's a good dog, and really smart. Sometimes it even feels like he's a person. Like he's listening." *No, c'mon! I'm just a dog!* A frown flashed across his face. "Maybe that's a dumb thing to say, though." *You also aren't dumb!* I felt bad for pretending, but I shouldn't have acted the way I did when we first met, either. I was conflicted.

Dr. Jake watched Tonio seriously. "I don't think that's dumb. One of the best parts of having a dog around—even one who isn't trained like Buster—is that feeling of having a friend. You shouldn't feel embarrassed talking to him. I bet he's a good listener."

"Yeah! That makes sense. I think I like it, but we only just got to take him home this morning, so I don't really know yet." There was something different in the way Tonio talked to Dr. Jake from the way he talked to me. I tried to listen closer and figure out what it was.

"Could you tell me what you hope Buster will help you with?"

"Sure. Um, I think having Buster with me will make me feel a little safer walking around town on my own. I'm usually scared I'll have a panic attack when I'm by myself, and if I do, I might do something stupid like fall and hurt myself or not realize where I am and walk out into the street."

What is it? I wondered. *Something in the way Tonio smells, in the rhythm of his voice. Why does this feel different?*

"Buster's trained to learn how to lead me back home and to move people away from me so I can have space during a panic attack. With Buster, I bet I'll be able to go everywhere and not feel scared!"

"That's a good, big goal." Now Dr. Jake's sound had changed. He could tell there was something different in Tonio's voice, too. "Anything else?"

"Uh . . ."

There, I thought. *A flicker in his eyes, like he's searching for the right thing to say.*

"Sometimes I don't talk to people, because I might say something stupid, or I might get anxious while I'm talking to them, and then they'll know something's wrong with me. Other kids . . ." He trailed off and didn't finish the thought. "Buster has a trick where he can help me leave a conversation if I give him a little signal. Plus, I guess people like to talk about dogs. So I can talk about him if I don't have anything else to say, and maybe I'll make some friends."

"All of that sounds really great, and I hope you do try some new things with Buster at your side. Speaking of which . . . have you considered speaking to that boy? Devon?"

Tonio's face twisted in fear. He recovered quickly, but I saw it. "Oh, uh . . . what about?"

"You've talked about feeling guilty, and about your fear of returning to school when summer's over. I believe talking things through with him—apologizing, maybe—could help you feel more comfortable. Our mistakes are almost never as huge as we make them in our heads."

A few moments of silence. Dr. Jake watched Tonio for the first, then checked his notes during the next. "Last session, we talked about some tools you could use to fight intrusive thoughts—those ideas that pop into your head, maybe out of nowhere, and spark a worry that can lead to an anxiety attack. Do you remember that?"

Tonio nodded. "You said that even though they sometimes don't make any sense, or aren't based on anything real, my anxiety tells me they're true."

"Right. And you can tell those thoughts, 'No!' as soon as you realize what they are. You can try to think about whether something is *logical*, whether your worry is based in fact, or whether it's just a thought, and doesn't have to be true. Do you remember any of your intrusive thoughts since our last session?"

I hadn't heard of these before, but I knew exactly what Dr. Jake was talking about, because I'd seen it already: When Tonio had sneezed on first meeting me, he'd had an intrusive thought: *I must have sneezed because I'm allergic to dogs.* Even though he already knew he wasn't allergic, his anxiety said it must be true, and he started focusing on it too hard, which started the bad circle. I wagged my tail, proud of myself for figuring it out, and waited for Tonio to tell him about the sneeze.

But instead he said, "I don't think I had any this week. Not that I remember, anyway."

Dr. Jake wrote a little note on his pad of paper.

"Really? Maybe you could start by telling me about one of your panic attacks, and work backward to what might have triggered it."

Tonio shrugged. "I didn't really have any panic attacks this week, either." My tail stopped wagging. I stopped chewing my ball. *That's* what felt different. He was *lying*.

"That's unusual. Are you sure?"

"Yep. I'm sure."

Dr. Jake was clearly surprised. He watched Tonio for a moment before responding. "That's great news, but let's talk about some more strategies for the next time you have one."

I was too stunned to listen to the rest of the session. Tonio was lying to a doctor! Even I knew he wasn't supposed to do that. And if he was lying about his panic attack, he might have been lying about everything. That would mean that he wasn't planning on going new places, wasn't planning on making friends, AND didn't really think I could help.

I was going to have to prove him wrong.

— 3 —

Dinner was an awkward time for the Pulaski family—or, I should say, dinner was a bunch of awkward times for the Pulaski family. Tonio's parents loved to cook together; it was a family rule that every day, at least for dinner, Tonio would join them in preparing and eating a meal. They even figured out a meal plan as a team at the beginning of the week, no exceptions.

But it wasn't that simple. Tomorrow Grocery, the store Mr. Pulaski owned on Bellville Square, had started staying open late to compete with the big store that had recently appeared on the edge of town. He didn't like to make his employees work late every day, so to be a good boss, he would often work until midnight organizing produce and gossiping with customers.

Mrs. Pulaski worked from home designing websites, but her office had so many *Do Not Disturb* signs on it—and she came out of it so rarely during work hours—that it might as well have been on another planet. If Goggle (Google but for divers) needed a brand-new font for their logo made by hand *by tomorrow morning, we're really in crisis mode here, thanks so much for your help,* she would lock herself in her office until it was done.

And Tonio—well, it was summer, so Tonio had appointments with Dr. Jake and then didn't leave the house much otherwise. I was trying to figure out how to change that.

If Mr. Pulaski was going to work nights, then they'd eat dinner early. If Mrs. Pulaski was pulling extra hours designing for Gobble (Google but for Thanksgiving supplies), then they'd eat dinner late. But when *both* were happening, things got a little weird. Sometimes dinner was at noon. Sometimes it was at nine (if Tonio was still awake). My first unusual "dinner" with the family was at six the morning after it was scheduled to happen.

"The Gargle account really likes the latest draft," Mrs. Pulaski was saying. She had finally burst out of her office an hour before, triumphant and hungry, and had woken the rest of us up for dinner. A few sleepy seasonings and a pot of coffee later, she was devouring a pile of steak and mashed potatoes while Tonio and Mr. Pulaski stared at their plates queasily.

"That's . . ." Mr. Pulaski had only come home three hours before. He forgot what he was saying and his eyes drifted closed.

"Great?" Tonio suggested. Mr. Pulaski nodded, or maybe just nodded off. Tonio secretly dropped a little piece off his plate, and I caught it out of the air. I'll chew on anything that's even *touched* a steak, any time of day.

Mrs. Pulaski's fork clinked against her plate. She was staring at Tonio and chewing, deciding what to say. Finally, she said, "I love you, Tonio. Do I tell you that enough?"

"I think so."

"Good. I was reading this summary of a book that looks *amazing*—a book about kids, I think, but also just about people, you know, and it said that most of us don't hear nice things enough. That's probably true."

"You just read the summary?" Tonio asked.

"Yes, but I think that was good advice already."

They sat in silence for a few moments before Tonio realized Mrs. Pulaski was waiting on something, because she was making a cartoonish grumpy face. His face reddened, and words tumbled out of his mouth in a jumble. "IloveyoutooMom. Sorry."

She looked disappointed for the tiniest second— her eyebrows pulling together and her mouth tugging down—but then she grinned and wiped her face with a napkin. "That *does* feel great. And I didn't even have to buy the book! What a deal. Honey?"

Mr. Pulaski picked his face up off the table. Mashed potatoes held one of his eyes closed. "Mm?"

"I need to get some sleep. Are you done with your dinner?" Mrs. Pulaski was already picking up the plates while Mr. Pulaski was trying to remember how to nod. "And, Tonio, *please* take Buster to the dog park today. He tore up a roll of toilet paper yesterday, and I think it's because he's been stuck inside."

(I will neither confirm nor deny that accusation.)

Now Tonio was staring at the table, face still red. He wasn't listening to what his mom was saying, but she wasn't waiting around to notice. His parents left the room together, and I stood up so I could get a good sniff.

Tonio was breathing just a little bit harder than normal, through his mouth. His eyes were zoning out, so I could tell he was lost in his head thinking about something. I could hear his heartbeat up this close, too—it was faster than it should be, but not *pounding*. He wasn't having a panic attack yet, but he was lost somewhere. Stuck in a thought. I needed to help him out of it.

I kicked off the floor onto my hind legs, careful not to slip on the tile, and pushed both of my front paws into his stomach. He didn't do anything the first time, so I bounced off and pushed harder.

"Ow! Hey!" Tonio's eyes finally snapped over to me, and his face scrunched up, confused. I kept my paws on his stomach, and after a few seconds of confusion, he leaned over and put his forehead up against mine, his curly hair tickling my ears. "Oh, wow. Thank you. How did you know?"

(I would like to note, *for the Court*, that this was

entirely within my training as a service dog. This technique is perfectly normal and was not overstepping my position even a little bit.)

"What happens now?" Tonio asked. "Do you just stay there?"

I stared at him.

"Do you want a treat?"

My ears swiveled on their own and my tail gave two good wags before I forced it to stop. I needed to stay strong. I know what you're thinking—a Good Dog would have wanted the treat. And you're right—a regular Good Dog. But as a service dog, I had to stay focused and committed to my work. If I took a treat, I was admitting my job was done. And it *wasn't* done.

But I could *smell* those good treats in his back pocket . . . and when he grabbed the bag and started crinkling it, I felt my mouth betraying me with drool. I clamped my teeth shut and turned away when he brought the treat up to my face.

Tonio frowned. "What's wrong? You love these." I did love these. Little packets of chewy something wrapped around a perfect pouch of peanut butter—

No! I thought. I kept my teeth together and bounced up and back down on his stomach.

"Oof!" Tonio let out a breath of air. "Go easy. I'm okay, I promise." He scratched around my collar. "I just . . . I didn't even think to tell Mom I loved her back. And what kind of— Who doesn't—" He stopped, because he was getting lost again. Then he mumbled, "I don't think I'm a good person. I never notice things like that. Everyone is always so nice to me, and I just hurt their feelings. Even Mom."

The whole thing was a big misunderstanding, but Tonio didn't understand that, and now he was sitting here thinking he was a bad person.

"Maybe she's upset in her room right now. I should probably go apologize, or make it up to her, or—what if I haven't noticed other times, too?" He was back in the same mode from when he told the story, words spilling out like they were out of his control. For a kid who was usually so quiet, it was strange to watch—almost like he was fighting with himself, trying to stay under control and failing.

I couldn't just let him stay in the bad circle. I put both paws on his stomach and bounced again, to get his attention.

He lifted his head up just a little, and his mouth dropped open the tiniest bit. "You're supposed to notice anxiety, though, right? You stopped me because you could tell I was feeling anxiety."

He took one more deep breath. "I don't know. It's confusing. I need to ask Dr. Jake."

I could feel his heart rate falling, and his breathing going back to normal. He patted me a few more times, and I pulled my legs back down to the ground.

Tonio stood up and gave a big, long stretch-and-yawn, like I do after a good run—I guess being anxious can wear you out. "You've been stuck in here with me for a while, huh?" he said to me. "Mom's right. We should go to the park." My tail wagged. He held the treat out again, and my willpower was spent. I snapped it up immediately, and he laughed. "Good boy, Buster. Good boy!"

I followed him back up to his room and had to resist barking with excitement. Tonio was right: I *was* a good boy. And so was he! But being good was about to get a lot more difficult, for both of us.

Frisbee!

"So let's review." Pronto checked his notes, typed onto a laptop modified for use with paws. "You were adopted by a human who was, by his own admission: a bully, a liar, *and* someone who made up problems out of nothing. Which part of that was I supposed to take as . . ." He clicked back in his notes. "Tonio being a 'good boy,' as you said?"

Buster felt his insides boiling at every word out of Pronto's muzzle. "You don't get it!" Buster barked. "You didn't see him!"

Lasagna placed a paw on Buster's. "He's trying to make you mad," the corgi explained quietly. "You don't have to fetch just because he's throwing."

Pronto went on. "What we're seeing is that he made his problems up, and you fell for it. You decided you needed to 'save' him, when the only person he needed saving from was himself."

"What an interesting point, Pronto!" Lasagna proclaimed with a squeak and a cheerful tail wag. He tilted his head at Buster. "Was Tonio making up his own problems?"

"No!" Buster barked, frustrated.

"Okay." Lasagna subtly twisted his front paws and twitched his ears in the Underspeak for *trust me*. "It does look like that, though, right? On the outside, it seems like Tonio is worrying about nothing."

A small whine escaped between Buster's teeth. "Yes, on the outside, it can look like Tonio is making things up."

Lasagna tilted his head and swiveled an ear in a way that meant *but*.

Oh! Buster's ears shot up and his tail stiffened. "But . . . the problems feel real to him. Anxiety is like . . ." He searched for a way to explain to all these dogs. "Anxiety is like if you smelled a cat, all the time, even if there had never been a cat anywhere near you. Your brain would always be yelling, *Cat! Cat! Cat!* Even though you knew there wasn't one around. It's like if there was a part of your brain that kept telling you, every second, that someone had thrown a Frisbee." Buster nodded, and his tail started wagging on its own. He'd found it.

"You didn't see anyone throw a Frisbee, and you know deep down there isn't one, but every bone in your body is saying, *Jump! Catch it! Find the Frisbee! Where did it go?!*" He saw some dogs in the crowd nodding, understanding. "You might even get used to it! You might be totally sure, on a conscious level, that there's no Frisbee. But then maybe you're really tired, or you had a bad day, and your brain yells, *FRISBEE!* and before you have a chance to think about it, you've jumped up in the air to catch a Frisbee that doesn't exist, and everyone is looking at you weird, like 'Why did you just jump over nothing?'"

"I see." Lasagna looked over at his opponent. "Does that make sense to you, Pronto?"

"Absolutely not." The husky made a dramatic exasperated face. "Antonio is a child! He doesn't have anything to worry about. And he's certainly not chasing Frisbees."

"Not an *actual* Frisbee!" Buster knew the other lawyer was only pretending to not understand. He hoped that telling more of the story would help convince the judge.

Buster's Testimony

Bellville Square is the center of all life in Bellville, South Carolina. The center of Bellville *Square* is the Bellville Bell, which they named the town after. A long time ago, somebody branded the words *ring, ring* into the side of the bell, which looked neat but accidentally messed it up so it couldn't really ring anymore. Now it's just for display. I didn't know all of this on our first trip to the dog park, but I thought I'd go ahead and warn the Court so you'd understand why everyone in Bellville says "ring, ring" all the time. It was *extremely* confusing at first.

"Ring, ring, Antonio! How are you this morning?" A woman in a plaid shirt and big jeans waved at us as we walked through the square toward the dog park. Tonio smiled.

"Ring, ring, Mrs. Chambers. I'm doing all right."

"Looking forward to sixth grade?"

Tonio didn't have time to look as horrified as he felt, because he was interrupted by a yell so loud, so sudden, that my whole body reacted.

"SOMEBODY STOP THAT DOG!"

I felt a tickle in my hearing off to the side and turned my head just in time to see a puppy flying past, a little tricolor collie, inches from my face. He cocked his head, looked right at me, and winked.

A big necklace covered in diamonds glittered between his teeth.

The world sped back up. "Excuse me!" a girl yelled, diving past Mrs. Chambers. She didn't see Tonio until it was too late, tripped on his tennis shoes, knocked the leash out of his hand, and they both fell onto the sidewalk.

Before I even had time to think about it, I was chasing the puppy.

"BACK OFF, GRAMPS!" the puppy barked as he looked behind him, silver chain threaded around his lower teeth. "THE NECKLACE IS MINE!"

He dodged around Video Garden, out of the square. All four of my legs scrabbled on the pavement as I struggled to turn—I'm not a big dog by any means, more small-to-medium, but sudden turns can still be a challenge.

As we rounded the corner, I realized I knew this dog. Mozart was his name—I knew him from the shelter I'd been sent to by Dog Court the first time. Which meant the girl was Mia Lin, whose parents ran the shelter.

There was a fire escape on the back of Video Garden, and he used that to jump onto the roof. I leaped along behind him as closely as possible, and when I got to the

45

top, he ran to the edge of the roof to jump to the next one. "Stop!" I barked. "It's too far!"

He glared behind as he picked up speed, fluffy legs pounding the roof as hard as they could. I went into overdrive as his front legs lifted off the ground. I opened my mouth, ran the last few steps to the edge, and leaped.

I glided over him, and his head jerked up to look at me. The end of the necklace floated up like it was moving through Jell-O, and I reached out to clamp down on the opposite end of the chain.

The weight tugged my neck down and slowed my jump. I whipped my head around and flung Mozart as hard as I could. He flopped onto the roof and braced himself against the edge—while I dangled by the necklace over the side.

"I'm not—nngh—strong enough!" he whimpered. I scrabbled my paws against the roof.

I kicked my front paw up, up—and finally caught the ledge. With a tug from Mozart and a push on that leg, I rolled up onto the roof, panting.

"What"—I gasped—"are you doing with this?"

Mozart pounced on my neck and started biting, but he was too small to do any damage. "Rrr!! RRRR!!!!!"

"Hey, hey, now! Stop that!" I rolled over and pinned him easily under my front legs. "I just saved your life."

"I would have been fine," he growled. "Leave me alone."

I made a big show of flopping my head down over my

paws and resting my weight on his side. "We can just sit here all day, then. Until you tell me."

A low rumble came out of his throat for a few seconds, but then he sighed and gave up. "Mia said she needed money. So I was getting some."

"This isn't money. This is a necklace."

"I know that!" He batted at my face with his front paws. "But I've got ways. I was gonna sell it. That store has so many jewels! They don't need all of 'em."

"So you *did* steal it from a store." I shook my head. "You're not acting like a Good Dog."

"Like you're one to talk," Mozart spat. *"Miracle Dog."*

I winced. Of course, he already knew. Everyone at the shelter did. But it didn't matter; I was right. "I know you want to help Mia, but right now you're not helping. If she wanted you to do this, she wouldn't be yelling at people to stop you, right?"

He tried to snap at my ear. "She'll understand when I come back with cash!"

I snorted. "No, I think she'd understand even less if you did that." I looked him in the eyes. "Let's take this back, okay? We can talk about it more later."

". . . . ."

"Okay??"

". . . . . Fine. I'll take it back." He relaxed under my legs.

47

I wagged my tail. "Good. Let's go." I lifted my weight off him and stretched as I stood up.

"Gotcha, GRAMPS!" Mozart scooped up the necklace with his mouth and, before I could grab him, bolted to the edge of the building and jumped down, winking as he did. "Later, lose—"

"*Gotcha*, Mozart! Finally." Mia's voice came from below. I ran to the edge of the roof and looked down— she'd caught him, and he was wiggling uselessly as she pried the necklace away. "Now I have to go apologize to Louis. What has gotten into you?"

I was glad she found him, but something was missing. I couldn't quite put my claw on it, but something wasn't right. There she was, and there he was, and there the necklace was . . . but there was something I was supposed to be doing, right? What was it again?

My tail fell between my legs. *Tonio!* I was supposed to be watching him, and I'd just run off! Where was he? I jumped off the roof onto another dumpster with a loud *CLANG*, then ran past Mia and around the corner as fast as I could.

"Tonio?" I barked, even though I knew he couldn't understand me.

He was leaning against the side of the building, breathing heavy by the Video Garden window display that said *Grow into a New Movie Today!* As soon as he saw me, he burst into tears.

"Oh no, Tonio, I'm sorry, I'm so sorry," I whined, and licked at his face. Why was he crying? I was only gone for a second. "I didn't mean to leave you alone, I'm sorry."

"I didn't know what to do," he blubbered. "Everything happened so fast, and then Mia from school was here, yelling at me to help, and you were gone, and I didn't know if you'd run away for good, or into the street, or something—"

Whoa whoa whoa. All of that happened in his head just while I was gone?

"—and Mia kept talking to me, but I couldn't say anything, and so she was like, 'I guess I'll do it myself!'"

I tried to lick his face again, but he pushed me away and frowned.

"Bad dog. Bad."

You know how it feels to hear that. I lost all my energy to fight. As Tonio picked up my leash and started back toward the dog park in silence, I tried to think of anything that would make him feel better.

He made a little groany, growly noise in the back of his throat. "I don't know why I'm even talking to you, anyway. You don't understand what I'm saying."

I couldn't tell him that I was trying to help. I couldn't explain why I hadn't done my job right. And if he knew I was trying to catch Mozart for Mia, I'd be a Bad Dog, anyway, because I'd look smart. In the end, I was just a service dog who hadn't done his job. I'd left my human behind.

So, yes, I was taking my duty to Dog Court seriously. I could have found a way to tell him then, and probably would have made him feel better.

But I didn't.

— 5 —

The Lin Family Dog Shelter also functions as Bellville's only public dog park. People in Bellville are encouraged to bring their pets to the grounds of the shelter, which allows their dogs to roam around the farm as much as they want. This provides a service to the town (which is too small to afford a nice dog park on its own) and the increased activity and socializing means the Lins don't have to spend all day playing with the shelter dogs themselves.

Or, at least, that's how the humans see it. For us, it means Bellville is one of the most social dog communities in the country!

The farm itself was split into four main areas: the human area, which had the shelter's office building (a repurposed barn), a big toolshed, and the Lin family's house; the living area, where dogs slept and ate in an old stable; the "forest," a light clumping of pecan trees with a little creek flowing around them; and what used to be crop fields, which was now a wide spread of dust, mud, and weeds for dogs to run around and get dirty in.

An unpaved road led from the entrance to Mia's house

and the shelter's main building, so we started by walking along the edge of that. Tonio seemed to know his way around—I wondered when he'd been here before—and he steered us away from the buildings and onto the trails leading toward the forest. I looked around for Mia and Mozart, but couldn't spot them anywhere.

Over the course of our walk, his stress from the square gave way to embarrassment. When we reached the picnic tables between the pecan trees, he seemed to have forgiven me. He unclipped my leash and looked me in the face.

"Let's practice, okay? Stay." He stood up and left me by the bench, then walked a few feet away. "Now, come here, Buster!"

I ran over to him and sat down. He nodded seriously. "Good boy. Okay, stay." This time he went behind a tree, where I couldn't see him directly. "Come here, Buster!"

Easy as pie—and even okay for a regular pet! I ran around the tree and wagged my tail for a treat, which he gave me.

"I know you don't understand me, but I'm going to sit here and draw in my sketchbook. You can go play, but you have to come back when I call for you. Okay?"

I couldn't answer him, so I just wagged my tail at his voice. He knelt down and pushed his forehead into mine. "I'm sorry I got mad at you. I should have held on to your leash better."

My tail drooped. *No, Tonio, it was my fault.*

He pulled a little sketchbook out of one of the many pockets in his shorts and sat down to draw the creek bubbling beside him. I sniffed around slowly at first, to show I was hesitant to leave him alone, but I think he really did want a moment to himself. So I wandered over to the nearest dogs—a group of runners just finished with a race, cooling off in the water and the shade—and asked them not to bother him. Dogs who love exercise are usually pretty chill, and this group just nodded and splashed some water around.

Something interesting had to be going on, somewhere in the park! I planted my feet, closed my eyes, and tuned my ears toward different crowds to listen in on their conversations.

A referee made tough calls over an impromptu wrestling tournament in the dirt field: "Illegal mouth grab! Yellow card! Watch yourself, Leila!"

A book club discussed their latest pick over by the stable's water fountain:

"I'm sorry, I just didn't like it. Is that okay? Is it okay that I didn't like it?"

"No. I mean, yes. I mean, you're wrong, but it's okay."

The sound of lightning-fast typing from . . . somewhere? "You're good, WagCorp. But I'm better." The clacking of that keyboard reminded me that Mozart had said he had a way to sell the necklace. Which meant, probably, someone in the shelter was helping him. My best guess was Jpeg—and she was also the only dog I knew who could type so fast. I decided to follow the clacking to its source, deeper into the forest.

I found her pretty quickly, hiding behind a big tree with a computer she'd built herself stuck in a hole. From far away, it would just look like she was digging.

"All right, bonewrangler2016," she mumbled at the computer, "let's see if you're serious." Then Jpeg, a Shiba Inu with a dark brown coat and a face stuck constantly smirking, tilted her head toward me, her paws still slamming down quickly on her keyboard (which only had two big buttons). "Oh, hey, Buster. Welcome back, ya big nerd."

"Hey, Jpeg! What's up?"

She spun a sphere on the side of the computer with her nose to send the cursor flying across the screen, then clacked the keys some more. "Some rare bones showed up on the Bark Web. I'm trying to win the auction, 'cause I know a buyer who'll want them."

That gave me an idea. "Hey, if I, uh . . . if I wanted to sell something, would I talk to you about it?"

She gave me a sharp look. "Depends. What are you trying to sell?"

"Oh, I dunno." I sat down in front of her and tilted my head, flopping my ears in a way I hoped looked innocent. "Just normal stuff. Like maybe . . . diamonds? Would you sell those?"

She gave me an even sharper look, closed her computer, and switched to Underspeak—a sign that we were talking about something she didn't want anyone to hear. She twisted her paw, flapped her ear, and posed her tail in a series of directions that meant *I don't know what you're talking about.*

I'm not talking about anything! I posed back. *Just asking a question!*

Jpeg bared her teeth to show she disagreed. *You're talking about whether I would sell the diamonds that Mozart tried to steal from a store in town, and I don't know anything about that or what you're talking about.*

I rolled my shoulders and twitched my ears with my tail posed for extra exclamation points. *You obviously do know!!! You just said all the details!!!!*

No idea what you're talking about, she underspoke emphatically. *I don't know what a diamond is, and I definitely wouldn't have sold any if Mozart brought them to me, no matter if it was for a good cause or not.*

That was interesting. *What cause?*

I DO NOT KNOW WHAT YOU ARE TALKING ABOUT. Jpeg opened her computer back up and resumed typing. Apparently our conversation was over. I wandered toward the fields to watch the wrestling tournament and think.

"Buster Pulaski?" a voice growled real close to my ear.

I jumped. A medium-sized dog with a dark brown coat and beige splotches had somehow kind of snuck up beside me. She looked me over with a serious expression. "I'm Officer Sergeant, your new pawrole officer. And this is my partner, Officer Grizzle. Care to see our credentials?"

A tiny gray dog with a long body like a dachshund but a much fluffier coat had come up on my other side. He bared his teeth up at me, as if daring me to cross him. Just to be safe, I sniffed their butts. They were legit. "'Officer Sergeant'?" I repeated.

The splotchy dog looked embarrassed. "I know. A human named me Sergeant. And then when I started working for Dog Court . . ." She rolled her shoulders in a shrug. "The two of us keep an eye on Bellville, so we wanted to introduce ourselves." She fixed me with an unwavering stare. "There will be *no more funny business* like the stunts you pulled in the city. Is that clear?"

"Clear as a glass door, Officers. I could walk right into it."

Officer Sergeant, surprised by my joke, barked out a small laugh. I tried to wag my tail to keep up the energy, but she dropped back to a stony expression. "We're here to keep an eye on you, but we're also here to help. If you need anything, or you see anything suspicious, just let us know. Got it?"

"Got it."

"BUSTER!" I turned to see Tonio walking out of the trees, hands cupped around his mouth. When I turned around, the officers were gone.

I trotted over to Tonio's feet and licked his hands while he clipped on my leash. I was still trying to figure out what was going on with Mia and Mozart. And I was also trying to figure out how to help Tonio get out of the house more. Then I realized the answer to both problems might be *the same answer.* Friends get you out of the house! And if Tonio was going to make a new friend, why couldn't it just happen to be Mia?

The top of Tonio's sketchbook was poking out of the loose pocket of his shorts as we walked along the road. I waited for a few dogs to run past us, chasing one another, and while Tonio was distracted by the short burst of chaos, I grabbed the sketchbook between my teeth and dropped it on the ground, in clear sight of Mia's house.

He didn't notice, and my tail wagged the whole way home even though my stomach was flipping with nerves.

— 6 —

Tonio woke up buzzing. That's the best way I can describe it—I wasn't feeling an actual, solid vibration or seeing him bounce or anything, but the way he was acting from the second his eyes opened just felt like *buzzing*. He was tense, his breathing sounded shallow and difficult, and he wouldn't stop moving.

He'd describe this feeling later like something in his stomach had grabbed his throat and was shaking it, just enough to make him feel uncomfortable. Or like he was full of helium so the spot just under his chest was trying to escape his body. The feeling kept him from calming down, so he was awake before either of his parents and emptied the fridge to make a huge breakfast for everybody.

I didn't mind the sausage, of course, but his buzzing was infectious. I kept trying to figure out what was wrong, but eventually, I realized nothing was. Nothing outside of Tonio, anyway; his anxiety was using his body to say *something's wrong, fix it, something's wrong, fix it* over and over. But there wasn't anything to fix, so he was doing whatever he could think of to get the energy out.

His parents woke up, grabbed some coffee, pancakes, and eggs, and groggily thanked their son before disappearing back to work. Mr. Pulaski ran downstairs to open the grocery, and Mrs. Pulaski handed Tonio a ten-dollar bill and said something about allowance before disappearing into her office. Loud music with lots of electric guitar blasted behind the door seconds later.

I was stunned! My life before this hadn't encountered a lot of eleven-year-olds, but I was pretty sure it was unusual for a kid to just get up and do that for his family.

Tonio cleaned the dishes until they shined, but still his body buzzed. He took a shower, put on the same kind of T-shirt and shorts he always wore, and guided me into my service dog vest. I shook my body out, a big dramatic wiggle, like I had the first time we met.

He tilted his head at me, then shook his hair back at me, little droplets from his shower spraying around. I wagged my tail and shook again, back at him. He laughed.

"You're so weird. Does seeing me wet make you think *you're* wet? That's goofy." I heard his pulse lower a little bit, though. Even a tiny distraction helped—good to know.

His energy redirected into his own room, where he

threw the buzzing at anything that could even barely be considered "mess." Laundry: folded. Desk: organized. He collected a few freshly drawn cards from his desk and opened his box. It took him a few seconds to find exactly where the new ones were supposed to go.

Tonio's finger ran along the top of the cards, lightly pushing them into a gentle flipping motion. He stopped on Om, the Martian Dragon, which looked like a powerful card. He'd worked very hard on the scales and wings but apparently given up on the face, because it was left blank.

I nudged his hand when he froze, staring at the card. I didn't know what was going on with it, but if it was something bad, I needed to distract him. He looked at me, then back at the card, then nodded to himself— apparently making a decision—and tucked the card in the big, buttoned pocket on the front of his shorts.

I followed him back downstairs, and then outside into town. A few adults waved at Tonio as we passed, and I wondered for the first time why we weren't seeing any kids around. Shouldn't a town like Bellville be full of bored kids over the summer?

He was leading me to a store I hadn't seen before. Its name, Roll the Ice, was displayed in big letters next to a cone with three different dice in it (like three scoops of ice cream). The whole thing was supposed to light up, I realized, which is why I hadn't recognized it—almost none of the lights were working, so from Tonio's window at night it just said *h I*.

Waves of cold air rushed over me when Tonio pushed the door open, a welcome break from the South Carolina heat. "Ring, ring, little dude!" An older teenager with big, stylish glasses and a pastel-blue apron smiled and waved from behind an ice-cream scooping freezer. "Hey, the dog isn't—" She saw my service dog vest and smiled at Tonio. "Never mind. My name's Skyler, and I'm in charge here today. Ice or dice?"

Tonio looked surprised by the question. He stared at her longer than humans are usually comfortable with.

The teenager grinned and tried again, slower. "Do you need help with ice, as in cream, or dice, like game stuff?"

I felt Tonio heat up with embarrassment. I could practically hear him talking to himself, telling himself he was stupid for not getting it.

Luckily, Skyler had noticed Tonio's reaction, too, and wanted to make it better. "That's a cute dog. What's his name?"

This was something Tonio could handle. "Buster."

"That's a good name! Are you training him?"

"No. My parents got him for me." He swallowed and looked away from her uncomfortably. "Because I have anxiety."

Skyler nodded seriously. "That's cool. Me too."

"You . . . have a dog?"

"I have anxiety, too. Sometimes."

His eyes widened in surprise at this. Had no one else ever told him that before? She let him consider for a moment, until he mumbled, "I don't have it *sometimes*."

"That sounds tough." Before Tonio could say anything else, she continued. "But Roll the Ice is a stress-free space, so nothing to worry about here. What did you come in for again?" She made a face and said it in a way like he *must* have told her, and it was totally her fault for forgetting. I realized this was on purpose to make it easier for Tonio to answer, and was very impressed by how smooth it was.

"I want to look at Beamblade cards."

"You got it." Skyler took a long sideways step to the right. The glass display wall continued, unbroken, but instead of looking down into a freezer, it looked down onto individual cards laid out in sleeves. "You're the second kid to come in for Beamblade today! I thought everybody your age was off at Sticks and Bugs."

Discomfort flashed on Tonio's face. He didn't know what to say, so he just shrugged. Skyler didn't seem to mind. "The singles are in here, and if you want booster packs or deck boxes or whatever, they're behind you by the Spell of Togetherness stuff. And hey, let me get you a single scoop. On the house."

"You don't have to—"

"What's your favorite?" She didn't seem like she was going to take no for an answer.

"Cookie dough."

Skyler pulled some from the freezer and stuck it on a small cone for him. "There're some guys in the back playing Beamblade, if you want to join. I think that kid's still here." She gestured toward long tables in the back. I followed where she pointed and saw some younger adults playing with a kid around Tonio's age.

Tonio didn't even look. "Thanks," he said, with an expression that said *no thanks*. He moved his face up to the glass and scanned through cards like Cordurboy the Fabricant, with his wand of creation, and Nine-Eyes, hacker pirate of the Galaxy Wide Web.

Skyler had started messing with the register and wasn't looking at Tonio anymore. I saw him look from her, to the case, and back to her. He tensed up, uncomfortable with the idea of interrupting her. "Um, excuse me," he mumbled, too quietly.

She didn't look up. Tonio looked back at the case, clenched his hand tight around my leash, and headed for the door.

I wanted to stop, to tug him back, but that wasn't my job. I was disappointed, but it was his decision. He reached up to push the door open, then closed his eyes and turned back around. *Yes!* He took the few steps back to the register and tried a little louder.

"Excuse me, do you have Om, the Martian Dragon?"

Skyler's eyes lit up. "You're after the good stuff! A lot of people are looking for him right now, but I actually just bought one off of somebody this morning." She took off her ice-cream serving gloves, turned around, and flipped through a folder of cards in plastic sleeves. After a moment, she pulled one out and presented it for Tonio to see.

The image on the card wasn't like anything I'd seen before, and I understood immediately why Tonio wasn't able to draw it himself. Unlike the other Beamblade cards, which were mostly flat illustrations, Om's "face" was made out of a special kind of shiny foil that gave the effect of a void filled with glittering stars that moved when your head moved. It wasn't something you could copy with pens and paper.

"Most attack power in the set," Skyler said. "The foil's so cool, right?" Tonio nodded emphatically. "He's really rare, though. If you want to take him home, it'll be fifty-five dollars."

Oof. That took the wind out of Tonio's jowls. He shook his head and Skyler nodded, understanding.

From the back of the store, one of the adult players had started to argue with the kid who was playing.

Skyler called out, "Hey, now! I'm the one with the judge badge. What's going on over there?"

"Does Summon Advanced Familiar's ability work on

the Manabytes you use to cast it?" The adult's words sounded like absolute nonsense to me. Skyler looked a little confused, too.

"No," Tonio whispered. "Because the spell isn't finished until the familiar is on the field. It can't recharge Manabytes that aren't spent yet."

"No!" Skyler also said, then repeated what Tonio had said. After she was done, she looked down at him and whispered back, "You sure you don't play? It sounds like you know your stuff. Come on—just sit in for a bit and see how it goes."

I nuzzled the palm of Tonio's hand with my nose, and he scratched behind my ears while he thought about her offer.

Finally, he said, "Okay." She grinned, and we followed her to the tables in the back. She introduced the players as she went.

"You already know Phil, and that's Keegan. Laurie Ann went out for pizza, I think, and—oh, right. The new kid's name is Devon. Say hi, everybody! This is— actually, I forgot to ask. What's your name?"

"Antonio!" Devon, the kid Tonio's age with the gap between his front teeth, smiled a big smile and waved. "What's up?"

It was like an anvil had fallen on Tonio's chest. He dropped the rest of his cookie dough ice cream on the floor and took two steps backward.

"Are you okay, Antonio?" Skyler asked, a concerned look on her face. Tonio did the signal on his leg, so I pawed at him and whined a little.

"Sorry, I'm sorry. My dog really has to pee. I'm sorry!" And just like that, we were out the door. As soon as they couldn't see him, he was gasping for air. I gently guided him over to a bench by the corner so he could sit down and collect himself.

Devon, I realized, was the same Devon he'd thrown up on at yearbook signing—and the reason he was scared to go back to school. I couldn't believe that goofy kid with the sweet smile had such a strong effect on Tonio, but there were a lot of things about how Tonio's anxiety worked I was still learning to understand. I stepped up onto the bench and laid down over Tonio's lap, trying to add warmth and reassurance in some small way.

"I'm sorry," he whispered. I couldn't do much in response other than wiggle, but I wished he wouldn't apologize. I turned and licked his face. He pushed me away, laughing and making a "pwuh" noise. "I guess you don't care, huh? You're just having a good time outside." He smiled. "Thanks."

At least that was something. He glanced back at Roll the Ice, sighed, and started walking home. *We'll keep trying*, I promised silently. *Things are going to change.*

But first I had to figure out what to do.

⤐ 7 ⟞

Mr. Pulaski was going in for another night shift, so we had "dinner" again at four in the afternoon.

"I saw you had some Beamblade cards out," Mr. Pulaski said once the tuna casserole had been finished off. "You know, I've got a bunch of my old cards in storage, if you need 'em. *Gotta blade*, right?"

"That's okay," Tonio replied. "You don't have to."

"I know, but I will. A Beamblade card isn't meant to sit alone in a box. It's meant to *blade*! I wish I was still in college. I'd slash through all your life crystals in three turns, flat."

Tonio didn't answer. Mr. Pulaski shook his head like he was suddenly amazed. "You're such a good kid, Tonio."

"Dad, I—"

"No, no, I'm gonna be a dad here for a second and tell you how good of a kid you are! All our friends, everybody, their kids would yell, and scream, and throw tantrums. You never did that, never threw a tantrum, not once. Still haven't. You're almost a teenager now, sure, but I know you won't be any trouble."

He was trying to be nice, but something about his compliment rubbed my fur in the wrong direction. I could already tell Tonio was a lot of things—smart, for one. Observant, like I said. His art was good, and he cared a lot about how other people felt. But his dad was telling him he liked that he was *quiet*? That he didn't cause trouble?

I wondered if Tonio felt the way that I felt, when I was in Dog Court the first time. When I thought, *You just want me to sit and stay. To lie down.*

"Thanks, Dad."

"And once we get past this tough spot you've been in lately, everything will be fine. And we're almost past it. I can feel that, for sure." *Just say anxiety*, I thought, feeling protective of Tonio all over again. "And if you have time later, you should come by the store! I could show you how to use the sticker maker! I got it custom-made to look like the biometric scanner in *Aliens Everywhere, Part 2: '2' Many Aliens*." And just like that, he was on a roll: "It's famous because they didn't introduce it until part two, but if biometric analysis already existed in the universe, then half of the problems in part one wouldn't have even—"

The doorbell rang, saving everyone.

"I'll go see who it is!" Mr. Pulaski announced in a big action-hero voice. He patted my head as he passed.

A voice chimed through when he opened the door,

saying, "Sorry to bother you, Mr. Pulaski!" It was Mia! My ears perked up. I trotted over to get a better view right away.

"Mia! Good to see ya!"

Mia was wearing a green ribbon in her hair this time, matching a T-shirt featuring a centipede in a Bug Scouts hat (and one hundred boots). "Ring, ring! I was wondering if I could interest you in some Bug Bites." She lifted up a tray of snacks for emphasis, and her voice shifted into a serious, practiced pattern. "As you may know, the Bellville Bug Scouts work hard every year to bring you high-quality snacks and raise money for various activities. As you also know, all of these activities are out in nature. But like we Bug Scouts always say, 'Nature is Expensive!' so I am hoping you will buy some of these Bug Bites. How many would you like?"

Mr. Pulaski blinked. "Is that a real Bug Scout motto? I don't know that one."

But Mrs. Pulaski was looming behind him, hunger in her tired eyes. "Peanut Butter Beetles?"

Mia smiled and held up her cardboard tray of snacks. "Twenty dollars."

Mr. Pulaski's eyes widened. "For one box?"

"Prices are up over the summer. Of course," she said with a big smile, "you can always wait four months for the regular season."

"Well, all right. Always happy to help out the Scouts.

Laura, do you want any—" Mrs. Pulaski shoved Mr. Pulaski out of the way and slammed twenty dollars down on Mia's tray. She took a box of Peanut Butter Beetles and zombie-walked her way back to her office.

Never get in the way of her snack, I noted.

"Is Antonio home, by the way? He left something at the shelter."

"Antonio!" Mr. Pulaski called out. "Mia's got something for you!"

"Don't worry about it, Dad." Tonio was blushing as he got to us. He stepped around Mr. Pulaski and slipped out the door with me at his heels. It was only when the door was shut and Mr. Pulaski was gone that Tonio looked at Mia directly. "Why aren't you wearing the Bug Scout uniform?" he asked.

"I'm not really a Bug Scout. They're all at camp." She set the tray of snacks down on the landing in front of Tonio's door and leaned against the rail. "But people pay good money for this junk when you can't find it anywhere else. I bought a bunch of boxes in the fall and saved them up for summer."

"You lied to my parents?!" I don't think he even thought that was possible.

"So what? Your mom wanted them, and there aren't any *real* Scouts around." I'm sure Tonio wanted to argue, but his confidence wilted when he saw how sure she seemed. *Maybe I made the wrong call,* I thought, *getting her attention.*

Mia saw something in his face change, and she sighed. "I came over because I wanted to say sorry for yelling at you."

I noticed that this was not, technically, an apology.

Tonio said, "Oh."

She held out his journal. "Plus, you left this at the dog park."

Tonio took it from her, surprised.

Mia went on. "My best friend used to draw. You're not as good as her, but you're pretty good." She hefted up the tray of Bug Bites. "I'm at the shelter pretty much all the time. Usually over by the stable. There's always stuff to do."

Tonio's eyebrows pushed together. "I don't understand."

She sighed in frustration. "We're, like, the only kids in town, okay? And I saw how much you draw in that thing, so I know you don't have anything better to do."

My tail wagged. *A friend! She wants to be friends! I did it!*

"Better to do than what?" Tonio seemed genuinely confused.

Mia laughed again, harsher. "Okay, never mind. I get it. Sorry I lied to your dad." She turned around and started heading down the stairs. Tonio looked down at me, alarmed, and then realized I was a dog and could not help with this one.

"Wait!" he called out. "Get *what*? What do you mean?"

She didn't turn around. "I'll see you later, Tonio. Bye, Buster."

We stood there, together, and watched her walk away. Tonio shook his head and pushed the door back open for me. Fifteen minutes of staring blankly at his computer screen later, he finally spoke again.

"Does she want to be my *friend*?"

Now that Tonio knew Devon wasn't at camp and could appear anytime, he was extra careful about going outside. Before we left for our next appointment with Dr. Jake, he looked out his bedroom window to make sure the other kid wasn't walking around the square, and the whole ride there he slid down in his seat, like Devon could show up any second and stare right into the window of a moving car.

When we got to Dr. Jake's office, that tension was replaced with a different one: the fake-happy smile and weird vibe Tonio put out when he was trying to pretend everything was okay.

"You look a little tired, Tonio," Dr. Jake observed. I moved to him for a treat, and he had one ready in his hand. What a guy. "Is everything all right?"

He'd spent a long time thinking since Mia left. I didn't know what about, exactly, but I hoped he would at least talk to Dr. Jake about it this time.

"If I did something bad," Tonio said, "would you tell my parents about it?"

Concern flashed across Dr. Jake's face, and before he could say anything, Tonio was already talking again. "I don't mean that I did anything bad. But like . . . if you saw me doing something that you thought was bad, would you tell my parents or anybody about it?"

"We've talked before about how our sessions are confidential. Anything you tell me in here is between us, unless you or someone else is in danger."

"Yeah, but if you weren't my doctor. If we were friends."

"I would need more information to know for sure. But if there's something you want to tell me, I promise you're safe. I'm here to listen."

Tonio shook his head. "Oh, thanks, but I didn't mean anything specific. I was just wondering."

"Are you sure? If something's bothering you, I want to know. I care about how you're feeling."

He shrugged. "No, I'm just making things up, but do you think that if you hear about something bad, and you don't say anything or do anything to stop it, you kind of did the bad thing, too?"

A pause while Dr. Jake considered his answer. I found

the squishy ball and chewed on it again. To me, this sounded a lot like what Tonio had told me about what happened with Devon—he'd been concerned for Devon, because of the way those other kids talked about him, but never spoke up. And now, I realized, he'd seen what Mia was doing with the Bug Bites.

"There are a lot of reasons why you might keep a bad thing secret. Like if you are trying to protect someone, or if talking about the bad thing would only hurt some-body." Dr. Jake stretched out his long legs and leaned over more toward us. "Plus, if we made ourselves feel personally responsible for every bad thing in the world we heard about, we wouldn't have any time to be our own selves."

Tonio stared at the carpet.

"We don't always know what's 'good' or 'bad,'" Dr. Jake continued. "Not really. And looking for those labels will waste a lot of your time. But if you feel like you want to *do* or *change* something, to make life better for you or someone else, then I think you should listen to that feeling. That feeling tells you who you are."

— 8 —

I thought Tonio might try to stay away from Mia, but instead, he asked his parents if he could go over to the shelter-park the next day.

Tonio's parents had two vehicles: "the nice car" and "the truck." The Lins' shelter was down a dirt road on the north side of town, so Mrs. Pulaski decided to take the truck. The truck seemed to imagine bumps even on *regular* roads, so I spent the drive bouncing between them in the middle seat.

Mrs. Pulaski talked to Tonio as she drove. "You know, I got your dad into Beamblade back in college. He did what he always does and got *totally* obsessed with it. Memorized the cards, tried to collect every ultra rare." The car leaped two hundred thousand feet in the air, and my paws scrabbled on the scratchy seats for balance. "Didn't they change that? Are those called 'epic rare' now?"

Tonio's fingers tightened around his box of Beamblade cards. Before going downstairs, he'd written a series of questions and concerns on note cards—a list of everything he wanted to talk about with Mia, so he didn't get nervous and forget anything. He neatly ordered them in a box next to some of the Beamblade cards he'd drawn, which he must have brought just in case Mia was interested in the game, too.

"I think so," he said.

"You *think*? You'll have to know these things if you're ever going to be a Beamblade master!" Mrs. Pulaski smiled at Tonio, but he stared out the window with a tense expression and didn't acknowledge her teasing at all. She looked out the opposite window before he could notice her disappointment. I licked at her hand on the wheel, and she patted my head.

The red truck curved into one of its very slow but somehow still extremely jumpy turns. I spread my front legs and tried to wedge them under the humans' legs so I wouldn't go flying off the seat. A whine wriggled its way out of my jaws, despite my best efforts.

"Wow, he hates the truck, huh?" Mrs. Pulaski said.

Tonio looked at me sympathetically. "Sorry, buddy."

No problem, guys. I can handle a little—ugh—being thrown around inside the stomach of an angry monster.

Mrs. Pulaski leaned out the window to hit a buzzer and open the gate at the edge of the Lins' property. She parked close to their house, which looked like it was as old as Bellville itself.

"Do you remember going to the fall festival here when you were little?"

Tonio nodded, his eyebrows still pushing painfully into each other. "Did they stop doing it?"

"No, the festival still happens. We just—you didn't—" Mrs. Pulaski was trying not to say something, working her way around it.

"You didn't want to take me anymore."

"That's not it. Of course we wanted to take you. You just didn't seem like you wanted to go." She took her hands off the wheel and reached out toward Tonio's leg—but then put her hand on my head instead, and petted me. "Maybe we should have asked."

"Can we go back home?" The edges of the box were crumpling under Tonio's grip. Mrs. Pulaski and I both turned our heads to Tonio, surprised.

"We just got here!" Mrs. Pulaski said, echoing what I was thinking. "Don't you want to see your friend?"

"I'm feeling too anxious. I don't think I can."

My nose twitched as I smelled for details. His breathing wasn't relaxed, but he wasn't panicking. This wasn't an attack—it was anxiety, sure, but it was closer to regular fear.

"Oh, Tonio. Are you scared it won't go well? Making friends isn't supposed to be scary. It's not something you need to be worried about."

That's not helpful, I thought. *It doesn't matter if it's "supposed" to be scary. It is scary.*

"I can't do it by myself."

"You won't be by yourself. You've got Buster!"

I wagged my tail at my name. I nudged him. *I'll be right here.*

The truck didn't have an automatic unlock, so Mrs. Pulaski reached over to tug up the little nub. "You can do it, Antonio. She wants to be your friend because she already likes you. There's nothing to be scared of."

But she might not really want to be his friend, I thought. *Tonio's worried he made it up.* Tonio shook his head. "I can't. I can't do it. I don't even know why I'm here."

Mrs. Pulaski did try to touch him this time, but he flinched away. She put both hands on the steering wheel and watched a goat wander across the sunny field. It was bright outside, but the truck felt like it was under its own personal storm cloud. The goat turned and wobbled toward us.

"I'm sorry, Tonio." Mrs. Pulaski spoke to Tonio gently. "We moved to Bellville because your dad loved growing up here, and we thought it would be good for you to be somewhere smaller, but I think we might have just made it tougher for you." She sighed, and her hands tightened around the steering wheel. "There's a school in the city, with teachers who know how to work with kids like you. A lot of my clients live there, which is nice, and your dad could find something to do. We probably couldn't take Buster with us, but—"

This finally shook Tonio into speaking. "What do you mean? Take him where?"

She blinked. "To the city."

"We can't leave. You love it here."

"I do. But I could love it there, too, and if you can't go back to this school—"

"So it's my fault." Tonio's voice shot up louder. "We have to move because of me."

"I'm not saying we *have* to. But, considering every-thing, it might be the best choice for us."

This was not something Tonio had expected. His breath was catching, changing—I tried to squeeze under his arm to distract him, but he pushed me back at Mrs. Pulaski. The truck was tiny, so there wasn't very far for me to go, but I was stunned at his force.

"Tonio, please calm down. I'm just saying, maybe you need another environment."

I wanted to tell Mrs. Pulaski to stop talking, to give him some space, but the conversation was getting out of control too fast for me to do anything about it.

Tonio's face contorted into an angry, confused shape. "I don't need another environment!" he yelled.

His mother's grip tightened on the steering wheel. "Then what do you need, Tonio? I'm trying to understand."

"*I don't know!*" He untangled from his seat belt and tugged at the door handle. The truck door stuck until he kicked it and jumped out onto the grass. "I'm going to go play Beamblade." I leaped down after him and barked, but he didn't stop running.

"Antonio!" his mom yelled after him.

"I'll call you later!" Tonio shouted back. He stumbled on a pile of logs but caught himself before he hit the ground and kept on moving.

He threw up behind the barn. His box fell open when he dropped it, and the note cards blew around in the wind. I whined and bumped against his ankles while he gagged.

Suddenly, Mia was there, in overalls and a wide black hat, smirking at Tonio. "Is this what it looked like when you threw up on Devon Wilcrest?" she asked. The ball of fluff named Mozart peeked out from the crook of her arm, his tongue lolled out.

She caught a note card in the air. "'Are you like Robin Hood or like Catwoman?'" She raised her eyebrows at Tonio. "I don't understand the question. They're both awesome."

Tonio rested his forehead against the wall. He was breathing heavy.

"I'm going to get you some water," Mia said. "Be right back." Mozart wriggled out of her arm as she walked away. I stepped in front of him and bumped him back with my paw before he got to Tonio.

"Hey!" Mozart barked. "Owie!"

I folded my ears down and stamped my foot for quiet. If he was going to talk, I wanted him to use Underspeak. I wasn't allowed to bark like that, as a service dog. He ignored me and kept yipping.

"What's that kid doing? Smells good! He sad or something? Mia will fix it. She's good at cheering people up, no problem!"

I twisted my tail and shifted my posture. *This is kind of her fault.*

"Her fault?" he yipped. "No way! Mia's the nicest, coolest human there is. Whatever's wrong with him must be *your* fault."

I hated talking to puppies.

It's not my fault, I said. *I'm trying to help.*

Tonio groaned and dragged himself along the wall. I stepped over to him and licked his face. He patted my sides and slid down to sit in the grass.

"Help how?" Mozart was still yipping. "Looks like you're just standing around to me!"

I'm doing my job.

"Oh, you are? That's cool. I guess your job is to not do anything? Hey! I want him to pet me, too!" Mozart hopped up into Tonio's lap and put his little paws up on Tonio's shoulders.

"You're so pretty," Tonio said. "Look at your big

poofy chest." Mozart puffed up his chest proudly. Tonio scratched at it, and I rolled my eyes—puppies have it so easy! But at least Mozart helped calm Tonio down.

I decided to ask Mozart a question, since he was in a good mood. *Why is Mia working so hard to get money?*

"None of your business, old man! It's a secret."

If you tell me, maybe I could help.

He bared his teeth, but it was more cute than scary on his tiny face. "We don't need your help!"

"Here." Mia was back. She held out a water bottle and looked down at me. "Okay if I come through?"

I stepped out of the way, and Mozart hopped in circles around Mia. Tonio took the water and gulped it down while Mia looked around at the cards.

"Your handwriting is cute. 'Are Bug Scout cookies the only thing you lie about?' 'What's your favorite movie?'"

"I was—I'm—" Tonio was already embarrassed. I sat down and leaned my weight against him. "I wanted to know if you were good or bad. I thought that would help. But it was stupid."

She looked amused. "Good or bad at what?"

"At . . . like, all around."

"Oh, that's easy. I'm good."

"If you were bad, you would also say that."

"Okay, but I'm not."

Mia stared Tonio down. He took another drink of water.

"Can we go somewhere else?" she asked. "It smells like throw-up over here."

"I'm sorry," Tonio mumbled miserably. "I should go home."

Mia was already walking toward the stable. "You just got here! Besides, I need your help."

"My help?" Tonio was surprised. He pushed off the ground and quickly gathered up the cards that hadn't ended up in the splash zone. "With what?"

"My dads are busy, Leila spent all morning rolling in mud, and it's hard to give her a bath by myself."

"Leila isn't a bad dog or anything, but she has *so* much fur," Mia explained when we got to the stable. She was right—Leila was part mastiff, part Saint Bernard, part everything huge and fluffy. And she was absolutely caked in mud. "She's the sweetest dog on the planet, absolutely perfect, but if anyone's ever going to adopt her, she has to be clean. It's like she knows when humans are coming and gets extra dirty."

Leila winked at me—or at least I think she did, under the dripping gunk and thick fuzz. *Almost like it's on purpose,* she underspoke to me with a twitch of her nose and tail.

You're making the humans waste time cleaning you on purpose? I asked, surprised. Mia tossed Tonio a bottle of shampoo and walked to the stable's wall to hook up the hose. *Why don't you want to be adopted?*

All my friends are here. I like the wrestling league, and I don't like leashes. Leila wagged her tail when Mia started blasting the hose without warning. Tonio had to dive out of the way before he got soaked.

But you'd probably stay in Bellville, I argued. *And you could still come here to wrestle sometimes. Is that really it?*

You're nosy! Even for a service dog. You know that?

"I don't want to be adopted, either!" Mozart yipped, oblivious to Leila's tone. She laughed as he jumped in front of the hose's stream, trying to catch water in his mouth.

You won't be, little pup. You're Mia's favorite.

"That's *right*!" Mozart said. Mia turned the hose off and showed Tonio how to start scrubbing the shampoo into Leila's fur. "And she's gonna take me with her when she leaves."

Leila swatted him on the snout as my ears perked up.

Leaves? I asked. *To go where?*

See? Leila underspoke. *Nosy.*

"Nunya biz, old man!" Mozart barked. "It's a secret!"

Don't worry about it, Leila added. As if to emphasize the point, she flexed and shook out her fur, spraying sudsy water all over the kids. Tonio sputtered in surprise, Mia laughed, and after a second, Tonio laughed, too.

"It seems like you throw up a lot. You're not sick, are you?" Mia asked once they'd settled into a rhythm and were working their way through opposite sides of Leila's mountain of hair. "I can't get sick right now."

"No, I'm not sick. Not like that."

Mozart slammed into my front leg while dashing around. I grabbed his neck in my mouth and set him to the side. He recovered immediately and tried to jump onto my back.

"'Not like that'? Meaning . . . ?"

"I have anxiety."

Mia leaned over to look at him suspiciously under Leila's stomach. "Is that contagious?"

A smile dug through Tonio's stressed face. "No, it's not like that."

"Okay, well, I'm tired of asking you to explain what you mean, so you can either tell me or we can just sit here and clean the dog."

Tonio blushed, embarrassed. I shook off Mozart and moved over to nudge him supportively. "It's, like, a brain problem. Where I get really worried. But . . ." Tonio checked Mia's face to see if she was actually interested, or just being nice—or, worse, getting ready to make fun of him. She was watching him seriously, so he continued. "But when it's bad, I feel it in my stomach. Or in my throat. It can hurt, or make me throw up." He paused, then added, "I don't really throw up a *lot*."

85

Mia made a face like she wasn't sure she believed him about *that*, but she said, "Did you have any other questions you wanted to ask? On your cards?"

Tonio considered. "Why did you ask me to come back here?"

With a *crackle*, Mia unwrapped a ball of Crunchsquish gum (*First You Crunch and Then You Squish*™) and popped it in her mouth using her bare, soapy hands. I winced at the combination of flavors this must have created, but she didn't flinch. "I dunno. I just did."

The look on Tonio's face reminded me of robots in movies when you tell them something that doesn't compute. "But you came all the way to my house."

"I came to your house to drop off your sketchbook," she pointed out. "Everything else I just thought of right then."

Something about the way she said this caught his attention and gave him an idea for what to say next. "Do you still talk to Sloan?"

I'd never heard that name before, but Mia's head snapped up to look at Tonio, with the least-chill expression I'd seen on her so far.

"Why are you asking me that?" she said defensively.

"You were best friends."

"Yeah, but why do you care?"

"She was nice. I thought you might know if she was okay."

"Of course she's okay. She's always okay." Mia turned the hose back on and waved Tonio out of the way to wash off the shampoo. "She's the person who taught me that quiet people like you are paying attention, too."

"Is *that* why you asked me to hang out?" Tonio pressed. "Because I'm quiet?"

Mia looked uncomfortable for the first time as they rubbed Leila with some old towels. Leila and Mozart had both stopped playing around and were taking concerned poses as they listened to Mia.

"I don't know," she said. "I thought you'd be like Sloan, maybe."

"Do I—"

"But you're not anything like Sloan." Suddenly, Mia seemed frustrated. "She doesn't have to ask a bunch of dumb questions; she just knows what to say. And she doesn't have anxiety, either."

"I'm sorry," Tonio said. "I thought you'd like talking about her."

"Of course I like talking about her!" Mia glared. "You don't get it. I knew this would happen."

Knew what would happen? I underspoke to Leila. She didn't answer me. I nudged Tonio, but he was frozen, surprised by Mia's sharp tone. *She must really miss her friend*, I said to Leila.

We all do, she answered. *But we're handling it. All*

87

right, Miracle Dog? You take care of your human, and we'll take care of ours.

Handling it? I asked. *What does that mean?*

"I don't need other friends, okay?" Mia said to Tonio. "I asked you to come because I didn't want to wash Leila by myself. You can go anytime." She shoved her hands in the pockets of her overalls and walked away with a stomp that was a little too intense to match the casual way she tried to hold her posture. Mozart followed behind at her heels; Leila watched her go with a sad droop to her tail.

But Tonio swallowed and raised his voice. "Do you know what kind of dog Buster is?" he almost-yelled after Mia. "I think he might be a vizsla, but also maybe some poodle or something."

She stopped and turned her head around to answer. "No way. Terrier, maybe, but poodle?"

He whispered loudly through nearly clenched teeth. "I just think there might be some poodle."

Mia put her hands on her hips and shook her head. "That's ridiculous. Don't you know anything about dogs?"

"No!" Tonio almost-cheered, relieved she had turned back around. "I don't know anything about dogs *at all!*"

Her chin pushed up into the air. Her Crunchsquish gum popped. "Well, you can help me feed the dogs, if you want. And I can tell you about them."

Tonio's hands clenched and unclenched around his box of cards. "Okay," he said. Mia started walking in a different direction from the one she'd been heading in a moment before, and Tonio moved to follow her. I stuck to his heels, tail wagging with pride.

Chasing Details

"Pride. Interesting word choice, Buster." Pronto stepped out of his bumper car, thick coat rippling over his intimidating muscles. He walked along the front of the Court's audience confidently, making Lasagna waddle around in a circle to watch him. Buster didn't bother. "Because right now I feel the opposite of pride. I feel *shame*. Shame that so many of my fellow dogs are ignoring our sacred laws to try to make a few children happy."

Lasagna hopped back around to look at the judge. "Your Honor—"

"I've been *very* patient," Pronto interrupted. "I cannot allow Buster to continue misleading the Court without offering the Law's perspective."

The judge nodded. "Make your point, Speaker."

"Do you know what human happiness looks like?" He turned to the crowd. "It looks like a puppy, adopted into a family for its cuteness, and then abandoned when it grows up. It looks like a greyhound, forced to race until the humans stop making money. It looks like Laika, may she watch over us always, sent to space alone with no hope of return. They take our childhoods, our strength, and our lives for their happiness." The husky shook his head sadly. "When they know we have minds, they'll try to take those, too."

A sadness swept over the expressions of the crowd, and a few dogs arched their noses into the sky in the traditional salute to Laika. Lasagna and Buster saluted, too, but Buster's head was bursting with frustration. Her name in Pronto's mouth felt gross, especially because he was just using it to get people mad at Buster.

Pronto continued. "Human happiness is temporary, and they never try to fix it themselves. They always try to get someone or something else to do it, and these children, Tonio and Mia, are no different. Instead of pulling themselves up and dealing with their own problems, they're begging at all sorts of tables: first other humans', like therapists and friends, and then, when that doesn't work, they turn to us. You fell for it, Buster. You and Mozart and Jpeg and Leila. Mozart's just a puppy, of course, so maybe he can be relocated, but for the rest of you, The Farm seems the only correct option."

"One case at a time, Pronto." The judge's pose was serious. "We're here to talk about Buster."

"I *am* talking about Buster, Your Honor," Pronto insisted. He stepped back into his bumper car and hit his paw against the dashboard. "The Court didn't punish him severely enough last time, and now there are *three other* dogs turned Bad by his influence."

A dog's bark rose from the crowd, breaking the silence. "OKAY, BUT WHO'S SLOAN?"

Pronto's head shot around to glare into the crowd. "That doesn't matter."

Lasagna's tail wagged. "Actually, Speaker, I believe it does. Your Honor, he's trying to hide the details from us, because he knows they matter."

"WAS SHE, LIKE, A SPY? OR SOME KIND OF ROCK STAR?"

"Sadie," Pronto chided, "you're not supposed to yell in court."

"I'M NOT YELLING. I'M ASKING A QUESTION!"

"Thank you for your input, Speaker." The judge nodded at Pronto but made no expression of her opinion. "Buster, you may continue."

A deep breath. A nod. "Well, Your Honor, Tonio had made a friend. I wish I could say that fixed it all, but . . ." Buster closed his eyes and tried to push back the hurt that came from thinking through these memories. "I messed up."

Buster's Testimony

Tonio came home exhausted. He returned his box of cards to its precarious position at the top of the stack and fell into his desk chair with a heavy *thwump*.

I thought he'd be happy. He'd spent the whole day with someone who might be a friend! But he didn't seem excited. He just looked totally worn out. Not the good kind of tired, like when you just want to spin around in three circles and lie down anywhere, but the kind where I was pretty sure he was thinking about something too hard.

Oh, right, I thought. *He hasn't even had time to think about what his mom said about moving yet. Today was a long day.*

After about half an hour of drawing, Tonio got up and walked back downstairs to turn off the movie his parents had fallen asleep watching. A nudge got them to stumble over to their bedroom, and on the way, Mrs. Pulaski pointed at the fridge. A magnet held a folded piece of paper and a sticky note in her handwriting that said *Tonio—Devin Wilkins (I think?) came by while you were gone. Left this for you.*

That set his heart pounding immediately. The folded paper dangled from his fingertips like a tissue someone else had sneezed in. Back in his room, he carefully unfolded it on his desk. I couldn't see what was on it from my four-legged spot on the carpet, but whatever it was definitely didn't improve his mood. He threw it away, then threw himself onto the bed. I hopped up to curl against his side.

His eyes drilled a hole in the wall, and I imagined him repeating that memory of yearbook signing over and over in his mind. After several minutes of staring, he rolled over to look at me, face clenched in focus. "I was fine, at school, until him," he said.

Talking was a challenge. He was trying, hard, to do what Dr. Jake had said to do—talk to me. Use me as a sounding board. I locked my eyes on him and tried to look encouraging. He continued. "I think it was okay because nothing ever changed. All my classes had pretty much the same kids. I knew the teachers because my parents know everybody." He rubbed at his eyes.

"And then Devon showed up last summer, and Sloan left over Christmas, and it was like . . ." He held his hands out in front of him, trying to form a picture in his mind. "Like opening a book I'd read a million times, but starting it and finding out everything was different."

I wished Tonio would talk like this to Dr. Jake. I was sure the doctor would have something interesting to say about it, or some way to help Tonio understand how he was feeling. All I could do was sit and listen.

"Miles and Parker weren't even mean before! They were kind of loud, but they weren't bullies until Devon moved in. And it was like that one thing changed *everything*. I didn't know how to talk to anybody anymore. What if they paid attention and noticed that I'm not . . . that I'm . . ." He shook his head and swallowed the thought.

"I know it's not Devon's fault. But I can't talk to him unless I tell him the truth. And if I tell him the truth now, he'll see that nobody tried to help him, especially not me!" His voice cracked, and he rubbed at his eyes again. "He'll have to go back to school knowing that he can't trust anybody. He'll hate me."

If that were me, I thought, *I'd want to know.* Tonio's anxiety was trying to convince him that he could read Devon's mind, that the bullies' actions were his responsibility, AND that he could tell the future.

Tonio sighed. "Maybe we *should* just move." I rested my muzzle on his side and huffed, because I couldn't do anything else. He reached up to scratch me around my collar, but I barely even leaned into it. "Thanks for listening, Buster."

But I'm not helping! I wanted to yell. I kept thinking about this while Tonio got ready for bed, then fell asleep. Once I heard his breathing settle into a sleeping rhythm, I gently rolled off the bed and made my way over to the trash can.

Devon's paper was a flyer for a Beamblade tournament at Roll the Ice. *Standard Rules, Ancient Cards Allowed, Three-Hundred-Dollar Prize!* it yelled with garish 3D text. *LEGENDARY Battles! AWESOME Refreshments! EPIC Inclusive Environment for All Ages and Skill Levels! GOTTA BLADE!*

At the bottom was a sticky note covered in cute, bubbly handwriting:

Hiya, Tonio! I hope you're feeling better—Skyler said you got sick or something because of the ice cream. I hope it's the ice cream, and not looking at my face! (ha, ha.) (but if it is looking at my face you'd let me know, right?) Anyway ~~I wanted~~ *since you left and didn't get to play* ~~Beabl~~ *Beamblade with us, I thought you might want to come to this instead. Maybe if you feel better? I hope you can read this, I wrote too big at the beginning and now I'm not even sure I can read these tiny letters. –DW →*

There was an arrow pointing to the back. I unstuck the note with my nose to flip it over onto its back. *That stands for Devon Wilcrest!!!!*

I knew if Tonio was going to go back to school, he needed to talk to Devon and tell him the truth. I could help *both* of them if I could figure out how to get Tonio to the tournament.

All of a sudden, I had a plan. I triple-checked that Tonio was sleeping, then nudged the power button on his computer with my nose. I hopped up onto his desk chair, but the force of my jump wheeled it away from the desk, so I had to reach my front paws down on the floor and walk my way back over. Another bump with my nose turned on the monitor.

Human computers are so hard to use. I slapped at the mouse clumsily until I opened up the browser, then input the secret codes we all know by heart, no need to repeat them, to log into the Bark Web. A few clicks navigated me to the DogHouse chat rooms, and I checked my list of friends. Since it was still early in the night, I figured most dogs wouldn't be online—but if there was one person I could count on to always be logged on . . .

WELCOME TO THE DOGHOUSE V.3.9:
WHO LET THE DOGS IN? WE DID.
CREATING PRIVATE ROOM . . .
INVITING SELECTED FRIENDS . . .
NICE! CONNECTED. USERS IN ROOM:
FireBuster, dotpng

dotpng: what
dotpng: hello

FireBuster: hwlko jhp[eg, 8i aMUsinbg a jhum,an cxompOuterr.

dotpng: lol omd

dotpng: are you using a smartphone

dotpng: is the keyboard six inches wide

dotpng: how are you so bad at this

FireBuster: wwhgat dsoes ommds m eewan/

dotpng: it means oh my dog

dotpng: i made it up

dotpng: here i have a program that will help correct your typing

dotpng: you'll get a popup in a second just click yes

FireBuster: wk

FireBuster: sdkfjldlsfan

dotpng: haha just kidding it makes it worse

FireBuster: bu

dotpng: and it presses enter at random times, hahahahaha

FireBuster:

dotpng: here this one actually will help

dotpng: omd i can't believe you clicked it again

FireBuster: 2lvbv

dotpng: those clowns are pretty scary though huh lmto

dotpng: that stands for laughing my tail off. i made that one up too

dotpng: sorry i scared you with a clown video

dotpng: i know i'm the wolf who cried boy rn but you can really click the next one

FireBuster: .,.,.,.

dotpng: haha im sirius

dotpng: get it? the dog star

dotpng: i guess you wouldn't know but dog puns are cool again

dotpng: basically just use one paw to hit the keyboard and the other to hit the space bar to confirm which letter you meant

dotpng: it's kinda slow but you'll get used to it

FireBuster: Thank you, Jpeg. This helps a lot. I am messaging you because I want to tell you about something.

dotpng: ok

dotpng: one second i have to hack into the united states government

dotpng: im in

dotpng: ok what's up

FireBuster: There is a Beamblade tournament at Roll the Ice in a week.

dotpng: the card game?

dotpng: what about it

dotpng: also I don't think you appreciated my joke enough

dotpng: i said i hacked into a whole government

dotpng: while you were typing one single sentence at the speed of three grandpas all trying to type at the same time

dotpng: (which makes them slower)

dotpng: i really did hack into the government though

FireBuster: It has a 300 dollar prize, and I know y'all have been looking for ways to help Mia make money.

dotpng: no wag

dotpng: (as in way)

dotpng: (ok that one was weak)

dotpng: i don't think mia knows how to play BB though

dotpng: oh wait i get it

dotpng: your boy does. the one who always looks like he's trying to chew with his eyebrows

FireBuster: I think it could be good for both of them. And it's easier than trying to find a secret way to give her your money.

dotpng: you're right about that

dotpng: she doesn't have a bank account, and ive only really got bitecoin anyway

dotpng: ok i found the flyer on their website

dotpng: ill print it out and try to put it
somewhere, but no guarantees

dotpng: she kinda does what she wants

FireBuster: The scary clown video just popped
up again! It's not funny!

dotpng: hahahahahahahaha yeah dude you
should stop clicking strangers' links

FireBuster: You're not a stranger!!!!!

"Buster?" I was surprised by a soft voice from behind me. *Oh no! Tonio!* I had to think fast.

"Wuh—uh, wuh—" he sputtered.

Even being *around* a moment like this was bad news for me. I'd already been to Dog Court once already. If Tonio realized what he was seeing, I'd be . . .

Well, I'd be here. Telling this story. But I didn't get caught this time.

As soon as I realized what was happening I started acting wild, barking and jumping. I grabbed the keyboard with my mouth and tugged it to the floor with a growl. "RRR!" I roared. "RRRRRR, I'm just a DUMB DOG who HATES COMPUTERS!"

"Hey, uh, down! Down, dog!" Tonio wasn't used to giving real commands. He lifted both hands awkwardly and twisted his wrists while taking slow steps toward me. "Don't break the computer, please!"

"What IS THIS THING?!" I ran around to the power cord and pulled it away from the wall, hopefully in a way that looked like an accident, to wipe everything from the screen. "WHATEVER IT IS, I HATE IT!"

"Buster, no. Down! *Bad dog!*" That was what I was waiting to hear. Tonio thought I was just a bad dog, doing something random that an animal does. He plugged the computer back in and picked the flyer off the floor. He looked at me with a wary expression, clearly concerned with how this *particular paper* ended up outside the trash can and uncrumpled.

"What are you doing?" he asked. I couldn't meet his eyes, so I pretended to suddenly be very interested in sniffing his shoes. "Hello?"

He got back in bed and stared at me. I curled up by the window and pretended to have one of those running dreams, but my heart was pounding until he finally fell asleep.

— 10 —

"RING, RING!" Mia threw open the bedroom door before either of us was awake the next morning.

"The front door was unlocked," she explained when our eyes were open.

Tonio blinked at her, groggy. "Yeah?"

"Mhm." A quick pat on my sleepy head. "Hey, Buster." I yawned gratefully. She held out a copy of the tournament flyer while Tonio sat up, clutching his blanket up to his throat like a princess in a movie. "Have you seen this?"

"Devon gave you one, too?"

"What? No. It was sitting on top of the food I give the dogs. Three hundred dollars! Just for playing a game!"

"*Winning* a game," Tonio corrected.

Mia waved her hands around dismissively. "I saw the word Beamblade in your journal a lot." She grabbed a shirt from Tonio's closet and threw it for him to catch.

"How much of my sketchbook did you—"

"You have to teach me!" She opened one of his drawers—much to Tonio's dismay—and rummaged through it. "Do you only own cargo shorts?"

I watched horror crawl across his face. "Are cargo shorts . . . *bad*?"

"This is Bellville. How many people are actually going to compete, like four?" She threw one of his identical pairs of shorts onto the bed. "If we both enter, that's twice the chance of winning."

Tonio tossed the blanket off and found a bandanna to push his morning hair back. "The rules are all on the internet."

"I guess, but I can't practice on the internet. And I want to *win* the tournament, like you said. So I need more than just to know the rules." Mia sat on his windowsill and looked out over Bellville Square. "Plus, I looked it up, and Beamblade cards *cost* money, which is ridiculous. I thought you'd probably have some."

Yes! I thought. *They'll practice together and become better friends. And then he won't have to be scared of talking to Devon. Everything's working out exactly like I planned!*

"I don't have any cards," Tonio confessed. Her face fell, and his eyes widened. He didn't want to disappoint her. "But my dad does, I think. In storage."

"That's perfect! Where is he? Let's go ask him."

Tonio's eyes worked on finding the exact corners of his room. "He's busy, at work, so I don't really want to bother him . . ."

Finally, Mia noticed how uncomfortable he was

acting. "What's your deal?" she asked. "I thought you liked Beamblade."

"I do." His hands clenched the fabric on the inside of his (huge) pockets. "But I can't do the tournament."

"Why not?"

"My anxiety."

"Still?"

Tonio was so surprised at her response that he half laughed.

"Uh, yeah. I guess, still." He could tell she wanted more, so he looked for a clearer explanation. "I just can't. Devon will be there, and I don't want to . . . you know."

Mia nodded seriously. "You don't want to give him another Mountain Dew bath."

Tonio gasped. "I co—I didn—I do *not* drink Mountain Dew!"

"Okay." Mia walked through the open doorway and started down the stairs while she continued. Tonio had no real choice but to follow her, and I stuck to his heels. "I get that. Totally. So you don't have to do the tournament! I'll actually *play*. You'll supply the cards and teach me. I won't split it fifty-fifty with you anymore, of course, but I'm sure we can work something out."

Tonio paused at their front door—her intent was obviously to go straight down to the grocery and ask Mr. Pulaski, but Tonio wasn't sure.

"Come on!" Mia put on a pair of sunglasses and tucked her hands into the pockets of her jean shorts. "There's gotta be something you need money for, right? Something hopefully a lot less expensive than three hundred dollars?"

He does, I thought, and I watched him realize it, too.

"There's this card—"

"Perfect!" She grinned. "Let's go find your dad."

"Welcome, traveler, to the groceries of tomorrow!"

A short fiberglass man in a cartoonish space suit held a ray gun above his head but wasn't looking where he was pointing it. *Dangerous.* I could tell his smile used to be as bright white as his spandex, but a thin layer of grime had settled over it in the—I gave a long sniff— more than ten years it had been there.

A few feet away from the welcoming spaceman was a silver UFO with a green plastic "tractor beam" dangling fresh peaches in a way that made them look like they were being lifted from the basket. *OUT OF THIS WORLD PRICES*, a sparkling sign proclaimed.

The building was unusually dark for a grocery store. Tonio's dad had stuck to the sci-fi theme so tightly that most of the lighting was LED strips and black lights. An electric globe hung from the ceiling, and the oceans beamed a soft white glow around the cat food and laundry detergent.

Mr. Pulaski wasn't working the registers, but he wasn't difficult to find. He was more than happy to unlock the storeroom for us to get his old cards.

"Your cards are all called ancient cards now," Mia told him.

Mr. Pulaski made a face like he'd been punched in the stomach. "They're already *ancient*?"

Mia pulled down a box that he pointed at. "Luckily, this tournament allows them. Even the *extremely* old ones like these."

Tonio patted his dad on the back and tried to soothe his distress. "You're not that old, Dad. They just use that word because it sounds cool."

While they looked through the storeroom to find all the cards they could from Mr. Pulaski's college years, I had my mind on other things: a plan to prove to Tonio, once and for all, that I was just a normal dog.

So far I had made two big mistakes. One: I'd given myself away a little too much when we were in training. Two: I'd let Tonio see me on the computer. The first one I had to do, but the second was a real problem. I had made a mistake, and I did *not* want to go back to Dog Court. No offense.

Tonio was a smart kid, and if he connected the dots, I'd be in trouble. To keep everything under control, I needed to break out the Big Three: mail, toilet, and chocolate. As you probably know, the Big Three are the easiest and most reliable way to prove to a human that there's nothing to be worried about from us dogs. Just in case you didn't learn it in puppy school, I'll explain.

One: barking at the mail carrier. There's no reason to bark at any mail worker once you know they're perfectly nice people just doing their jobs, so it stands to reason that any dog barking at the mailman must not understand things like *jobs* or *nice* or *mail*. They must just be a dog, and not someone who won a prestigious award from the Dog community for their book of original poetry.

Two: drinking from the toilet. An act so utterly disgusting, so completely demeaning, that someone would only do this if they were absolutely desperate or didn't understand what a toilet was. That's another strong point toward "I'm a dog," and a strong point away from "I have the equivalent of a human master's degree in civil engineering."

Three: eating chocolate. This one's risky, but basically foolproof—if a human catches you eating this pure poison, not only will they think you have fewer than zero brain cells to rub together, they will also be so nervous about the possibility of throw-up on their rug or expensive trips to the vet that they'll forget whatever else they're worried about, like whether or not you've been doing research on radioactive isotopes in a secret lab under their backyard.

It seemed like I'd have a few days where Tonio and Mia would spend all their time practicing Beamblade. We wouldn't be leaving the house much.

It was time to get into some trouble.

— 11 —

First on my list was mail. I'd never met the person who delivered mail to the Pulaskis' house before, but to work myself up to a good bark, I imagined a monster: fifteen feet tall with bright red eyes from all the caffeine they had to drink to get up so early; huge, muscular arms and giant hands to throw heavy boxes from the road to the door; a bag full of paper cuts and a truck full of secrets. Even imagining them was making the fur on my neck stand on end.

I'm gonna beat this monster, I thought when I heard someone approaching the door. *I'm gonna bark so loud they SCREAM. Or at least go away . . . FOR A WHILE!*

Tonio frowned at me as the doorbell rang. "What's wrong with you, Buster? Your hair's all weird." I didn't answer because I had to stay in the zone. *This package is going BACK TO SENDER!*

"Uh, I'm going to open the door now, okay?" *I'm gonna scare them so bad they become an emailman! Snail mail? More like WAIL MAIL, from all the screaming they're gonna do!!!*

Tonio opened the door, revealing a smiling woman

standing next to a probably three-year-old boy, both in post office uniforms. "Ring, ring," the little boy mumbled bashfully. "I'm deli—devi—"

"Delivering," the mailwoman suggested.

"De*liderving* the mail today with my mom, because I want to be the best mailman ever when I grow up. Here is all of your letters!" He held a few pieces of junk mail out carefully, like they were precious and delicate.

This was the monster? I was supposed to bark at *this*? The boy was smaller than I was, and his mom was obviously very busy. Yelling at them could hurt his feelings and ruin their whole day! What if I scared this kid so bad he gave up on his dream of being the best mailman ever??

It didn't matter. This was for Tonio. I couldn't take care of him if I was stuck on The Farm, and so he had to believe I was an animal. A Good Dog wouldn't know the difference between a monster mailman and an *extremely cute, so sweet, aww, look, he said thank you and shook Tonio's hand, and he gave me a treat, what a good boy, goodbye! Have a great day! You're ALREADY the best mailman ev—*

They were in their truck and driving away before I realized the door was shut and I'd missed my chance. Tonio scratched me behind the ears and headed back upstairs to draw while I laid down, pitifully, in front of the door.

So much for step one, I thought. But all was not lost! I still had two more chances.

"Blademasters—that's us," Tonio read from a starter guide Mr. Pulaski had given them, "lead their Heroes to battle on the Aethernet. Using a combination of hero, tech, and spell cards, each Blademaster seeks to drain all the other players' Spirit Batteries."

Mia rolled her eyes. "The lore of this game is all over the place. Plasmogast the Devourer's card says he eats Spirit Batteries to survive, and so he's a bad guy." She spun around in Tonio's desk chair. "Does that mean every Blademaster is a bad guy?"

Tonio shook his head. "Plasmogast eats the *whole* battery. Blademasters just take the energy, and they can be recharged later."

"Of course. Obviously." She opened one of the deck boxes and dumped cards out on the desk in a big pile. "When do I get to make my deck?"

"Well, first you have to know what kind of deck you want to make."

"Whichever one is the strongest!"

"It doesn't really work like that." But I saw Tonio smile and make a note in his sketchbook—*probably fire element deck?* He was happy for the chance to really help someone.

Mia groaned and gestured for him to keep reading the guide.

Next up, I had to drink from the toilet. Obviously, water from a toilet isn't exactly healthy, but it's mostly survivable. The hard part of this one was definitely to get *caught* drinking—Tonio's bathroom was down the hall from his room, closer to his parents' room, and when he was working at his drawing table, he sometimes wouldn't move until he *had* to go.

Worse, he kept my water bowl in the kitchen very full, all the time. I could lap up just a little water and he was there, immediately, pouring more back in to keep it filled to the brim with that fresh, crisp life juice. Tonio was a good owner, and so I didn't have a good excuse to drink out of the toilet unless I drank all that water first. I was trying to prove I was a dog, not get into real trouble—I couldn't just spill it all over the floor for no reason!

While Tonio was distracted, I headed downstairs to work on drinking the water. I figured I'd come up with a plan to get Tonio's attention after at least that step was done. Mrs. Pulaski was downstairs on the phone, and Tonio mostly had been avoiding her since their conversation in the truck, so I knew he wouldn't come down and refill my water bowl anytime soon.

"Yes, thank you. It says here you've got a counselor who specializes in helping with school-related anxiety." Mrs. Pulaski clicked around on her laptop. "I was wondering if you could tell me a little more about what that looks like."

She's really serious about Tonio switching schools, I thought.

The first few seconds of lapping up water were easy. I love water. *I could drink water all day*, I thought, until a few seconds later, when I really felt like I had had enough water for right now, and should come back later to drink the rest of the water.

No! I resolved. *Why would a dumb dog drink toilet water when perfectly good bowl water was available? I have to appear desperate.*

"So you have places he can go if he gets upset? And you'll try to get him over his fear *completely*?"

Halfway through the bowl and I felt like I was drowning. *Lap lap lap lap lap lap lap.* The sound annoyed me, and I was the one making it! Three-quarters through and I had to take a break, dry off my tongue. Crying a little wouldn't help get the water out, right? Probably not.

"No, I know that—I'm not saying I need a guarantee. But he's been dealing with this for a while, and I want to find someone who can help him move past this."

I powered through the last quarter of the bowl and sniffed at it while my stomach gurgled. *Ugh.* But it was empty, and now I just needed to take a few more gulps from the toilet bowl. No problem. My trip back upstairs was slow and sloshy, which gave me time to think of a plan.

In puppy school, they made it sound so *easy*, like humans were always standing around toilets waiting to catch us grabbing a sip, but I was beginning to realize the Big Three were easier barked than done. The more I considered, the more I thought the best option was to wait in the bathroom until Tonio had to go, and drink when I heard him coming down the hallway. He and Mia were debating over exactly what cards to put in their decks and were very much in the zone, which meant it might be a while. But I could handle it.

The tile of the bathroom was cold under my paws. I sniffed at the toilet—such a complicated series of scents, so much information about Tonio's family. Mr. Pulaski was getting over a cold, Mrs. Pulaski had eaten a *lot* of Cheese Bobs, and Tonio was having stomach trouble. Tonio had a lot of stomach trouble, which is apparently common when you have anxiety.

No sign of Tonio after ten minutes, and I was starting to feel all that water I'd drunk. I'd have to go to the bathroom soon, but it could wait. If Tonio took me out, we'd go downstairs, and he'd see my water bowl and refill it. I wasn't leaving until I drank from the toilet!

Fifteen minutes and nothing. I focused and in the other room could hear the quiet flipping of cards. *Come on, Tonio!*

Twenty minutes and I was getting desperate. I really needed to use the restroom, but this plan was important. The Big Three were foolproof, right? This would work, if Tonio would just come out of his room.

Flip, flip. "What about this one?"

Shuffle shuffle. "If you take out one of your other spells, yeah."

I had overestimated my ability to hold it and now I was desperate to pee, in the house, and there was *no* way I was going to have an accident on the floor. How embarrassing!! There was only one choice: I had to use the toilet. Tonio wasn't coming, anyway, and this way I'd be able to keep waiting until he did.

One quick jump onto the toilet. I balanced all four paws on the seat and did my business.

"What's that noise? Buster?" Tonio had heard! *Oh no.* I tried to finish up fast and then, panicking, hit the flush lever on the toilet. *He can't see what I've done!*

Tonio pushed the door open wide as the toilet was finishing its flush cycle, and I was hopping off and trying to look innocent.

"Did you just flush the toilet?"

I couldn't meet his gaze—I was too embarrassed. After a second with no answer, he patted his leg for me to follow, and we went back to his room.

Two failures. One more chance to prove I was just a boring dog.

"So cards are based on the five Beamblade Elements: Fire, Water, Air, Earth, and Gravity. They each have a different color that's on all the cards." Tonio continued to insist that they should go over all the rules *before* they started to play, and Mia was protesting this method by getting bored and asking unrelated questions.

"Why don't you ever show these in art class?" She held up a handful of Tonio's card drawings. "I had no idea you were so good."

"Those are just copies." Tonio flipped over a few of his dad's cards to illustrate the different elements. "And I don't want to look like I'm too far ahead."

That got a big grin from Mia, who pointed a card at him in accusation. "You *know* you're better than the rest of the class!"

"That's not true," Tonio sputtered, embarrassed. "I can only draw what I see. So, each of the elements has a different play style, and you can also do a combination of—"

"Why is that bad?"

"Doing combo decks? I guess it's not, if you know how to balance—"

"You know what I meant!" she snapped. Tonio gulped.

"The people who draw Beamblade cards draw all kinds of things that aren't real. I'm not really creative like they are." He shrugged. "Squirrels are boring."

"If you say so." Mia pointed at the Beateor spell, which the card described as a "musical missile." "I want to do those cards. The red ones."

Tonio smiled to himself, his guess confirmed. "Those

117

use Scorched Manabytes, and they're all about strong attacks."

Mia immediately began searching through Mr. Pulaski's boxes for all the red cards. "What about you?"

Tonio's hand hovered over the four remaining cards. "I don't know," he finally admitted. "I like all of them."

"Well, what do the other ones do?"

"Green uses Buried Manabytes, and it's all about growing over time, and defending. Blue is, like, the spooky one. Its Manabytes are called Drowned, and there are zombies and ghosts and stuff, ways to get cards back that you've already used. Yellow is Windswept, and they're all about a ton of tiny, fast creatures and spells. Grays are called Suspended Manabytes, and . . ." He picked up Principia, the Galaxy's Reflection. "I think I'll do these."

"Great!" Mia spread out all the red cards she'd found, in a big fan on the carpet. "Let's find the good ones."

❧ ❧ ❧

Last on the list was eating chocolate. I couldn't *actually* eat it, but I had to look like I was *going* to eat it, just in time for Tonio to swoop in, save me, and convince himself I was nothing more than an adorable four-legged best friend.

I knew there had to be chocolate in the house *somewhere*—Mrs. Pulaski loved all kinds of snack food, so I knew I could find a bar of chocolate. Or at least some baking chocolate. Or hot chocolate powder. Or *something*!!

I sniffed around at the doorway to the kitchen (with my farsmelled nose it was easier to search the kitchen from there than digging around in the cupboards) and realized, to my dismay, that the only chocolate smell in the entire kitchen was leftover Halloween candy from the year before, still stuck in a jack-o'-lantern at the back of the highest shelf in the pantry. It would be tough to get to, and the candy would be disgusting by now.

I don't have to eat it, I reminded myself. *Just pretend like I'm going to.* I balanced on my hind legs and grabbed the pantry door's handle with my teeth—it folded open easily with a tug. My nose was overwhelmed with all the smells—Cheese Bobs and Pretzel Bobs, cans of beans and tuna and Noodle Hoops, that half-eaten box of Bug Bites, all kinds of breakfast cereal, and more different flavors of potato chip than I even knew existed. (Flaming hot lobster? Really?) My tongue fell out of my mouth on its own, dripping with hunger. *What am I looking for again? Oh, right. Chocolate.*

Tonio's mom was back in her office and Tonio was upstairs with Mia, so they didn't hear me push a chair from the dining room table to the pantry's open door. I leaned back onto my hind legs and flopped my chin down on the highest shelf. All the forgotten snacks made their way up here—veggie straws that must have been too healthy for Mrs. Pulaski, a whole box of orange StarChews (the worst kind, obviously), and my prize, abandoned in a plastic pumpkin.

Even on my tippy-paws, I couldn't quite reach the jack-o'-lantern all the way in the back. I braced both front paws on the shelf and pushed up with my chin, wriggling until I got my back paws on one of the lower shelves, a little higher than the chair. I pushed my neck forward and snagged the pumpkin's handle in my teeth.

A few quick tugs pulled the pumpkin to the edge of the shelf, but I wasn't going to be able to hold on to it and climb down. I chewed gently on the plastic handle, thinking, when I heard footsteps running down the stairs—Tonio! I had to put the chair back!

"Buster? Are you down there?"

One more jerk of my neck and the pumpkin went tumbling to the ground, sending StarChews, Crunchsquish pops, Sour Power Blasts, and fun-sized Beantangle chocolate twists sliding across the floor. I threw myself down after them and put both front paws on the chair, pushing hard with my back legs to get it to the table.

Tonio's footsteps turned the corner right when I made it—but I'd turned the chair around on the way there, and now the back was up against the table. *It'll have to do.* I flipped around and looked for a Beantangle chocolate twist—*there!*—scooped it into my mouth and held it gently between my teeth so the logo was clearly visible.

Tonio looked around at the mess of candy all over the floor, the backward chair, and me. I posed with my chin up, ears folded, tail between my legs to look perfectly embarrassed. *You caught me!* I tried to say with my eyes. *Now save me from my very dangerous decision to eat poison!*

But nothing happened. Tonio just put his hands on his hips and tilted his head. "Are you going to eat that, or what?"

This was not what I'd expected.

"Go ahead. Eat it!"

I don't know what Tonio was thinking, but he had me trapped. If I really tried to eat it, he'd probably stop me, so I needed to commit and bite down on the wrapper. But what if he *didn't* stop me? Even a little bit of chocolate could mean a really bad time for me. I wasn't sure I could risk it.

The front door clicked unlocked, and Mr. Pulaski carried a handful of boxes inside. He pushed past Tonio into the kitchen, set the boxes down on the counter, then looked down at me.

"I brought you some more—oh, geez! Tonio, he can't eat chocolate." Mr. Pulaski leaned down, grabbed the wrapper from my mouth, then started throwing candies back in the jack-o'-lantern.

Tonio stared me down from under his curls. "I know."

"How did he even get to this? You need to keep a

better eye on him, or he'll get hurt." His dad was on a roll now, and he smelled sweaty and tired. "And you need to take him outside more so he doesn't go looking for new ways to entertain himself. Take him for a walk right now and play with him tomorrow, okay?"

"Okay." Tonio was still staring directly at me. "And you're right. I think I do need to watch him better." He grabbed my leash from a peg by the door and clipped it to my collar. "Come, Buster!" Mia joined us downstairs, and we headed out for a walk around the square together, my tail between my legs. I tried to sniff poles for too long and tangle up his legs with the leash enough times to seem annoying and normal, but I had a sinking feeling he wasn't fooled at all.

After our walk, the gaming continued. Tonio made it very clear I wasn't to leave his sight, so I watched as he and Mia played.

Mia's hand slammed down on the cardboard play-mat. Tonio had drawn little rectangles for where all the different cards should go at different times, and she'd placed a new one in the Battle Server spot. "I use all my Manabytes for MIGHTAS, THE GOLDEN BARBARIAN!" She boomed his name proudly. "He's got cool bracelets."

"You don't have enough Manabytes," Tonio pointed out. "You need three."

"Auughhhhhguughhhh. Okay, let me think." Mia put

Mightas back in her hand. It lasted long enough that Tonio felt like he needed to fill the silence.

"Do you ever feel like dogs might be . . . like, smart?"

Oh no.

Mia shrugged. "Well, yeah. Dogs are super smart."

"I mean *human* smart."

"Are you trying to distract me? It won't work! I'm going to—" She flipped through the cards in her hand. "I'm about to totally win." She raised a card in the air triumphantly, then huffed and put it back in her hand. "I can't do anything else. Your turn."

I'd started out with two mistakes, and now I'd made five. Tonio kept glancing over at me suspiciously while they played. I'd really messed up this time.

— 12 —

"TOOOOOOOO-NII-OOOOOO! Come DOOOOOOOWN, PLEEEEEEEASE!"

We walked down to the grocery and found Mr. Pulaski had loaded up two wagons with over a dozen plastic bags, tied and labeled with names. I turned my head away to sniff—they were full of produce, laundry detergent, canned food, even cat food.

"We're trying something new: delivery! Nobody else takes groceries right to your door . . . and especially not by *rocket ship*!" Mr. Pulaski posed proudly next to his wagons, which I realized he'd painted silver. He'd attached swim flipper "wings" to the sides, antennas made of foam and wire on the front, and plastic cups to build jet engines on the back. That was commitment!

"That's a great idea, Dad." Tonio poked at an antenna, and it wobbled. "I didn't know you could make stuff like this."

"Are you kidding? I made a lot of the decorations in the store! Your mom and I used to go to tons of conventions; we'd build costumes and everything. You knew that!" He clapped Tonio on the shoulder.

"No, I didn't." Tonio frowned. "Why did you stop going?"

"Just got busy, I guess." Mr. Pulaski lifted his cap off his head to scratch at his hair, then rested it back down. "Anyway, more people signed up than I expected, so I need your help delivering these today. They're all in walking distance, and I even drew up our *galactic trade route*! Figured it'd be good exercise for Buster, too."

Tonio's eyes widened. "Uh, I don't know. It's gonna get kind of dark soon, right? Are you sure it's safe?"

"It's only four thirty!"

"And those look kind of heavy. I don't want to slow you down."

"I can't pull two on my own. You'll be a huge help!"

"I just don't know if you really want me around while you're trying a new—"

"Antonio, come on. Don't be lazy. You're coming."

Tonio's head tilted down so his hair dangled over his eyes. "Yeah, sorry. No problem."

His dad didn't get it. Tonio wasn't being lazy—he was nervous about messing things up for his dad.

But he didn't say anything else. We went along with the plan and soon were off into Bellville Square, following the route on Mr. Pulaski's clipboard.

"Where to first, Captain?" Tonio tried to make up for his hesitation by playing along, and Mr. Pulaski beamed.

"Mrs. Morris requires two bags of dog food, pasta noodles, meat sauce, and one *secret item* delivered directly to Planet Garden Gnome." Tonio laughed, and when we got to Mrs. Morris's house, I saw why—her whole yard was filled with gnomes in a variety of sizes, from the little ones who hid in her flower beds to a giant one by her door that was almost as tall as Tonio if you included his hat.

An old woman with crinkly skin and a giant wig answered the door and smiled at us. "Well, look at you boys. Ring, ring! Having a good evening?"

Mr. Pulaski shook his head. "Evening? It's not even five o'clock! What has gotten into everyone today?"

"Well, when you're my age . . ." Mrs. Morris winked and laughed. "And look at this cute little dog. He's yours?" Tonio nodded. She leaned down to pat me on the head. A corgi peeked out from around the doorframe and—oh, that must have been *you*, Lasagna. I didn't realize we'd met.

The old woman turned to go inside, then abruptly spun around and whispered to Mr. Pulaski, *"Did you get what I asked for?"*

"I did! Yep! It's all in there."

"Good." She smiled at Tonio again. "Good night!"

On our way back through the garden gnomes, Tonio had to ask. "What was in there?"

Mr. Pulaski shook his head somberly. "You don't want to know."

Most of the deliveries were like that—Mr. Pulaski

led us to places like Dr. Lozada's house, which was locally famous because a tree was growing inside it, right through her living room and out the roof. ("She never cut it down because it started growing after her grandfather passed away," Mr. Pulaski explained. "So it's special to her. A bunch of folks—your grandparents included—chipped in to help fix up the house so it wouldn't fall over, back when I was a kid.")

We stopped by the Coats' house, and all eight of their young kids (five were quintuplets!) ran out at once to barrage Tonio with questions and tug on my tail. We met the Farnell family—Mr. Farnell was one of Tonio's art teachers in elementary school. He asked if Tonio was still drawing, and said he was one of the best students he'd ever had—even though, I knew now, Tonio wasn't showing his teachers everything.

"Did you hear that?" Mr. Pulaski asked.

"He was just being nice," Tonio mumbled, but he was smiling.

Tonio started out nervous, but by the time we were on our eighth or ninth delivery, he'd relaxed. This was easy work, and nobody expected much from him except to pull the wagon. Plus, his dad seemed so happy—it was a good time for them.

Somewhere between Mr. Farnell and Cheryl Barger, the owner of Nice Slice Pizza, I noticed we were being followed. A medium-sized dog with a dark brown coat and beige splotches was trying to look casual as he kept pace with us across the street, and a tiny gray dog with a long body like a dachshund but a much fluffier coat was tailing us from about fifteen feet behind, never any closer or farther.

The officers, I realized. *Sergeant and Grizzle.* While Tonio and Mr. Pulaski laughed and talked, I twisted my ears and focused my attention away from them. Officer Sergeant was growling, just a little, under her breath. Quieter than a human would hear, but enough for my ears. It wasn't an aggressive growl—she was asking if it was safe to approach.

I huffed out a tiny cough-bark. *What's going on?*

Three small barks and a whine. *Can we ask you a few questions?*

I kept my tail up and my posture confident, but my stomach did a flip. Could they have heard, somehow, that Tonio was onto me? Were they here to take me away? I didn't have a choice: I huffed *okay*. The splotchy dog trotted across the street, and the fluffy one bounded extra hard to catch up to us.

"Oh, hello. Strays?" Tonio asked. Mr. Pulaski shook his head.

"No, they've got collars. And they're fine—lots of people let their dogs out around here, 'cause it's not a busy neighborhood."

"Is it okay if I let Buster say hello?" Tonio asked. "He's probably bored of just paying attention to me all day, and you're here." Mr. Pulaski considered, said sure, and Tonio leaned down to unclip my collar. I fell in step with the officers.

"Sorry for surprising you like this," Sergeant said. "We've been hearing some things lately that are making us a little nervous, and just want to check if you know anything."

Phew, I thought. *So this probably isn't about me.* I couldn't let my guard down completely, though, in case this was some kind of tactic to make me relax.

"Sure," I huffed. "How can I help?"

Officer Grizzle took over. His voice was very high and tiny, but the energy behind it made him sound a lot more serious than Officer Sergeant. "From what we understand, your human has been spending time with the human Mia Lin. Is that true?"

"Yeah, that's true."

The little dog bobbed his head affirmatively. "And from what we understand, she often has a puppy with her, correct? A tricolor collie who goes by Mozart Lin."

"Yeah, that's also true." I tilted my head and twisted my tail into a question. "What's this about?"

"*We're* asking the questions here, citizen!" Grizzle snapped. Sergeant lowered her nose apologetically.

"Have you seen Mozart engaging in any Bad Dog behaviors, such as: performing tricks without being taught them, responding directly to human language as if he understands, or otherwise suggesting intelligence to his human or other humans?"

The officers were right to be investigating, but I still didn't want to get Mozart and Mia in trouble. He was so young!

"I don't think so." I said. "He's just acted like a puppy around me."

"TELL THE TRUTH!" Grizzle barked.

Tonio glanced back at us. "Are y'all okay?"

Sergeant bopped Grizzle on the nose. "Calm down. You'll blow our cover." We trotted along quietly until Tonio stopped paying attention. Sergeant spoke again: "Since you two are friends, if he—"

"We're not really *friends*," I argued, "and he doesn't listen to me!"

"Yeah, but you've been through it. You know how serious this is. Try to get that across to him, okay? So we don't have to." Sergeant stopped walking, and Grizzle stopped a few steps after that.

"What happens if I can't stop him?" I called back. Sergeant looked uncomfortable, but Grizzle yipped ominously.

"We'll protect Dogkind however we have to."

Tonio patted his leg and jingled my leash. "Come, Buster. We're going back on some busy streets."

The sun really was going down when they delivered their last bag of groceries, so Tonio was sort of right. Evening smells and sounds settled over Bellville, from the smoke of dinner grilling in backyards to the buzzing of the town's few streetlamps switching on around the neighborhood. Tonio was relaxing—the job was done, and a good distraction from his worries about Devon and Mia—but his father was acting strange.

Mr. Pulaski was clearing his throat more than normal, just tiny ones, like he was getting ready to speak but then didn't say anything. Twice I caught him open his mouth in a silent moment and shut it again. Finally, a few blocks from Bellville Square, he found the words.

"So your mom talked to you, I gather." The wagon's wheels whistled along the sidewalk. Tonio knew what he meant but didn't answer right away. "She said you didn't like the idea so much." Again, no answer. Tonio kicked a pebble on the ground. "Why not?"

"I don't know how *you* could even think about it. You love Bellville. It's our home."

"Our home, huh? It hasn't seemed lately like you like it so much. Always in your room, saying you don't want to go back to school. There is a lot to love about Bellville, sure, but maybe it's not the right place for you."

"That's not—" The words jumped out of Tonio's mouth immediately, but he caught himself and swallowed the rest of his sentence. "Yeah. Maybe."

"No, come on." Mr. Pulaski stopped walking, let the handle of the wagon drop. The spaceship's foam antennas vibrated with the impact. "Tell me what you're thinking, buddy. I can take it."

"It doesn't matter."

Mr. Pulaski scratched under the edge of his hat. "You know, to me, it does."

"Let's just go home, okay?" Tonio pulled his wagon back into motion.

Mr. Pulaski crossed his arms. "This spaceship isn't going anywhere until you tell me what you're thinking, young man! Buster, stay."

"He's trained to listen to me. He's not going to—" Tonio was wrong. He needed to talk to his dad. I sat down on the ground. Tonio wasn't very strong—he wouldn't be able to pull me if I didn't let him. "Buster, come."

I stayed.

Mr. Pulaski wheeled his hands around each other, a *keep going* motion. "I'll start your sentence over for you: 'That's not . . .'"

Tonio looked from his dad to me to the wagon. He sighed. "That's not what it is," he mumbled. "You guys always talk like I'm like this on purpose, but that's not true. I don't *want* to be in my room all the time. I don't *want* to be scared. But I can't help it. All I do is ruin things."

"Oh, Antonio." Mr. Pulaski stepped forward, and Tonio flinched backward, dropping the wagon handle and my leash. "That's not true."

"It is. You don't want to leave. Mom doesn't want to leave. You're only even talking about it because of me."

Mr. Pulaski took a few more steps this time, and Tonio didn't move away. He pulled his son into a hug and squeezed. "We want you to be happy. Anything that will help you is worth it to us. You don't have to worry."

Tonio hugged him back, but his face went blank. *Mr. Pulaski doesn't get it*, I thought. Of course Tonio was going to worry. He was always going to worry.

"Feel better?" Mr. Pulaski asked.

I whimpered, and Tonio picked up my leash. They both grabbed their wagon handles and started walking.

"Yeah," Tonio said. "Thanks, Dad."

But I'm pretty sure he felt worse.

— 13 —

Tonio laid down in bed as soon as we got home, but by the time I fell asleep, I still hadn't seen him close his eyes. The next morning, he was awake before everyone else in the house again, buzzing in the same way he had been last time, and cooking everybody breakfast.

I don't know what was going on in his head because he wasn't talking to me, but his body was acting like he was jogging—his heart was irregular, and he was sweating a lot (though that could have just been June in South Carolina). I tried to get his attention a few times, but he would just move me out of the way with his foot and go back to pushing eggs around in the pan.

I still didn't understand this part of anxiety. It wasn't a kind I was trained to deal with as a service dog, and it wasn't one I knew how to help Tonio with as a person. His body added a layer of fear over everything and wore him down, little by little. I knew this kind *could* turn into a panic attack, though, so I tried to stay extra on guard, all the way up until he was unclipping my leash and waving for me to go out into the dog park.

"Go on!" he said. "I'll be okay. Go play with some other

dogs." I realized with a sinking feeling in my stomach that this was the first thing he'd said to me all morning. He opened a box of cards he'd brought and started trying out different combinations for Mia's deck.

I told myself I could deal with it later if I had to. For now, I needed to take the time I had to find out what was going on with Mozart and Mia.

A quick listen to the sounds of the shelter didn't point me toward Mozart, but there was a huge commotion in the dirt field, so I headed over there to investigate. Dozens of dogs were pretending to be doing all sorts of activities while *really* watching a tug-of-war unfold in the center.

Two lines drawn in the mud showed how far the knot in the middle of the rope had to move before one team or the other won. A bunch of dogs I didn't recognize— a team of pets, I guess—stretched and gnashed their teeth on one end, while Leila and a small team of other shelter dogs huddled quietly and talked about strategy.

I found Jpeg at the front of the crowd, mud painted on her face to mirror the markings in Leila's fur. "YOU CAN DO IT, LEILA!" she barked.

"No computer today?" I asked, nudging up beside her. "That's unusual."

She shrugged, curly tail wagging pleasantly. "What can I say? I love the sport."

A retriever walked up to her and muttered, "I'll put

one bitecoin on the new kids. There's no way Leila can keep up this streak."

Jpeg yipped a laugh. "If you wanna lose money, be my guest!" She swept her paw along the ground, and I looked down to see a tablet, half-buried in the dirt, keeping track of bets. *Of course.*

"All right, teams. Mouths up!" A border collie named Charmander liked to referee sporting events around the shelter, and she was the undisputed best. "Three . . . two . . . one! PULL!"

Leila was twice as big as the next-closest dog, and apparently that meant her team had one fewer member—but that didn't seem to be a problem for them. The visiting pets strained against the shelter dogs, but their feet started sliding in the mud almost immediately. A few seconds later and the knot was hovering near the line on Leila's side of the mud—and with a huge tug that toppled even her own teammates over backward, she finished the match and made it look easy.

"Game!" Charmander called. "Home team wins!"

Jpeg cheered. "YES! THAT'S MY GIRL!" Leila winked at her, and Jpeg waved her over before turning to the retriever from before. "Just press your paw print here to confirm the transfer, *thanks so much.*" He patted his paw down on the tablet forcefully and wandered away with the rest of the crowd, tail tucked between his legs.

Leila came over to nuzzle up against Jpeg and bop me on the nose. "Hey there, Miracle Dog. Enjoy the show?"

"I think so. It was over so fast." I tilted my head in a question. "Are they always that short?"

"No way." Leila flexed, but you couldn't see any change under her big, curly fur. "I'm the best around here."

"Then why does anyone come?"

"I guess they think I gotta lose sometime."

Jpeg tilted her chin up proudly. "No chance. You're never going down!"

Leila laughed and pushed her away with a paw—it was supposed to be playful, but she was so strong even a gentle push sent Jpeg stumbling sideways. "She just likes that she can make the odds against me more extreme every time."

"*And* I like seeing you win." Jpeg smirked at me. "Uh-oh. Looks like Buster's got his serious face on. What's up, nerd?"

The opening was there, and I didn't bother pretending she was wrong. "I want to know what's going on with Mia. For real this time."

Leila tensed up, standing straight and towering over me. "I told you, we're handling it."

"Not very well!" I protested, then lowered my voice. "Dog Court officers came to talk to me about Mozart. Whatever y'all are doing, it could get me in trouble, too. And I helped out—I told you about the tournament."

I shifted onto my back paws in a begging position—embarrassing, but I wanted them to know I was serious. "I deserve to know. And if it could affect Tonio, I *need* to know."

They exchanged glances. "Okay," Leila finally said, "But let's go somewhere more private. Jpeg, you take him to our usual spot. I'll go find Mozart."

We walked together out to the far edges of the shelter property, right up near the fence. Jpeg flipped over a totally normal-looking rock to reveal a keypad, which she dialed a code into. A hatch in the ground slid aside, revealing a laptop underneath. *They really must be all over.* She popped it open and tapped away while we waited for Leila and Mozart, who was hopping around, angry.

"We *can't* tell him!" Mozart yipped in his little puppy voice. "How do we know he won't tell on us?"

"Good question." Leila looked me right in the eyes. "Did Dog Court put you up to this? Are you trying to get us in trouble?"

I bared my teeth. "Absolutely not. I just want to help."

"What do you think, Jpeg?"

She shrugged. "He's a nerd, but he's not dumb. And besides—" She flipped her laptop around and showed all of us the screen. One tap and it started playing a video.

Me, squinting and lit only by a screen. My paws tapping

138

at a keyboard. "Buster?" Tonio's voice. *My face shot to the side, and I froze.* "Wuh—uh, wuh—" *he babbled, and I jumped away from the computer screen.* "RRR!" *I growled, and you could see the edge of a keyboard flopping around in the dim light.* "RRRRRR, I'm just a DUMB DOG who HATES COMPUTERS!"

"Hey, uh, down! Down, dog!" *Tonio's nervous hands wiggling across the screen.* "Don't break the computer, please!"

"What IS THIS THI—" *and then the video cut out.* Jpeg turned the laptop back around.

"It's a good thing you clicked that last link I sent you. Gave me your webcam's direct feed." Jpeg shook her head and clicked her special keyboard quickly. "If he tells the officers, I can show them this. Caught red-pawed by a human *on the computer*, like some kind of amateur!"

My heart dropped down into my stomach. *I'll never click a link again in my life.* "Please don't show anyone that," I whispered. "I can't get in trouble again. Please."

"What do you think about that, pup?" Leila knelt down onto the ground to look Mozart in the eyes. "Can we tell him?"

He bobbed his little nose in thought. "Okay," he decided. "But if he ruins anything for Mia, we send it." He looked at me and held out his cute paw, too big for his tiny body. "Shake?"

I took a long breath, decided I had no other choice, and shook. "Good boy," he yipped seriously.

"Good boy," I repeated, to seal the deal.

Mozart looked up at Jpeg, who looked at Leila, who looked back at Mozart. Mozart shrugged and took the lead. "She's leaving. *We're* leaving."

"Leaving . . . where?"

"Leaving Bellville. We're going to Cold Dorito."

"Colorado," Leila corrected.

"That's what I said! Sloan lives in Collared Rat-o, and so we're going to go there, too."

I narrowed my eyes. "Like on vacation, or . . . ?"

"No." Mozart rolled his eyes around like I was being dense. "Like *forever*. Mia doesn't like it in Bellville anymore, because Sloan's not here, but Sloan *is* in Code Lyoko." He said it all with the simple energy of a puppy—this was the truth, and it was obvious. My tongue flopped out of my surprised mouth.

"She's *running away*? And you're *helping* her?" I know there were a lot of things I could have thought in that moment, but my first worry was about Tonio. He was just now finally making a friend, and because of me, it was someone who was already on their way out of town. He'd be devastated, it would give him even more reason to hide from school, and it would all be my fault. "Tonio and Mia *just* became friends, and now she's leaving?"

"He'll make other friends."

"So will she! How could you—" I should have found this out sooner. I shouldn't have told Jpeg about the tournament. They should have *told* me that—

No. I squeezed my eyes shut and tried not to fall down the same kind of spiral I'd watched Tonio go down. He didn't need me to freak out, too; he needed me to focus. And right now, I still needed more information.

"Are you okay?" Leila asked. I nodded.

"So this is why she's been saving money," I said. "For the trip." Now it was their turn to nod. I took another deep breath and tried to consider it from their perspective. They wanted to help Mia, right? I thought about what I always wished people would do for Tonio: ask questions. Dig deeper before they thought they knew the right thing to do. That's what I should have done in the first place, before I messed with both of their lives. "Why does she want to leave? What's wrong?"

"It's not really about what's *wrong*," Leila started. Jpeg pulled the top of her laptop down to look over it and help explain.

"Bellville's fine. The Lins are great. The problem is that Mia just doesn't *care* about any of it. She cared about Sloan."

"Mia's so sad now." Mozart flattened himself onto the ground and rested his chin on his paws. "She's been sad *the whole time I've been alive*. Even though I'm cute and she loves me!!!"

141

I thought about how quickly Mia had lashed out about Sloan, and how many times her tough front had cracked through in front of Tonio. She was definitely carrying around some big emotions. "But why Sloan?" I pressed. "Why is she worth running across the country for?"

"Not many people are patient, with Mia."

"That kid never stops moving." Jpeg smirked. "She's always got big ideas, big plans, and she drops them and starts new ones on a dime. It's a lot to keep up with."

"It's fun!" Mozart yipped.

"But also, sometimes, exhausting. Sloan never acted like she was a problem, like she was 'too much.' Mia needs that in her life." Leila tugged Jpeg into her stomach for a big hug. "It's not fair that they can just separate kids like that. I'd never leave Jpeg for the world!"

"Back atcha, you big jock." Jpeg grunted. "You're squishing me, though."

"She can't just show up at Sloan's house, though, right?"

Mozart's ears flattened defensively. "Why not? People get adopted all the time!"

"Yeah, dogs do, and humans that need families. But Mia has a family—and you don't know that Sloan's parents are able to take care of another kid."

Leila looked confused. "But when they lived in

Bellville, Mia was over at their house every day. They were together all the time."

"That's different." I realized that Jpeg and Leila had spent almost no time with humans. They'd been in this shelter or another their whole lives, and Mozart was barely four months old. I'd lived with, and learned from, humans since I was a puppy, so this situation seemed obvious to me. "If she goes, they won't let her stay. At best, she'll be there for a few days and then they'll make her come back home, which will cost more money and make everybody feel bad, especially her parents."

"You don't know that!" Mozart growled. "Mia needs to be happy again!"

"Y'all have to trust me. This is a bad idea."

"He's lying!" Mozart turned to Jpeg and Leila. "This is just because he wants Mia to stay with his boy."

I sighed and closed my eyes again. *Think.* "Okay, how about this? Jpeg, do you know Sloan's email?"

"Of course."

"Why don't you contact her anonymously, and say what's going on?" I paced back and forth in front of the group. "If she tells Mia it's okay, and that she should come, then great, I'm wrong, but at least then Mia isn't showing up by surprise. If she says not to come, you'll see that I'm right."

"No way!" Mozart yipped.

"Mia might have a good reason for not mentioning it," Leila started, but I could tell her heart wasn't in it. She was listening to me.

I tried to speak as kindly and gently as possible. "I think Mia hasn't told Sloan her plan because she knows it won't work. And either way, you have to stop helping her find money. The Officers are onto you, and Mozart will get sent somewhere *far* from Cold Dorito if you're not careful."

Three tails twitched in thought. Then, after a moment, Jpeg said, "I'll do it." She pushed her laptop open and went back to click-clacking.

"I don't like this," Mozart grumbled.

Leila sighed and patted the top of his head with her paw. "Buster's right, little one."

"I think . . ." I tried to find the right words. "Sometimes it's easy to do what someone *wants*, but you have to help with what they *need*."

"BUSTER?" Tonio had his hands cupped around his mouth and was calling from the edge of the forest. "BUSTER!"

"I have to go." I nudged Mozart, who was glaring unhappily into the ground. "I'll see you soon, okay? Everything will be all right."

"Whatever."

Jpeg nodded goodbye over her computer, and Leila sat back on her hind legs to wave like a bear.

I trotted up to Tonio. He clipped on my leash, and we walked home without a word. He looked so tense . . . I wished there was something I could do, but I had to leave my faith in the plan. *I'm doing all I can*, I thought. *All a Good Dog can do, and then some.*

I just hoped it was enough.

— 14 —

I'd spent a lot of time around Mia now, and I noticed right away something was off when she got to Tonio's the next day. She wasn't *lying*, exactly, but she sounded strained. Like she was working really hard to sound like she normally did—and not quite making it. Her eyes were just a little puffy, and red.

Tonio noticed, too. "Are you okay?" She looked away, self-conscious for the first time I'd ever noticed, and waved a hand back at him like he had said something ridiculous.

"I'm fine!" It sounded perfectly convincing, if you didn't know Mia. I tilted my head in confusion, then realized Tonio had tilted his head at the exact same time.

They sat down in his room, and Mia immediately began shuffling her cards. Tonio grabbed one of his new decks and tapped the corner of the cards against his leg a few times before finally saying, "I need to tell you something."

Mia's eyes shot up, fake smile melting away and a sudden force in her gaze. *"Did you tell her?"* she snapped.

Oh no. Jpeg's email must have gotten through. I hadn't even considered that Mia might think Tonio had—

"What?" Tonio's confusion was so genuine it couldn't possibly be a lie, and I saw Mia relax right away. "Tell who?"

"Sorry, nothing." She counted seven cards and fanned them out in front of her. "I've just had kind of a bad morning. But this is fun, and I just . . ." She swallowed and rubbed at her eyes. "I just want to have fun. For a second. What were you going to tell me?"

Tonio's heartbeat spiked up through the ruff. Excuse me, roof. "Never mind. It can wait."

What was *he going to tell her?* I wondered. His face didn't give me any hints. What was I missing?

They played a few turns of the game in silence, and Mia won very quickly because Tonio was distracted. "You had Auntie Virus in your hand and didn't play her? Why not?"

"Oh, I just—I didn't realize that I could—"

Mia rolled her eyes. "I'm fine, Tonio. You don't have to let me win."

He blushed. "You just seemed like—like maybe you were—"

"Don't." She shuffled her cards and splayed out another starting hand. Tonio reset the hand-drawn cards they were using to represent Spirit Batteries. "That's annoying. I want to play the game for real."

"Okay." His blush rose through his whole face and ears. "I'm sorry."

They played another game, but this time, Tonio was so clearly stuck in his head that he made some *really* bad moves, and Mia kept stopping him and having him redo his turn so he wouldn't just lose. Around the tenth time he'd apologized, she tossed her cards down and stared at him. "Do I just need to go home? What's the deal?"

He didn't—or couldn't—look up from his deck. He swallowed, squeezed his eyes tight, then finally forced them up to look at her. I thought, *What could be so bad that he—*

"I think I'm moving. At the end of the summer."

Oh.

Mia's posture stiffened straight up and back, like a snake trying to scare someone away. Her face didn't change, but her eyes looked like they were going to drill directly into Tonio's head. "Are you messing with me?"

"No, I—"

"Because it's not funny if you are." Her words came out poisonous, disgusted. Tonio shrank and looked away.

"My parents think it's the best thing if I go to a new school."

Mia's face settled back into a bored expression, even though I could tell she was choking down some *very* strong feelings under the surface.

She said, "Okay," and then stood up to leave.

"We can still play," Tonio tried, voice weak. "The tournament is less than a week away, and I'll still—"

"No thanks." Mia shot him a quick, meaningless smile. "I only needed your help to get the money. And now—" Her face broke, and some of that anger came back into her expression. "Since I *don't need it anyway,* who cares? We weren't really friends, either way."

A sharp inhale from Tonio, who was trying his best to seem calm, like her, and failing. I looked back and forth between them, desperate for something I could do or say, but I was just a dog. I was a dog in the middle of two kids who didn't really know what the other was going through, and didn't know how to ask.

I felt Tonio's heartbeat hammering in his chest as he searched for something to say. Every option probably looked bad from where he was.

When Mia realized he wasn't going to say anything else, she shook her head and turned away. "You *should* move!" She yanked his door open and didn't look back. "This place is the worst."

I expected a panic attack, so I stood up immediately and turned to throw myself on Tonio's lap, trying to distract him from his anxiety—but his face had the same scary look it had after talking to his dad. Worse than panic, and worse than sadness: nothing.

"At least you're here," Tonio said, and that would have made me feel better if it hadn't sounded so empty. He scratched me behind the ears and took several deep breaths. Eventually, he stood up. "Let's go downstairs, okay, boy? I want to try something."

— 15 —

Three plastic cups sat, upside down, in a line on Tonio's carpet. One of them covered a treat—Tonio showed me when he placed it underneath—and the other two were empty. A stopwatch clicked in Tonio's hand. "Okay, get the treat, Buster!"

I was being tested. Of course I knew the center cup held the treat—he'd put it there right in front of me. But this was only one part of an intelligence test, the kind we're taught how to fake when we're puppies. I figured it was safe to answer this one correctly, and quickly. I knocked over the center cup and ate the treat.

"Good boy!" That's what Tonio wanted: a fast response. Proof that I might be as smart as he was imagining. Next he threw a towel over my head, and I shook it off immediately. (There were two other options, each dumber than the one before: Wait a while before shaking it off, or never take it off and whine until a human did.)

The internet is full of all sorts of tests like this, and I know how to handle them. Getting a slightly above-average score would make sense, since service dogs should be smart—but I needed to stop far short of perfect.

We went downstairs. He kicked a treat under the coffee table, where I'd have to get it with my paws. "Get it, Buster!"

This was one I needed to fail. I sniffed at the edge of the table—the treat's smell mixed in with years of tiny flecks of food and dust created a big mishmash of feelings in my nose, which delivered them extra blurry since I was so close. I made a big show of trying to stick my nose under the table, then pulled it out and looked at Tonio to whine.

His face shifted, just a little, into disappointment. *I'm sorry, Tonio*, I thought. *But I have to be a dog.* Even now—and I want to stress this for the Court—I didn't *plan* on doing anything.

"Try this. Look." Tonio leaned over and used his hand to grab the treat. He showed it to me, then put it back under the table. "Now you go."

This one was tougher. I probably could get away with having learned this just now, from him, and suggest that I'm an especially smart dog. But if I *didn't*, if I failed again even now, that would probably put everything to rest in Tonio's mind. He'd believe I was just a dog.

So I failed. I leaned my nose down again, sniffed, and whined some more. I even patted the ground with my paws for good measure. "Yeah, those! Come on!" Tonio patted the ground with his hands, too, and pushed his hand under the table. "You can do it!"

I can't do it, I thought. *Let it go.*

"Come on." He grabbed the treat and showed it to me again, more urgently this time. His voice sounded strained. "You can do it. Good boy. Get the treat." I poked at the table with my nose once more, then sat down and looked at him with the most confused expression I could muster. He bit his lip.

"Okay. So not that one. Let's try this." He wasn't even writing my scores down. He grabbed a couple cardboard boxes with the Tomorrow Grocery rocket ship on them from the recycling pile and carried them upstairs. He cut out one big cardboard wall, cut a hole in the middle, and wedged it between the other two boxes. "Come here. Sit." I followed his hand and sat in front of the box.

"Now look at me." I watched him through the hole in the box. "Good." He placed the treat down on the other side of the cardboard, then stepped back. "Now get the treat!"

I was impressed he'd taken the time to build the whole thing, but this was another test I'd seen before. The best score would be to walk around the box right away, and the worst would be to plow into the cardboard and push it to the treat. I opted for a middle ground: I stared at the treat through the hole, tried to stick my nose through again, and when that didn't work, I sniffed around the bottom of the box until I found the edge by "accident" and trotted over to the treat.

Tonio watched me eat the peanut butter rolled up in crunchy something with a look of horror on his face. "I thought . . ." He pushed his bandanna up higher on his head, tugging the curls back. "At the training center, you *listened*! You knew I was worried about allergies and you talked me out of it. And you were on the computer, and—"

His voice caught, and I heard the breath shift that marked the beginning of a panic attack. *Oh no,* I thought. *After everything with his dad, and then Mia, this is what does it?*

Tonio's finger pointed at me accusatorily. My tail tucked between my legs. "You pretended to eat chocolate, and then you used the *toilet*, and I'm pretty sure you were going to bark at the mail until you saw there was a little kid, and—" He coughed, like he was trying to get something out of his throat, then clenched and unclenched his fists so tight his nails left marks in his palm. The more he spoke, the more my adrenaline surged. He'd noticed everything.

"Nobody else sees, but you are *always* watching the face of whoever is talking in a room, which is *not* a normal dog thing." I didn't even realize I had been doing that, but he was right. His voice rose, angry. "And when you're around other dogs, you barely do any normal dog stuff, you just bark and wiggle at each other like . . ." Tonio swallowed. "Like you're . . ."

154

His mouth twisted and his eyes narrowed to fight off tears, but they started flowing anyway. "I'm crazy. This whole time—" His chest heaved. "This whole time, I was making it up." He stood up and walked around, gulping down air as hard as he could. "Like you're *talking*? I'm so *stupid*!"

When he yelled the word *stupid*, something in my brain clicked.

What do I do?

On the one paw, dogs. We'd kept our secret for thousands of years, mostly, and I didn't want to be the one to decide that should change. Everyone has their own ideas about whether we should reveal ourselves to humans, or stay hidden forever, or some combination of the two—but I had always stayed out of it. I just wanted to do a good job, maybe have an adventure every once in a while, do some good in the world.

On the other paw, I thought about Tonio. He needed someone, *anyone*, to really pay attention to him. Even someone like me.

I thought about the baby I'd saved in the fire. Dog Court wanted me to leave the baby there. Dog Court wanted us to let Mia fly across the country on her own. Dog Court wanted me to sit and stay. Dog Court didn't want *any* of us to do *anything*! Maybe, I realized, I *couldn't* do good without picking a side.

Tonio needed me to tell the truth, and Dog Court—all

of you—wanted me to lie. To keep my head down and be a Good Dog. No matter what I did, I was making a choice. I wanted that choice to be one I could live with, and seeing the pain in his face, thinking about everything he was going through, the answer was obvious to me:

I needed to tell Tonio.

But how? I couldn't talk, not like a human. And I had just spent a lot of time trying to convince him I wasn't smart. I considered everything in Tonio's room: his bed, his window, his art, the painting supplies, the . . .

Oh.

Oh.

I knew what would do it, for sure.

First, I had to help Tonio calm down long enough to get his attention. He stopped pacing and sat on the floor against one of his walls, hair pressed up against a painting of the Video Garden. I dipped into my psychiatric service dog training and flopped over onto his lap. I put pressure on his legs and licked at one of his hands to try to distract him from the panic attack.

The most important part of getting through it, like always, was patience. He petted me a little, and when he stopped I stood up and pushed on his stomach to remind him to breathe. He would be getting dizzy from his shallow breaths by now, which had the potential to scare him more—panic attacks try to convince him that he's going to pass out completely, but he wasn't going to. And even if he did, I was there to watch him and make sure he'd be okay.

Once that thought got stuck in his mind, and my physical reminders helped him get to deeper breaths, he calmed down over the next several minutes and moved out of panic into a calmer sadness. *Now*, while he recovered, I needed to make my move.

"What are you doing?" he asked, wiping his eyes with the bandanna. *That really needs to be cleaned*, I thought, but couldn't worry about it that second, as I was busy pushing the cardboard wall over in front of him. "There aren't any more treats in there."

Treats weren't my goal. Not this time. I stepped over to the side of his bed—he followed me with his eyes—and grabbed the little plastic box Tonio had put one of his Beamblade decks in. I trotted over to him and dropped the box in his lap.

"Why're you giving me this, Buster?" He started to stand up. I shot a look at him and gave a small but serious huff-bark. *No.* "Uh, okay."

Mia's deck was still shuffled and her hand was still spread out on the floor from earlier, so I grabbed the deck and loose cards with my teeth and dragged them to the other side of the cardboard wall with the slot in it. Tonio and I could see each other over the top, which was exactly what I wanted—I wasn't able to get the cards back into a perfect stack, but this was better because I didn't have opposable thumbs, anyway.

"Buster, you're acting really weird." I pulled the seven-card hand one at a time and flipped them faceup in front of the wall so he couldn't see what I had. He leaned over to look on my side of the cardboard. "Seven cards? That's . . ." He shook his head. "Did I pass out? Is this a dream?"

I barked again. *No.*

"You want to play Beamblade?" His dubious look didn't drop, but he opened his box of cards, shuffled them in his hands, then pulled seven of them from the top.

I barked again, wagging my tail. *Yes.*

Tonio closed his eyes and took a long, deep breath.

"Okay. You can go first." Tonio, being a human, was able to just *hold* his cards. "We need something to represent the Spirit Batteries, so . . ." He opened his little pouch of treats and placed six of them in two neat rows—three for each of us.

A trading card game was perfect: It required reading, critical thinking, math, an understanding of complicated rules, and an abstract understanding of what it meant to "win" and "lose." Regular animals don't think in those terms—but humans do, and so do we. This was the best way to convince him—and it was fun, too.

I had a Flaming Manabyte card in my hand

(Manabytes are the energy you use to summon heroes and cast spells), so I pushed it through the slot so Tonio could see it. He built the playing field for us on his side, and turned the Manabyte card so it faced me. I needed a hero card to protect me, so I pushed through Flashlord, the Power Spark, who cost one Flaming Manabyte to summon.

Tonio shook his head. "That's how you play the game. Yep." He looked back at me, and I watched him to make sure he wasn't freaking out. "Is this really happening?"

I hope this wasn't the wrong choice, I thought. But the look on Tonio's face—all fear and sadness gone, replaced with a sincere interest (and just a little confusion)—was worth it. This was a mystery for him to solve, and I knew he could do it.

Heroes can't attack on the first turn, so I tapped the top of the cardboard to show I was done. A Windswept Manabyte summoned Vera Descent, the Glittering Acrobat, for Tonio's side—she wasn't as strong as Flashlord without other cards helping her. I'd picked Mia's deck for myself because even though she put hers together haphazardly, at least she stuck to "the strong cards." Tonio still hadn't committed to a final design for his decks, so they weren't as consistent.

Back on my turn, I put another Flaming Manabyte on the table, but all the rest of my cards were too expensive, because Mia overloaded the deck with high-power heroes. I could only attack with Flashlord, but since he had 3 power and Vera Descent had 2, I thought I'd be okay.

Tonio dropped a spell card, Stormbomb, which was free as long as you had at least one Windswept Manabyte on the field. It added 2 power to Vera for the rest of the turn, making her stronger than Flashlord—but defending heroes can't kill attacking heroes, so nothing happened and the fight canceled out. I whimpered a little, disappointed that Flashlord didn't win, and Tonio's eyes widened.

"No way. There's *no way* you know how to play Beamblade! You're a dog!"

I lifted my ears and tilted my head, letting him decide for himself whether or not I was playing Beamblade. He stared me down, then sighed.

"Okay. I guess it's my turn." He drew a card and placed a Drowned Manabyte. He placed a tech card next to Vera Descent—Nanobot Wand. She got a permanent +1 boost to her power, but since we would tie if he attacked, he passed his turn to me.

I placed a third Flaming Manabyte and used all three to play the spell card Summon Familiar.exe. Flashlord got a dragon familiar with 2 power who would fight with him in any battle. They attacked, and Vera Descent was defeated. I ate one of Tonio's treats, and he ran his hands through his hair in disbelief.

"Wait, okay, what's dog for *yes*?"

I bobbed my head—Underspeak for *yes*.

"And *no*?"

Since there are a couple different ways, I taught him the most basic and bared my teeth, just slightly.

"Got it. Have you been smart this whole time?"

Yes.

"Okay. So . . . were you lying to me just now? With the test?"

Yes.

"Why?"

I tried to think of a way to tell him, but he didn't know enough Underspeak. I bared my teeth and bobbed my head at the same time to express that it was a more complicated answer than I could do right now. I also tapped the cardboard, to show that it was his turn, because I knew that he could work through this life-changing news a little easier if he was distracted by the game at first.

And also because I was winning.

He dropped Cordurboy, the Fabricant and equipped him with Self-Driving Armor, which took out Flashlord. I countered with Mightas, the Golden Barbarian, and cast a Refresh spell on Cordurboy, which reset his stats and got rid of the armor. The next turn, with five whole Flaming Manabytes (lucky draw), I was able to activate the Red Beamblade, and Mightas, the Golden Barbarian, TORE THROUGH Cordurboy with ONE CLEAVE. As I ate the final Spirit Battery, Cordurboy unraveled down to his last stitch, which blew away in the winds of time, *forgotten for eternity*! BEHOLD THE GREAT AND TERRIBLE POWER OF A BLADEMASTER!!!

Uh, excuse me. Sorry. (It really is a good game.)

"You beat me," Tonio mumbled as he stacked his cards back up. "I just lost a card game to my *dog*, which is, well— It means—" He stopped. I watched a series of emotions run across Tonio's face and was briefly scared I had triggered another anxiety attack. But after a quick pinch on his arm and a glance out the window to see if anything seemed dreamlike, he eventually settled on a nod.

"I was right. You *have* been paying attention like a person does, because you *are* a person." He stood up and put a hand to his forehead. "Wait, are you a human that got turned into a dog? Or a dog that someone did evil science on?"

No.

"So, all dogs are like you."

I mean, I'm a unique individual, but— I nodded. *Yes.*

"You've been forced to be around me all the time for weeks! You must be so sick of me by now. All I do is sit around here and draw, and I didn't talk to you enough, and when I did talk, all I did was complain about my life, and—"

I barked to interrupt and jumped up onto Tonio's desk chair. I grabbed the bottom of a marker awkwardly in my teeth and held it out to Tonio. He reached out and pulled the top off for me.

Holding a marker this close to my messed-up nose was *not* pleasant, and it overwhelmed everything else with its sickly sweet scent. I tried to hold my breath and maneuver my head to write words on some leftover cardboard on the floor—also not an easy task, as you know. After half a minute of working, I finally wrote out, legibly:

I like you.

"But you didn't have a choice. They took you from that shelter and trained you to help me without ever knowing what you wanted, and now you've had to be around me, and I've got to be one of the worst dog owners ever. I'm sorry, I—"

I had continued writing as soon as he started talking, and he finally noticed my sentence.

I'm here because I want to be.

Tonio stared at my marker scribbles uncomfortably. Here I was, telling him the truth about one of the biggest secrets on Earth so he would believe me about this small one, and his anxiety wouldn't let him. He couldn't just accept that I liked being around him—that I found him valuable on his own.

"It's time to go!" Mrs. Pulaski called from downstairs. *Oh, right. His appointment with Dr. Jake is today.* Tonio jumped at the reminder of the outside world.

"We have to tell my mom!" Tonio whispered. "There's no way she'll send you back to the shelter if she knows you're smart. And maybe we won't have to—"

My hackles rose and I bared my teeth. *No!* I grabbed the marker again and wrote one word: *SECRET.*

"Then why'd you tell me? I'm horrible at secrets. She's going to—"

"Antonio! Come on!"

Tonio stuck the cap on the marker and I pointed to the word again. *SECRET!*

"We'll talk about this more later." He picked up my harness and leash, then looked at me. "Do I . . . ? Should I still . . . ?"

I patted my feet on the ground impatiently. *Yes!*

He slid the harness on and clipped the leash to it. "Is that okay? Is it too tight or anything, or . . . ?"

I answered by pawing at the door. Tonio needed to go to therapy, and to be honest, I was feeling anxious myself—no human had paid this much attention to me before, or expected me to answer questions and have opinions. Plus, all the dangers of my decision were starting to sink in: I had just given a very dangerous secret to someone I *knew* hated lying, and who was easily distressed.

The best I could hope for was some time to help Tonio with the things I couldn't before: I could be a real friend, could help him face his fears, and could maybe get him on track to have a better life . . . if I wasn't caught first.

No Place for Bad Dogs

The crowd exploded when Buster paused—loud enough that Pronto didn't jump in to say anything. Everyone in the court had been surprised by Buster's direct accusation, which was an obvious insult to the judge. *Dog Court didn't want any of us to do anything.* Some were angry; some were considering the truth in his words. Dogs in both groups had seen their humans through hard times and chosen not to help them.

"Why should *his* humans get help, but not mine?"

"THAT STORY MADE ME SAD!!"

"He's right. If I had been there for her . . . maybe things would have been different."

"NO ONE TOLD ME THIS WAS A SAD STORY."

"They can help themselves. What's a human ever done for me?"

"IT WOULD HAVE BEEN BETTER IF SLOAN COULD DO MAGIC OR SOMETHING."

When the noise began to die down, Lasagna jumped in. "Thank you, Buster, for explaining how you got to this point. I am sure the Speaker for the Law will be ready with his counterarguments, his fury, his demands for Buster's guilty verdict to come *right away*!" The corgi's tail couldn't help but wag—he was *excited*, which made Buster feel a lot better. *At least one of us is*, he thought.

Lasagna continued. "But I'll save Pronto the breath and the time, because the story doesn't end here. Buster broke the law, but the *effect*, the *change* that came about for these kids, must be taken into account. Otherwise, how do we know whether his choice was worthwhile?" Lasagna jerked his nose toward the crowd but kept his eyes on the judge. "And I have a feeling they want to hear, too."

"Do they?" Judge Sweetie asked. She ran one claw lightly along the hood of the bumper car.

"Our society has no place for Bad Dogs!" Pronto tried to maintain his confident demeanor, but the cracks were starting to show. "Buster has told his story and confessed to his crime. If you let him continue, you're not putting him on trial anymore—you're putting all of Dog Law on trial. I cannot stand for that."

The judge regarded him coolly. "Well then, I suppose, Pronto, that you will have to sit."

Pronto's jaw dropped in surprise. Buster's ears twitched with just the tiniest bit of delight. *Maybe I like this judge*, he thought. *And maybe we have a chance.*

Sweetie looked back to Lasagna. "As a judge of the Court, the case *is* clear. Buster has violated the law, and

I have no choice but to recommend he be sent to The Farm." *Well, never mind. I* don't *have a chance.* "However, as this is the first case of direct human communication I've seen in many years, I'll admit that I'm curious." She crossed her paws, one over the other, and bobbed her head, as if agreeing with herself. "Continue."

Buster's Testimony

— 16 —

Under the warm lamplight of Dr. Jake's office, with colorful toys for humans (and a few for me) scattered around and the smell of books permeating everything, I decided not to worry about what *could* happen. How was I supposed to help Tonio if I was spending all my time worried about myself?

"Uh, my last week has been, well—" Tonio chewed on the inside of his cheek. "Pretty good."

I lifted my head and looked directly at Tonio. He looked at me with a startled face, like he'd remembered all over again that I was listening.

"Last time you were here"—Dr. Jake folded his long legs over each other—"you were deciding whether or not to speak up about something. What did you decide?"

I watched Tonio's face remember that session and try to think of a simple answer for everything that came after. "I didn't say anything," he answered. "And I think that was the right choice."

"And how have you been feeling this week? Any big news? Positive or negative changes?"

"Not really," Tonio lied. "Just a long week."

"Your parents contacted me, asking for recommendations for therapy in the city." Dr. Jake was prompting Tonio, giving him something to talk about. "They said they'd talked to you about the possibility of moving away from Bellville."

"Uh, yeah. I guess that did happen." Tonio tugged at one of his curls. "It's not a big deal, though. I'll be okay."

"That's a really big change! I think anyone would be nervous to move to a totally different place." Dr. Jake was doing a really great job not looking frustrated, but I was starting to get used to him. I could feel the shift in his mood. He knew Tonio was lying, or was at least pretty sure, but didn't want to scare him by mentioning it. Tonio had to decide to tell the truth himself.

Or, I realized, *I can help him.*

"Thanks. I've been doing pretty well lately, so . . ." I looked right at Tonio and barked. One short, sharp one. "Ah! Sorry, I—" He knit his eyebrows together.

"No problem. You okay there, buddy?" Dr. Jake scratched my ears. I licked his hand, then looked back at Tonio. I knew he would understand right away—he was a smart kid. "Did your parents say why they want to move?"

"Uh, I guess because the store's having some trouble. Dad's been trying to make it better with deliveries and stuff, but that's pretty much—" I barked again. Both humans looked at me. "Buster, what are you doing?"

170

"Maybe he can hear something outside?" Dr. Jake offered. "I hope we don't have mice in the office."

I rested my head down on the floor and kept watching Tonio. *I'm just a bad dog, doing random things a dog does.*

Tonio narrowed his eyes at me. "No, Buster. Stop." He turned back to Dr. Jake. "I think . . ." He glanced down at me. "My parents think maybe the best thing is to switch me to a different school."

"And how do you feel about that?"

"It might be a good idea." I can always tell when Tonio's lying now. I folded my ears back and rumbled a low growl from the floor. "Maybe I should just put him outside."

I bared my teeth just a little at him, where Dr. Jake couldn't see. *No.*

"Don't worry about it." Dr. Jake gently patted my head. "He doesn't seem worked up. Just noticing something we're not noticing. I don't mind."

"*I* mind. But—" Tonio sighed. "I don't think it will be any better at a different school. I'm just not good at making friends or talking to other kids. They'll all think I'm crazy no matter where I go." Tonio spoke like every word of this was a challenge to get out of his mouth. "I don't want to go back at all."

"What do you think will happen if you go back?"

"The kids will think something's wrong with me!"

"Why will they think that?"

Now we were getting somewhere. Even just a little bit of honesty from Tonio gave Dr. Jake something to work with. Tonio's eyebrows pushed together while he thought of an answer.

"Because I know I'll have a panic attack sometime."

"Panic attacks don't mean you're 'crazy.' They happen to almost everybody at least once in their life. They just happen to you a little more often, and they started earlier than they do for most people."

"The other kids don't know that. I'll be the weird kid who freaks out all the time."

Dr. Jake's head tilted. "Why do you care if they think you're 'the weird kid'?"

"It's embarrassing!"

Dr. Jake's expression was gentle, but he pushed again. "Why is it embarrassing?"

Tonio looked surprised. He stared at the floor in silence for a few seconds, and Dr. Jake waited patiently. "I don't understand."

"Why is it bad for someone to think you're weird?"

Tonio opened his mouth, closed it, then pushed air through his nose, frustrated. "Because it's bad! I don't know!"

"It's a hard question. How about this: Let's say another kid sees you have a panic attack. What are you worried they will *do*, not just *think*?"

"Make fun of me," Tonio mumbled.

"What happens if they make fun of you?"

"I get embarrassed."

"That's how you feel. What happens, what *really* changes, when they make fun of you?"

Tonio considered. "They won't want to be around me. Or be my friend."

"I see." Dr. Jake made a little note. "So you want them to be your friends."

"Well . . . yeah. I want people to like me. Doesn't everybody?"

"Sometimes. But if you don't go to school, doesn't that mean there's no chance they could like you? They won't even know you."

Tonio wriggled on his beanbag. "Yeah, but not knowing me is better than thinking I'm messed up."

"It sounds like maybe there's something else that you're worried about, then. Something that could happen other than losing friends."

"I don't know." Tonio wasn't lying this time—he really didn't know. "I can't think of anything."

Dr. Jake nodded. "I believe you. Remember, anxiety is trying to protect you. It's not a bad guy; it's more like a good guy who is working too hard. In small amounts, worry helps you do your homework on time, or help the people you care about. But in big amounts, like you feel sometimes, it can keep you from doing anything at all. Sometimes it protects you so well that you don't even know what it's protecting you from."

"So you're trying to figure out why my anxiety is protecting me?"

"Exactly. That's why our sessions work best when you give me honest, detailed answers—I can help you figure it out, because I'm good at asking questions." Dr. Jake smiled at Tonio. "You're good at asking questions, too, so I think you'll catch on fast."

Tonio's face turned red—he was embarrassed but smiled back. *Good*, I thought. *He'll see that Dr. Jake doesn't just want him to seem better. He wants to help him for real.*

"I understand, I think." Then a thought hit Tonio, and I saw a glimmer in his eyes. "It's like a mystery! We know *what* anxiety is doing, which is making me feel worried—and we know *where* it's doing something, because it's the times and places I feel anxious. But we have to figure out the *why*."

I felt relief from Dr. Jake. He had been trying to help Tonio see this for a long time, and had finally found the words to make it happen. (With a little help from me, of course.) I grabbed the chewing ball and kept listening.

"That's exactly right. Do you have any guesses about why?"

"Maybe. When I think about it very hard, I start to feel anxious, and that can make me feel kind of sick."

"Focus on your breathing and take your time. I'm here for as long as you need me."

Tonio closed his eyes and took a few deep breaths. After a minute, he opened his eyes. "Do you have a piece of paper? I think better with my hands." Dr. Jake gave him a pad of paper, and Tonio started writing. I didn't peek over—I wanted to give him privacy and not distract him by reminding him about me right now.

"Okay," he said after a few minutes, with a few breaks to close his eyes and breathe again. "I have some theories."

"Let's hear them!"

"Okay. When kids see me having a panic attack, they might think there's something wrong with me for real, and they might start being nice to me just because they think they're supposed to. I don't like when people lie to me, because I usually can't tell. So I'm scared that I won't know when people are lying, and then I'll be embarrassed when I find out." He paused. "But that's just being embarrassed again. And you said to think about why that was embarrassing. In this case, I think I don't want to be wrong. And also I don't want people to talk behind my back."

"We can still ask *why* on both of those," Dr. Jake

pointed out. "So let's pick one to focus on. You don't want people to make fun of you *and* you don't want people to talk behind your back. What happens when people talk about you?"

"More people think there's something wrong with me, and if more people think that, then even people I don't know will already think there's something wrong with me, and so I can't ever know if anybody is treating me like a real person, or if they are all being nice to me just because they know I'm not normal. Like my—"

Tonio froze. The concerned look on his face made me risk moving over to flop my head onto his lap. I couldn't help it. "Like my parents," he mumbled finally. "They don't act like they used to, and I don't want everyone else to act like that, too."

"What's different?" Dr. Jake asked softly.

"They changed everything for me. They used to throw parties and have friends over all the time. They used to play card games, and my mom was in a *band*." Tonio's voice quavered, and his eyes filled up with tears. "I'm sorry. One second." His breaths were shallower, too, and I could tell his anxiety was spiking.

"No need to apologize." Dr. Jake handed him a few tissues. "Remember that anxiety works extra hard when you're close to it. I think you're on the right track."

After another shuddery breath, Tonio continued. "I know they changed some things when I was little, but they changed more because of my anxiety. And now they even want to *move* because they think it might cure my anxiety."

For the first time, I saw Dr. Jake look genuinely stunned. "They said that to you?"

"Sort of." Tonio rubbed at his eyes. "I know that's why."

"That's a lot of pressure to put on you. I'm sorry to hear that." He wrote a little note down in his book. "You know, Tonio, I've talked to your parents about something, and now that I think of it, I might not have explained it to you very well." He tucked his pen into his book and closed it over to focus completely on Tonio. "Anxiety isn't something that you can *cure*, exactly, and panic attacks are something even doctors don't totally understand yet. Lots of doctors and scientists are still trying to figure out why they happen to some people more than others. What we *can* do is make sure you have ways to keep it from interfering with your life."

Tonio frowned. "So I might never get better? That's not fair."

Dr. Jake shook his head. "You'll definitely get better. And sometimes, with enough work and time, anxiety disorders can shrink down so small you hardly even notice them anymore. But it's likely you'll have some amount of extra anxiety for your whole life—and you're right that it's not fair." He looked down at his book. "I wish I had realized sooner how much your parents have been looking for a *cure*, because that's not the right idea at all."

"I'm sorry I didn't tell you."

"Oh, no, that's not what I meant." He smiled at Tonio. "You haven't done anything wrong. And I'm really proud of how hard you've worked today."

Tonio blushed again. "Thank you." I licked his cheek, and he remembered I was there. He scratched my ears and whispered, even tinier, "Thank *you*."

"I'm going to talk to your parents soon. I won't tell them anything you've said, but I am going to try to find out more about this move—and try to remind them of what our treatment is really about. I think they need to hear from you, too."

Tonio's eyes widened. "What?"

"You should tell them what you've told me today. The parties, the card games, your mom's band. If you want them to do those things again, you should tell them. I think they're trying their best to help you, but don't know how."

"Like anxiety!" Tonio realized. "They're trying to do something good, but doing it too much."

Dr. Jake smiled. "You're a really smart person, Tonio. And you're very kind. If you talk to them, if you tell them what matters to you, I know they'll listen."

Another deep breath, another swallow. "I'll think about it."

I wished I had hands so I could give Tonio a real high five. This was *amazing*. To wrap up their session, Dr. Jake asked Tonio to do more of what he'd done that day: Find a place where he was feeling anxious, try to solve the mystery around it, and write it all down to bring to therapy the next week. For the first time, Tonio seemed genuinely excited to think about his anxiety.

Dr. Jake seemed happy, too, as far as I could tell. He liked his job, and he liked Tonio. (I also liked him, and now it wasn't just because he had such good treats.) Tonio had taken a really strong step toward feeling better—all because I stopped trying to be a Good Dog.

But we still had a lot to talk about. And I had no clue what was coming.

— 17 —

The door to Mrs. Pulaski's office wore at least fifteen *Do Not Disturb* signs slapped on at various angles, including the handwritten one hanging from the handle. I'd never been inside before, but she opened the door for us when we got home from Dr. Jake's—Tonio had asked to borrow a tablet.

"There's definitely one around here somewhere you can use!" Mrs. Pulaski swept a pile of old snack food wrappers into her trash can. The room smelled like salt, sugar, ink, and the tiniest whiff of a candle she must have lit to try to combat the snack food dust. "Just have to find it."

Tonio began collecting old cans of soda and sparkling water, piling them in his arms to take to the recycling. "Do you need help, Mom?" he asked. "I don't mind cleaning up in here."

She dismissed that idea with a wave of her hand. "Oh, no, I'll get to it after I finish this project. Once the Gargle site is done, I'll take a bit of time off, get everything organized." She sniffed at a bag of Cheese Bobs, apparently decided they were still good, rolled the top shut, and shoved them in a drawer.

"Really? You never take time off."

"Well, I'm trading emails with a few clients right now, so I'll probably be doing *something*, but less, for sure." Tonio's face looked like that was about what he expected. "Hopefully something other than websites for a little while. I'm bored!"

I looked around at her walls and saw posters for a bunch of old bands—Blip Gloss, AARCTIIC TUUNDRAA, Typorgaphy Error, Our Elaborate Misconceptions . . . Her office walls were a catalog of famous bands from the last twenty years. It didn't take me long to realize why. All the posters had the same signature in the bottom right: *L(squiggle)P(squiggle)*. Laura Pulaski. She'd designed all of them.

"Aha! Here we go!" She found a tablet lying on one of her desks under a printed-out design with handwritten notes scribbled all around it. "I hardly use it, so you can keep it in your room. The charger is . . ." She rummaged in a drawer and pulled out a cord. "This one will work. I'm glad you're interested in digital work! Let me know if you need any help, okay?"

Mrs. Pulaski was excited to see Tonio interested in the kind of art she was making, too—which was making him feel nervous, because he was basically lying about why he wanted the tablet. "Okay, Mom. Thanks."

Music rumbled from under her door once we were out of it, loud enough that I was sure even Tonio could hear it until we shut the door to his room—that was normal, though. She liked to work to music. Sometimes she even sang.

Tonio waved the tablet at me triumphantly as we walked up the stairs. "This will be perfect!" he said once his mom's music made sure she wouldn't hear. "It might take a little bit of practice, but you can type on here, and we can talk for real. Wait—" He stopped with his hand on the doorknob and turned to me. "You can't just talk, right? I never really asked."

Nope. I tried to imitate the way a human speaks: "Aargggeeeohm!"

"Got it." He pushed open the door and plugged the tablet into the wall. We watched while it charged enough to turn on; then I unlocked it with a swipe and opened up an app to type in. "That is so weird."

What is? I typed slowly, with the pads of my paws and a lot of backspacing.

"Watching you use technology! You're a dog!"

I'm not very good at it. You should see Jpeg.

"Jpeg? The Shiba at the shelter? She's—" He blinked. "Of course she is. They all are. You're *all* smart." I gave him the space to process. "What about other animals? Birds?"

No.

"Squirrels?"

No.

"Cats?"

I winced. *It's complicated.*

"How is it complicated?!"

We think they have an Underspeak language like we do, but it's different from ours, and they don't seem interested in talking to us.

"Can you teach it to me so we can talk without a tablet?"

I'll try. You can learn to understand, I think, but probably not speak it.

"Why not?"

You don't have a tail. Or the right kind of ears.

"Are you going to get in trouble for telling me?"

I tried not to scare him. *Probably not. Maybe.*

"Then why did you tell me?!"

I wanted to help you.

"But *why* are you helping me?"

It's my job. I saw the look on Tonio's face—a disappointed look—and I tried to explain it better. *Not exactly job. It's like my purpose. Dogs aren't supposed to change anything about the world—we're just supposed to watch while humans do. Being a service dog is one of our only chances to make a difference, instead of just lying around and getting petted.*

"That sounds kind of nice. Not having anything to worry about, I mean." Tonio got a faraway look in his eyes, and I booped his nose with my paw.

It's not. Not for me, anyway.

"I hate making choices. It feels like ever since I was born, all I've done is get in the way." Tonio sighed. "I wish you were a human instead of me."

I don't. Humans are gross.

Tonio grinned. "YES! I've always thought that! We're *so* gross. Like, fingernails? The worst." *Weird choice,* I thought, *but sure.* "Don't dogs, like . . . eat poop, though?"

There's good stuff in there sometimes.

"THAT'S EVEN GROSSER THAN FINGERNAILS!" he yelled, the loudest I'd ever heard him get, with a big smile on his face. I wagged my tail, glad to see his mood swing over into something more positive. "I thought that would be one of the fake dog things!!!!!"

We spent the next few hours going over everything. I told him how I'd never met my parents, about my old firehouse, about Dog Court. I told him about the Big Three, the journal, the tournament flyer, and finally about Sloan. When we got there, I knew I needed to apologize.

I wanted to help you and Mia, but I didn't do it the right way. I didn't get all the information first, and I made decisions for both of you that weren't my decisions to make. I hadn't thought very far ahead, but in the moment, I suddenly knew what I wanted. *I don't want to do that anymore. I want to be a team.*

"A team," Tonio repeated. "What do you mean?"

There's a voice in your head sometimes, I know, that makes you feel bad. That says you aren't enough, or that you're doing things wrong. I want to be another voice, a good voice, to help you fight that one.

"But a team means we're working together. How could I help you? I'm just—" I was already typing a response, so he stopped to read.

You don't know how good it feels to talk to a human. To really get to be who I am. That's enough for me.

"No," Tonio argued. "It's not." I tilted my head back, surprised at how quickly he answered. "Sorry. I just mean—well, I mean no, it's not, but I should have said it nicer, maybe, because . . ." He squeezed his hands into fists, then released them. "If you're a real person, your life can't just be about me. That's not okay."

This was why I liked Tonio. He was right—it wasn't fair to either of us if I told him the truth and then kept making everything about him. He'd feel too guilty, and . . . I wanted to be a person, too, didn't I? If I was honest with myself, that's part of why I told him. That's why I wanted to help people. I wanted them to see me. The thought made me uncomfortable—I'd gone my whole life hearing people tell me to sit and stay—but I knew, deep down, it was true.

Thank you. But I don't know right now. If I promise I'll think about it, will you let me help you first?

Tonio bit the inside of his cheek, then nodded. "Okay, sure, you can help me. But what does that even mean? My parents say we're leaving, so that's that. What else am I supposed to do?"

I couldn't just tell Tonio what I thought he needed help with—I needed to be better than that. So I asked him something instead.

If you could change anything, I typed, *what would you change?*

"I would get rid of my anxiety."

Yeah, I agreed.

"But Dr. Jake said that might not ever happen, so I don't know." He kept making his thinking face, so I just waited. "I want Mom and Dad to stop changing things because they think it will make me better. I don't want to be scared to go to school. I don't want to get sick to my stomach every time I see Devon Wilcrest, and I want Miles and Parker to leave him alone. I don't want to have panic attacks anymore, and I want everything to be the way it was when I was eight again. I don't want to move. I want Om, the Martian Dragon, and I want Mia to feel better. I don't know."

It sounds like you do know, I tried.

"But I *don't* know. I don't know if any of that stuff is the right thing. What if moving would make my anxiety better, if there's a good school in the city? What if Mia shouldn't be my friend, because I'll just annoy her or hurt her feelings again?" His voice spiked up and down, but the words kept spilling out of him. "What if Mom and Dad are right, and if they go back to their old life, my panic attacks get worse, and then they get even more scared to do the things they like? And I wasn't so anxious when I was eight, but I also had, like, three ear infections, so probably it would be bad anyways, even if I did go back."

I tried to think, and to take everything Tonio said seriously. The unfortunate truth of the matter was that anxiety couldn't just disappear, and neither could his panic attacks—and making them go away wasn't an actual action he could take right now.

You don't want to move. Why not?

"I don't want my parents to have to go somewhere else just because of me. And I don't want to have to give you away!"

Are there any positive reasons? What do you like about Bellville?

"I know everybody here, and almost everybody is nice. I like that it's quiet." Tonio stretched and looked out his window. "I like the trees, and I like that it's mostly warm all the time, even though it's been super hot this summer."

What about school?

"I don't know. Everyone there is so *interesting*. Like, school on TV or in books or whatever, none of them are as weird as Bellville. And I've known all the other kids since I was, like, born."

What is Mia like? I asked. *At school.*

Tonio smiled—he liked getting to share all the stuff he'd noticed. "She is *so* loud! Well . . . was. When Miles and Parker started making fun of Devon, and they saw that some people liked them more when they did that, they also started looking for other people to make fun of, too, kinda. Once they said something rude about how Sloan was chewing on pencils all the time, and Mia basically threw them out of the class." He rubbed his finger on the corner of the tablet. "But then Sloan left, and she stopped talking."

What about Devon?

Tonio didn't like thinking about Devon too hard, but he closed his eyes and took deep breaths to fight back against his sudden jump in heart rate. "He's really nice. *So* nice. That's why I know he hasn't even noticed that they make fun of him behind his back, because he keeps trying to talk to Miles and Parker anyway. He tries to talk to everybody. He's not loud, and he's not super funny or anything. He's just nice. He tries to talk to everyone about everything, but they're all so weird about it." He sighed. "Even me."

Why?

"Because that's why they tried to make fun of Sloan.

Anyone who talks to him is a target, too." And Tonio didn't want them to pay attention to him.

What if Mia and Devon were friends? I asked.

The color drained out of Tonio's face, because he knew what I was *really* saying. "No. No way. I can't— What am I supposed to—"

It's up to you. I nuzzled his hand to show that I was trying to say this gently. *But their situations are both on the list of things we can try to change. Even if you're moving, I think you still want them to feel better. Right?*

He clenched and unclenched his fists, looked at his dog who could talk, and let out a long, pained whine. "It's a good idea. I hate it."

I just stared at him while he stood up and paced around the room. *He really is like a puppy*, I thought. *Just a little.*

"Fine, okay, fine." He put his hands on his hips and glared at me. "What do you think we should do?"

⊢ 18 ⊣

After a few Underspeak lessons, Tonio's insistence that
we practice all the possible conversations with Mia (I
have a pretty good impression of her now, I think, which
y'all have heard all night), a good night's sleep, and my
repeated reminders that I could *not* talk to him in front
of other dogs, we set out toward the Lin Shelter. It was
raining pretty hard, so Tonio brought a big umbrella for
us to walk under.

I kept asking myself if I was walking in a way that
looked like I'd spoken to Tonio. I had my ears and nose
on high alert for dogs—and Tonio, careful of my warning, didn't try to talk to me.

Even combined, Tonio and I didn't have much of a
plan exactly. Our first (and only) step was to try to get
Mia to go to the tournament—and hope that she got a
chance to really talk to Devon and like him. We didn't
want to trick anybody, and I'd resolved to not make
any more decisions *for* anybody else. I think now that
maybe that's one of the most important responsibilities
of a friend: You want to make it as easy as possible for
them to make good choices, but not choose for them.

And help them remember the good parts of who they are when they forget.

"Ah!!! Excuse me! Help!" Someone ducked under our umbrella, bumping Tonio hard but catching his arm to steady him so he didn't fall. "Sorry. It got bad so fast, and I just—" The kid grinned, showing off the gap between his front teeth. It was Devon. "Oh, hey, Antonio! Ring, ring, ring!"

The rain poured heavy onto the umbrella, tapping sounds so frequent there was no rhythm at all, just a big mess of noise. Tonio, overwhelmed by this sudden appearance, couldn't get anything out other than a nod.

"Whatcha doing?" Devon asked. Thunder boomed, and all three of us jumped. Devon laughed. "The playground is right over there! C'mon!"

No chance for Tonio to protest. Devon tugged his arm and pulled him off the road, dodging around puddles and muddy spots that were already forming. "I'm not allowed to go home yet, so if I get wet, I'll just be soggy all day!" Devon yelled over the rain while Tonio struggled to keep the umbrella over both of them. "Let's go to the gazebo!"

He pointed to a round thing with a roof, like a little hut with a low fence instead of walls, and they ran past swings and slides to get there. The roof was wide enough that only rain pushed by the wind got in, so the benches inside were totally dry. Devon threw himself down on one, took up the whole thing by lying across it dramatically, and laughed again.

He had an easy giggle, like he was ready to laugh all the time and anything could make it bubble over. I finally got a chance to really take in what he looked like, too, now that we weren't running away and I knew who he was. His skin was brown, and unlike Tonio's loose curls left to grow however they wanted, his dark hair was shaved into a stylish fade with little curls on top, close to his scalp.

"Did you know this was called a 'gazebo'? A wise old man, probably a wizard, taught me that last time I was here. He also gave me a sword and told me I was destined to be a *great warrior* who would protect the world from darkness." At Tonio's confused expression, he giggled again. "Just kidding. It was actually a four-year-old." He shrugged. "She was pretty cool, but I was like, 'How are you carrying such a big sword?'"

Devon kept watching him, expecting laughter, but Tonio just looked even more confused.

"I'm joking!!!!" Devon said.

"About which part?" Tonio asked.

"The word. This isn't really called a gazebo."

"Oh."

"I'm joking again!!!" He sat up while Tonio folded his umbrella and leaned it against the rail. "A little kid taught me the word last week. She said, 'Do you want to know the biggest word I know?' and of course I said yes, and then she told me what this was called. I asked if she knew the word *refrigerator*, and she said yes, of course, but when I told her that was a bigger word than *gazebo*, she kicked me in the shin!"

Tonio, at a loss for words, looked down at me. *It's okay*, I said. *I'm here. Talk.*

"You really can't go home?" Every word was a battle with Tonio's brain, the anxious part yelling *run run run run run*, but I could see now that he'd been right when he'd said Devon could talk to anybody about anything.

"Yep. We've got an 'outside rule.' My parents have meetings all day, and I 'shouldn't spend so much time playing games, Devon Isaiah!' So I usually just go to Roll and play games there instead." That little giggle again, happy enough with his own joke to keep going. "Oh yeah! You saw my note about the tournament, right?"

Tonio nodded.

"You *have* to come. Nobody told me that everyone was going to go to camp, so I feel like the last kid on earth most days. If you aren't there, it'll just be me and a bunch of grumpy adults like Phil. What's your dog's name, by the way?" He reached down to scratch behind my ears.

"Buster." Tonio's face turned red as Devon repeated my name, and I wagged my tail. "I don't really play," Tonio lied. I pretended to sniff around the bench Devon was sitting on and posed in the way that meant *Mia*. "But . . . Mia Lin might be there. So you won't be alone."

"Really? Mia plays?" He sat up and tugged at his earlobe. "That's awesome! I didn't know she was still in town, too. We can all play!"

"I said—"

"Okay, sure, maybe you don't play *yet*, but I've got a ton of cards and I can teach you, easy."

Tonio stared at the ground for a long time, long enough that Devon's expression drifted into concern. I tried to get Tonio's attention with a few poses, but he wouldn't move his eyes from the ground.

"Are you okay?" Devon asked.

"You don't have to pretend you want to be my friend." Tonio's voice was strained, and harsh. There wasn't really an Underspeak word for anxiety, so I had taught him a different combo of words to mean the closest I could get. *Bad brain!* I underspoke. Devon was a sweet kid, looking for friends. But Tonio's anxiety was filling in the blanks with a completely untrue story.

"Huh?"

"I threw up on you in front of everybody. I embarrassed you, and then I ran away at the game store, and then I ignored your note." Tonio's breathing was heavier, and he was barely speaking loud enough to be heard over the rain on the gazebo's roof. "I haven't done anything good. I haven't even been *nice* to you. It doesn't make sense."

Devon didn't answer right away, and Tonio kept talking, words falling out of him like he couldn't keep them held in anymore. "And *nobody* at school is nice to you. But you keep talking to them. You keep talking to *me*."

"I thought we could be friends," Devon said. "I'm sorry. I can stop talking to you, if you want."

"That's not what I mean!" Tonio croaked. He turned around completely to lean against the rail and tugged my leash, tied around his wrist, in the process. I moved closer to him and looked up to see him squeezing his eyes tight toward the rain. "I just don't get it."

Devon stood up and walked over to Tonio. He hopped up to sit on the rail next to where Tonio's hands were gripping it. "So it's okay that I'm talking to you?"

"I don't know," Tonio barely squeezed out. I nudged into his side, and his hand drifted down to run his hand along my fur. *Deep breaths,* I thought. *You can do it.*

"Okay." Devon leaned side to side, considering what to say. "Whenever Miles and Parker say dumb stuff at school, I always look over at your face."

That surprised Tonio. He opened his eyes and looked at Devon, confused. "What?"

"It's always like this." Devon raised one eyebrow and pursed his lips just a little in an *are you serious right now?*

kind of face. "So I know I'm not imagining that they did something stupid, 'cause I can tell you think so, too. And you never join in when anybody's being mean. But I know you're listening, 'cause you're always like—" He did the face again. "Or sometimes, it's like—" He brought his eyebrows together and dropped his jaw a little, a *very* familiar look of stressed surprise. "Those guys are the worst. But I'm pretty sure you aren't like those kids. I don't think you'd make fun of me, like they do."

Tonio brought his eyebrows together, and his jaw dropped a little.

"See?!" Devon grinned, and Tonio self-consciously tried to rearrange his face before he answered.

"You know about that?"

"Of course I know about that. They aren't, like, quiet about it. And also, if it makes you feel better, you should know yearbook signing was not the first time I've been thrown up on."

"Really?"

"One time, my best friend back in the city drank like a whole thing of chocolate milk before we got on a roller coaster, and as soon as we stepped off—" He waved his hand all over his face and chest. "Some of it got in my *mouth*. And actually, my baby cousin ran right up to me after getting off the trampoline and just blew it all over my shoes. Maybe I look like a trash can or something."

Tears were welling up in Tonio's eyes—tears of relief, I realized. "You don't l-look like a trash can," he said.

"Well, thanks, I—oh, are you okay?!" Devon stood up to catch Tonio, but he wasn't falling. Just sitting on the gazebo's wooden floor.

"I ruined your yearbook!" Tonio had been ready for disgust, anger . . . he'd spent so much time building this moment up in his mind—and building himself up to be a big bad guy in this kid's life. Now, seeing that Devon barely cared was a huge emotional release. Devon laughed and slid down next to him on the stair.

"They gave me another yearbook," he assured Tonio. "And it was a good excuse to give my parents for why there weren't any signatures." He opened his hands and made a *what can you do?* gesture. "Better than 'nobody likes me.'" Devon watched Tonio with what I could only think of as hope, and I realized Devon was nervous, too. He wanted Tonio to like him. Nobody had signed his yearbook, and his parents had changed his whole life around by moving. But Tonio was a chance at friendship.

I licked at Tonio's face. *Bad brain*, I said again, now that he was looking at me. He nodded and wiped at his eyes. "I guess I was more worried about it than you were. That makes sense," he admitted, "because I'm always worried."

"No sweat. For real." Devon hugged Tonio around

the shoulders with one arm. "I even still have the shirt! Washed right out." I cringed. Humans always think things have "washed out," because *they* can't smell it. I hoped his shirt was really clean. "I'm sorry you thought I was pretending."

"*I'm* sorry!" Tonio insisted, and Devon laughed again.

"Okay. We're both sorry. So we're even." It was such a smooth, kind gesture—I was impressed again at how good humans could be at helping each other out. Especially the kids I'd met.

As the rain relaxed to a drizzle, Tonio said, "I brought my cards. Could you look at my decks and see if they're any good?"

Devon pulled out his phone and looked at the clock. "Well, I'm supposed to be protecting the world from a great darkness at four, but—" At Tonio's confused face, he grinned. "I'm joking! Yes! Let's blade!"

We sat in the gazebo and went through Mia's and Tonio's decks. Devon said he'd let them borrow some of his newer cards to help get them ready for the tournament, and Tonio took careful notes in his journal of every tip about the game Devon said in his constant flood of words.

After Devon headed home, we tried to track down Mia, but she wasn't around. We did run into Skyler, the teenager from Roll the Ice. She was leaning back in one of the benches in the park and glaring at her own nose. Tonio turned to leave her alone, but she stopped him with a little smile. "Hey, kid! Ring, ring. What's going on?"

"Nothing," Tonio answered automatically.

Skyler nodded. "Cool." She sneezed a big loud booming sneeze into her elbow, then shook her head. "I came outside to get some air, but it turns out the air is poisonous! My allergies have gone *crazy* since I moved here."

I saw Tonio's little half nod. "My mom gets them, too. Where did you move from?"

"Chicago." She rubbed her eyes under her glasses, but pushed too hard and they fell off. She scrambled to catch them again before they hit the ground, then laughed. "Geez. I'm a mess today."

Tonio looked down at me, and I brought my brow up to show I was paying attention. Skyler seemed different from last time. Tired, at least, and a little bit sad. I, of course, couldn't resist finding out why someone was mysteriously sad, and it seemed like Tonio was feeling a little brave, too. Or maybe he just liked Skyler too much to ignore it.

"Are you okay?" he asked, sitting down on the bench next to her and scooting back to look up through his curls.

"I think so. Just one of those days where everything feels like . . ." She held her hands on either side of her head and vibrated them. "Too much. Adult stuff." Skyler

had told him that she had bad anxiety, too, sometimes—
I knew Tonio remembered—and that meant helping
her was part of my job! I hopped up onto the bench on her
other side and rested my head in her lap. She petted my
head slowly and carefully.

"I have days like that, too." Tonio sounded a little
defensive. "It's not just adult stuff."

Skyler laughed, not unkindly, and sneezed again.
"What are those days like, for you?"

Tonio considered her question seriously before he
answered. "It's like something in my stomach grabs my
throat and shakes it, so I feel sick but also like I might
choke." I was surprised he answered so genuinely—he
really trusted Skyler, and I understood why. She talked
to him like a person, without any fake layers. Like someone who cared about what he had to say. "Or sometimes
it feels like my brain has a thunderstorm inside of it.
Like everything's buzzing, and sometimes there's a big,
sharp lightning-bolt thought that's really bad."

"Wow." Skyler rubbed her hands together, clenching
and unclenching. "You're right. Not just adult stuff."
She looked up at the clouds, finally moving away from
Bellville's sun. "I think I'm having a thunderstorm day.
Any advice?"

"I dunno." Tonio looked down at me. "Maybe get a dog?"

Skyler grinned. "This little guy working out for you?"

"Yeah. He's helping a lot." I twisted my tail and dipped my nose in a little *thank you*.

"You guys are coming to the tournament, right?"

Tonio took a slow breath instead of answering.

"Come on! I don't like crowds, either, and I have to organize the whole thing. If I can do it, you can."

"It's not that." Tonio swung his legs back and forth on the bench, his feet only barely scraping the ground. "Well, it's a little bit that," he admitted. "I don't think I'm very good at it. And all I have is a bunch of old cards. And my friend was supposed to come, but I think she's mad at me. So if I come and she *is* there, which I want to happen, then that's kind of bad. But if I go and she's *not* there, that's kind of bad, too. And she might not go because she's avoiding me. So maybe I just shouldn't go."

"What about the positives?" Skyler asked.

Tonio frowned. "What do you mean?"

"You know all the bad stuff that could happen. But what's the good stuff?"

Tonio stared at her, brows knit together. "I mean . . . I guess, like . . ."

"You spend all that time thinking about the bad stuff, but haven't even thought about the good stuff?"

"The good stuff is obvious!"

"Well then, if it's obvious"—She spread her hands out, an invitation for Tonio to speak—"let's hear it!"

"Beamblade is fun." He tapped his fingers on the bench. "And I think everybody could become better friends."

"Have you told her that?"

Tonio groaned. "Everyone's always telling me I have to *talk* to people all the time. Can't I do something else for once?" He was joking, kind of. My tail wagged on its own. I was really happy to see Tonio like this—kind of relaxed, and talking so honestly. Skyler was amazing.

Her pocket started beeping, breaking the moment. "I gotta go back to work. It's in three days. Don't forget, okay?"

"I won't forget," Tonio promised. "But I don't know if—"

"You'll be there." Skyler winked. "And so will your friend. I believe in you."

Tonio wasn't sure what to say. "You too."

She held out her fist for a bump. "Thanks, kid."

We watched her go. Tonio shook his head in wonder, smiling. "That wasn't like me at all! Did you see that? I talked to Devon today, and then I went right up to an *adult*. And I helped her!" My tail wagged more. He was so genuinely happy—and so proud of himself, something I'd never really seen in him.

I was about to answer in Underspeak, but the wind changed and I smelled something in the air. Another dog. I looked up, and across the road, sure enough—

Officer Sergeant. Watching and listening.

What did she see? I licked Tonio's hand and didn't say anything else, but my heart pumped double time. I scanned back over the conversation and tried to see if I'd messed up. *Did I say anything? Did I talk back to him?*

But she didn't come any closer. Just watched, expression serious and ears alert.

Oh, Buster, I thought. *You have to be more careful.*

— 19 —

The next day, Tonio and I trudged through the puddles and mugginess of the morning to Mia's house, but all we found was one of her dads, who apologetically gave us a vague direction Mia had left in. Tonio was ready to leave, but I wasn't going to give up that easily. I led him over to our usual bench and posed for him to unclip my collar.

Be right back, I underspoke as small as I could. Tonio's head tilted a little—he was still getting used to seeing my movements as anything other than butt wiggles and toe taps.

I ran back to the house—it had been *ages* since my last good run, so I took the long way through the fields and got a little muddy—but didn't go up to the front door. I circled around it, ear pressed to the wall, until I heard the familiar shuffling of tiny paws and panting of tiny jaws. I stopped below the closest window, cracked open just a little bit.

"Mozart?" I barked. The movement stopped. No answer. "MOZART!"

When it became clear he wasn't going to answer me, I tried a different tactic. "Well, it's too bad Mozart's not here! Now who am I going to share all this delicious fresh-cooked bacon with?"

A tricolored nose immediately shoved its way through the crack at the bottom of the window. "I know you're lying," Mozart mumbled through a mouth held closed by the small gap. "I just wanted to smell fresh air! But there's nothing fresh about *you*, because *you stink*!"

A human voice groaned from inside the room. "Mozart, what are you barking at?" Nails, yellow polish chipped mostly off, slid under the window and pulled it up the rest of the way. Mia tucked her head out and frowned down at me. So she *was* at home! She made her dad lie to us!

"Hey, Buster." Her eyes were red and tired, like she'd slept too much or maybe not at all. Her pajamas had little elephants on them. "You wanna play?"

"NO!" Mozart barked. "I absolutely do *not* want to play with him!" She scooped him up with one hand, his kicking and wiggling as powerless as it was cute. "Let me go! STOP THAT!!!!"

"Have fun." Mia huffed and lobbed the ball of fluff out the window. Mozart screeched as he fell two and a half feet to the ground, and continued even after he'd landed on all fours, perfectly safe.

"LET ME BACK IN!" he howled. The window slid closed. I watched as he crumpled down onto his belly, ears and tail folded back and down, eyes glaring a hole in the wall.

"I came to check on you." I lifted my brow earnestly and tried to trot around to his face, but as I stepped, he rotated his body so I couldn't ever make it to the front. "And Tonio's been trying to talk to Mia."

"She doesn't want to talk to Tonio. And I don't want to talk to you."

"Why not?"

"Whaddaya mean 'why not?'" He mimicked my bark a little too well, honestly. Kids can be so good at making you sound stupid. "You ruined everything!"

I wanted to snap at him, to argue, but I made myself think before I spoke. I wasn't sure what the right thing to say was, but I figured Dr. Jake would probably ask questions. So I started there.

"What did I ruin?"

Mozart's head lifted off the ground, teeth bared in a sneer. "You know what you did!"

I dipped my muzzle in agreement. "I know what I did. But I don't know what I ruined."

The little body under that pile of fluff wiggled uncomfortably. "Yes, you do."

"Try telling me."

"No!"

"Why not?"

"'Cause it's obvious!!!"

"Not to me."

Mozart huffed and finally stopped rotating. "You're annoying."

"That's true." My tail wagged a little. "And I'll keep being annoying until you tell me what you're mad about." (I don't think Dr. Jake would have said that.)

A goat bleated in the distance while I waited for Mozart to answer.

"We had a whole plan." He whined. "She was going to take me with her. And you stopped it."

I nodded sadly. "But the plan wasn't ever going to work, buddy. You would have been back here next week, even sadder and in a lot more trouble."

"You don't *know* that."

"I guess not. But it seems pretty likely, right?" When he didn't answer, I sighed and lowered down onto the ground in front of him. He stared at the ground while his tail swatted the dirt, frustrated, but I looked at his eyes anyway. "I owe you an apology."

His tail smacked the ground, tossing up a little brown cloud. "For what?"

"Back when you stole the necklace, I said you weren't a Good Dog. And then when we were talking about Sloan, I acted like you were bad for trying to help Mia the best you could. Like you didn't know what you were talking about, just because you were a puppy. And that was wrong." He tilted his head away and looked at me

207

through the corners of his eyes, which I took as a good sign. He was listening. "I acted like I knew better even though I'd already gotten in trouble before for exactly what you were trying to do. But the truth is, I agree with you. Mostly. I *do* think we should help our humans as much as we can."

"So what?" He grunted suspiciously.

"*So*, you shouldn't give up just because this plan didn't work. We need to keep trying to help her, and Tonio, and all the humans. Even if we don't always get it right."

"You're saying I should steal more diamonds?"

"No!" I yelped, then saw the quirk of his tail and realized he was messing with me. "But she likes Beamblade. And she likes Tonio, I think, even if she's upset with him right now."

Mozart's ear twitched. "And she likes dollars . . ."

"And three hundred is so many dollars."

He nodded slowly. "What am I supposed to do about it?"

"I'm not totally sure. But do you think you could help her get to the tournament?"

"I'll think about it." All three colors of fluff lifted off the ground. He tilted his nose up into the air. "You're nicer than I thought. I'm sorry I turned you in to the cops!"

My tail stopped wagging, and my ears folded over. "You what?"

"I sent them that video of you on the computer yesterday. Actually, I thought you'd be arrested by now. But

I'm glad you're not!" He trotted past me, toward the front door, and waved one paw out to the side in good-bye. "Smell you later, gramps!!!"

I listened to him scratch at the door, which opened quickly to let him back inside. *So that's why Officer Sergeant was watching me*, I thought.

I closed my eyes and listened. I heard the bugs, the wind through the grass—and a suspicious absence of noise, a perfectly quiet spot not too far from me. Trying not to be obvious, I turned my head and peeked toward it.

Sure enough, there was Officer Grizzle, peeking out just barely from a pile of wood. I was being monitored.

Tonio started to say something to me when I came back to the table, but picked up on my body language right away and fell silent. We walked back home together, and now that I knew Grizzle was there, I could feel him tailing us the whole way. It wasn't until we were back up the stairs and behind closed doors in Tonio's room that I felt like I could finally relax.

"What happened?" he asked. "Are you okay?"

Nothing. I'm fine. Lying was easier when I was typing on the tablet. *Just got nervous, is all.*

— 20 —

"Here's a pen to fill out the sign-up sheet. Since you've never competed in a tournament before, I need your full name, address, and your Blademaster title here."

Tonio's eyebrows shot up. "My what?"

"Your Blademaster title!" Skyler smiled, reassuring and kind. "It's your name in the Beamblade world."

Tonio stared at the paper limply while activity bustled around us. Almost two dozen adults were crammed into Roll the Ice, adding an interesting musk over the smell of ice cream and cardboard.

The play room had burst from the back of the store and spread into the shopping area; displays were shoved to the walls to make enough room for the games. A few adults in blue aprons matching Skyler's were walking around, cleaning up ice-cream spills and helping people find places to sit.

"You can change your name online later if you want," Skyler told Tonio. "This is just so I can set up your account, and so I have something to call you tonight." She saw the look on his face and pointed to an open table. "Plenty of time to think of something. Just bring it to me before we get started. Is your friend coming?"

Tonio glanced down at me, but I didn't have anything to add. He knew everything I knew—we just had to hope that Mozart would really be able to bring Mia here somehow.

"I hope so," Tonio said.

"Me too. There are four rounds, single elimination, which means you can't win if you lose once. But when people lose, they always stick around to play, so even if you have trouble early on, you'll have people to play with. Does that make sense?"

Tonio nodded. "Are you feeling better today?"

She didn't have time to answer—a woman in line behind him caught Skyler's eye, and Tonio shifted out of the way so Skyler could focus on her job. He sat down at the table, and I watched the reality of the situation dawn on him: just him, in a room full of adults, about to have to compete in a game he'd only played a few times.

That wasn't *quite* the reality, though—he wasn't alone. I nudged him to remind him I was there. Some calm came back to his eyes, and he spoke just barely under his breath, like we'd practiced. "Maybe we can both have a name. Since we're a team."

I don't need—

"You were a fire dog, right? That already sounds kind of

Beamblade-y. What about Flame Wolf? Or Blaze Hound! Or . . ." He tapped the pen against his nose thoughtfully. "Okay. I think I got it." He scribbled something down.

I tried to stand up straight to see over the table—but he snatched the paper away. "It's a surprise! But now *I* need one." Something flashed across his face—a thought that didn't feel good. "There's nothing really special about me, though."

Bad brain, I warned. He nodded once, slowly.

In the back of the room, a little face with a big smile poked up above the sea of adults and yelled, "Tonio! Hey!!!"

There wasn't even time to answer before Devon was dodging and weaving through the crowd and dropping into the seat next to Tonio. He unzipped a shiny silver backpack—it looked brand-new—and plopped two boxes of cards in front of Tonio. "I brought all the cards we talked about. Not to brag or anything, but I'm *extremely* good at carrying stacks of cards from one place to another. I didn't even drop them."

"That's good," Tonio answered, heart already racing. Devon stared at him, wide-faced, waiting for a laugh. "Oh! You're joking! I'm sorry!"

"No, *I'm* sorry. Next time I make any jokes, I'll wear my T-shirt that says 'I'm joking.'" He popped open the clip on the boxes and poured the cards out. Tonio opened his box of cards and took the rubber bands off the two decks he'd brought. "I hope it's not too confusing to be playing with new cards all of a sudden."

"Not at all." Tonio shook his head. "We've been practicing with the ones I drew, so we're ready."

"Who's we?" Devon asked, meaning absolutely nothing by it, but Tonio was already sweating.

"Me," he started.

A sideways glance. "Right. And?"

"And . . ." I watched the wheels spin in his head. *Just say anything!* I thought, but didn't want to distract him with Underspeak. *Anyone at all!*

"My . . ." Bad start. His Mia? No. *Dad. Mom. Online friends. Just say anything!*

"Dog," he finished. I lowered my snout and pressed the top of my head against the table's leg. *We will never be able to keep this secret. What was I thinking?*

But Devon just laughed. "Cool." And reached over to scratch behind my ears. "I hope he kept you on your toes."

". . . . . . . Totally," Tonio said after one million excruciating seconds.

"These are so cool!" Devon gasped, looking at one of Tonio's drawn cards. He held up Tonio's version of Summon Familiar.exe. "Can I have this one? The dragon looks so cute!"

Tonio blushed. "Sure."

Devon did a short, excited dance, which Tonio

watched carefully—probably searching for a sign that it was fake. But there was nothing to find. That was Devon.

The last few cards found their spots while Skyler stood up on a chair to yell across the crowd, "We're going to get started in five minutes! If you haven't turned in your sign-up sheet yet, please bring it to me."

Five minutes, and no sign of Mia. *I shouldn't have trusted this to a puppy,* I thought.

With a quick scribble, Tonio finished writing his Blademaster name. I tried to catch a peek again, but he pressed it to his chest and barely let go even when Skyler was reaching for it. "Whoa," she said after looking at it.

"Is it bad?" Tonio asked immediately. "I can change the name. I just thought that—"

Skyler pushed the corner of her glasses to bring it back up her nose. "Your handwriting is really good," she explained. "That's all I meant."

"But is the name okay?"

She looked again and grinned. "It's intense."

"Is that bad?"

"No, I think it's cool." She pulled her phone out of her pocket and checked the time. "Is your friend here yet?"

Tonio shook his head. "Is there any chance you could wait a few more minutes? Just to see?"

"We have to get started. But . . ." Skyler consulted her clipboard. "If she *was* here, we'd have an uneven number of people, anyway, and someone would get a bye the first round."

"A bye?"

"It means someone has to skip, 'cause there's nobody for them to play against." She wrote a note down on her clipboard, then chewed on the end of her pen for a second. "I'll tell you what—I'll sign her up, and give her the first bye. She can fill out the sheet when she gets here. That's like thirty more minutes."

Tonio's eyebrows came together in concern. "Is that okay? If it's not fair, I don't—"

"It's fine. If she wasn't coming, everyone here would have to play, anyway." She held her phone up for Tonio. "Do you want to call her?"

"That's okay, I just—" I nudged him and underspoke, *Yes.* He gave me a confused expression, so I did it again, with an exclamatory quirk to my tail. *Yes!* "Uh, actually, that would be good. But I'm not good at phones. Is there somewhere private I could make a call?"

Skyler pointed. "Sure! Over there."

Moments later, Tonio and I were crammed into a tiny bathroom meant for one human. I sat on the toilet enjoying the smell, and Tonio leaned against the sink, staring pointedly away from the mirror and waiting for the phone to finish ringing. He put it on speaker so I could hear.

"Rrrring, ring?" Mia's dad Jeff answered.

"Hi, Mr. Lin. It's Tonio."

"Please, Mr. Lin is my husband." He chuckled. "Jeff is fine!"

"Uh, okay." The silence lasted too long. "Is Mia there?"

"Y'know, I don't think she is." He let out a sympathetic sigh. "Sorry about that, buddy."

"Is she okay?"

"Between you and me, she's been having kind of a hard time, and she won't talk to us about why. I appreciate you checking on her, though."

Tonio glanced at me, brow knit together. *Go on*, I underspoke.

He put his hand over the phone. "Do I have to?" he whispered.

It'll be fine!

Tonio squeezed his eyes shut and brought the phone back up to his ear. "ActuallyMr.Lincouldyouput Mozartonthephone?"

This silence lasted even longer. "The dog?" Jeff asked.

"Yes, sir." Tonio covered his squeezed-shut eyes with his free hand. I felt bad for putting him in such a stressful position, but we'd agreed this was our only chance to really find out what was going on. I fed Tonio the words to say. "My dog misses him, I think. He's been whining ever since I took him away from the park."

Tonio held the phone up. I gave a little whine for emphasis.

"That," Jeff announced, "is the cutest darn thing I've ever heard in my life. You got it. Mozart! Come here, boy!" He laughed. "Phone's for you!" There was the jingling of a collar and the ruffle of a phone being placed onto carpet.

"Hello?" I barked, making Tonio wince and Mozart whine sarcastically on the other line.

"C'mon, gramps. You don't have to yell."

"Sorry," I rumbled, embarrassed. Tonio stared at me, wide-eyed, like he was realizing I was smart all over again. "The tournament's already starting! Where are you?"

His little paws squished the carpet around the phone in a frustrated rhythm. "I've tried everything! I stole her left sock, I stole her right sock, I chewed on her left shoe, I chewed on her right shoe, I scratched at the door—all the normal stuff that always works! She won't budge!"

My ears flattened. That *was* the stuff that always works. "Okay, so we need a more complicated plan. Maybe we should ask Jpeg."

Static burst across the line for a second. Then, a new bark. "Ask me what?"

"Jpeg! How're you on the phone?"

She barked a little laugh. "Is that your question? You only get one."

Me-from-a-few-days-ago, the me who decided I wasn't going to meddle in people's lives anymore, was growling all over my brain again. But, uh, what is that saying? You can't teach an old dog to stop doing old tricks? I think that's how it goes, and therefore the thing I did next is *not* my fault, and I promise I have learned my lesson, mostly, but the truth was that Mozart couldn't talk to Mia directly. Maybe if he could, maybe if Mia knew how many friends she really did have, we wouldn't need to use tricks. But I wasn't ready to admit that I'd broken the law, so:

"We need a plan to get Mia to the Beamblade tournament, and we only have thirty minutes."

A keyboard clicked and clacked. "What's your budget?"

"Zero dollars?"

Click click click click click, like a backspace key over and over. "I see. So you want me to do this pro bone-o." She didn't sound pleased.

"It's for Mia!" I yelped. "You were just trying to help her like a week ago!"

"A lot can change in a week."

"No, it can't! You just wanted to make a pun and now you want to sound cool!"

KNOCK KNOCK KNOCK. "Is everything okay? It sounds like three dogs in there."

Tonio called back out, "Yeah," finally looking confident and ready with a lie. "That's just my stomach!"

"Your—that's y—" I heard whoever was behind the door take a step back. "All right, you . . . keep doing what you're doing."

Jpeg finally spoke again. "Okay, nerds, listen up. In two seconds, you'll hear the sound of a goat." There was a bleat, in the distance, from the other line. "And now the humans."

"Oh no, how did she get out again?" And now, louder: "Mia, we need your help getting Chompy back in the barn!"

Jpeg again. "Mozart, there's a friendship anklet on Mia's dresser. She and Sloan made them last summer, and she won't want to lose it. Once she opens her door, you need to grab it and take it outside. I'll make sure the front gate is left just a little open. I expect you can handle it from there?"

He yipped affirmatively. "Sure thing!"

"Great. Jpeg out." Another burst of static, and then the sound of a door opening. Mozart was already leaving, so I motioned for Tonio to hang up the phone.

Suddenly, silence. Tonio looked from the phone to me, and then at the mirror. "Have I been dreaming this whole time?" he mumbled.

No, I assured him.

"I can't do this," Tonio said, still staring at himself in the mirror. "This isn't the kind of thing I do. I can't talk to dogs and make friends and compete in tournaments. I'm not that kind of person."

You are, I said, and regretted how caught up in the plan I'd become again. I got so excited and forgot to be gentle with him. Too focused on myself, and my meddling. *You are because you're here. And you're doing it.*

"FIRST-ROUND PAIRINGS!" Skyler yelled from the store.

And it's time to go.

"Okay." He reached for the door, then let go of it. "I can't do it."

"I can."

"No, I can't."

Maybe you can't, I tried, *but can we?*

He watched my paws twist and took a slow breath. He nodded.

"Yeah. We can."

— 21 —

"And at table five, Keygator versus . . . Malbrain and Combuster!"

Devon cackled with laughter when Tonio stood up and sheepishly grabbed his cards.

"It sounds stupid," Tonio said.

"No!!!" Devon disagreed. "Combuster is *so* good." *I* liked it at least and wagged my tail to make sure everybody knew.

"You're just saying that."

"And table six: GriffinRider1 versus: Nevod, the First Techromancer."

"See? You believe me now? Mine's just as silly *and* just as good."

Now it was Tonio's turn to smile. "Yeah, I believe you."

Tonio's first real opponent introduced himself as Keegan. He was one of the younger adults in the tournament, with bright blue hair, five different piercings, and an entire rock collection's worth of crystals hanging from his neck. He was also, lucky for us, playing an earth and water deck, which was the worst possible combo against gravity.

"Malbrain, huh? And that fuzzy guy must be Combuster." Keegan played a Buried Manabyte and a Serverpillar. "Kinda scary. You sound like villains."

Tonio didn't answer—he hadn't even looked at Keegan yet—and silently played a Suspended Manabyte and a Sleep Pod on Keegan's Manabyte.

Basically, green decks are really slow—they plant seeds early in the game, hoping that they'll bloom into winning strategies later on. Adding blue—which is all about bringing destroyed cards back from the dead—is meant to be a check to make sure that if you lose important seeds, you can plant them again. But gravity is all about taking control of the board *as it is,* so if Tonio played right, he could make sure the seeds would never grow *without* sending them to the AfterFile, where blue can get to them.

That was, *if* Tonio played right. His nerves were already getting to him. He was trying to stay calm by pretending the other player wasn't really there, but it meant he wasn't paying close enough attention to what Keegan might be doing. Turn two the Serverpillar became ChrysalISP, so Tonio played cards to freeze it up, not thinking ahead to the fact that ChrysalISP took several turns to grow, anyway. Keegan was betting on that choice, and Tonio didn't have cards ready when HORROR.WAV crashed onto the battlefield.

"Nice!" Keegan cheered as he claimed the first Spirit Battery. "Got you this time, kid."

Tonio didn't look bothered at all. "Good job."

"Don't let me get the next one so easy, though, okay?"

Tonio blinked and finally looked up. "Huh? Don't you want to win?"

"Sure I do." Keegan shrugged. "But it's more fun to lose a tough game than to win an easy one. Show me what you've got!"

Tonio's expression softened. "My friend says that, too." He drew a card and considered it.

"Your friend is right!"

Now Tonio was watching Keegan and really analyzing the field. "I don't get it." He put down another Manabyte, and Checkmate, Gravity Runner. "She seems so frustrated and mad when she's losing, but she still says I'm supposed to do my best. But I don't care if I win, so why should I, if it makes people feel bad?"

Keegan pushed a ring on his lip back and forth, flipping a shiny stone in and out of his mouth. "Hmmm. Let me think." He drew a card. "Do you play video games?" And cast an update spell on HORROR.WAV.

"Not really." Tonio cast an Anti-Grav enchantment on the battlefield.

"Do you run?" HORROR.WAV flooded it in response.

"Not on purpose." Tonio contained the water in a Folder of Holding.

"Have you ever gone to an all-night party?" ChrysalISP burst forth into Luna Motherboard.

"I'm eleven." Tonio caught it in a Network. He sent Checkmate on attack.

"So???" Keegan sent HORROR.WAV to defend.

"We don't have a lot of all-night parties." Checkmate's ability activated, and she got a bonus in the Anti-Grav.

"*What* is the world *coming* to!" Keegan gasped. "Back when *I* was eleven, we—I—" He paused and looked at the battlefield. "Well, mostly I played video games, you're right. Good play."

"Thank you." Tonio collected a spirit battery.

"So, what *do* you do?" Keegan asked. He sent HORROR. WAV to the AfterFile.

Tonio considered this. "I draw."

"Perfect!" And didn't play anything. Just had to pass. "Sometimes drawing isn't fun, right? Sometimes you want to get to the end, when you've got something cool done, but you can't get there until you've done the hard part. It's kind of like that."

Another attack from Tonio. He won again and collected another spirit battery. "But at the end you don't have a picture or anything. You just lost."

"That's thinking too small! The picture isn't just that one match. It's all the matches." Keegan peeked at his next card and groaned. "Useless. Bad draw." He held his hand out, palm up, to pass the turn to Tonio.

"I'm sorry." Tonio looked down at the battlefield. He could win now, but he was hesitating.

"Don't be. I knew this deck might not have enough fighters in it. Anyway, all I'm saying is, one match is only the first line of the drawing. And even if I lose a million times, it's just more lines. Then, when I take what I learn and put all the lines together, that's the picture. And that feels *great*, even—and maybe especially—if it felt bad on the way." Tonio pushed his fighters out onto the battlefield, and Keegan sighed—he'd lost. "Maybe that's how your friend feels, too."

I'm not sure that's exactly how Mia thinks, I thought. But Tonio just nodded. "Maybe so." Keegan held out his hand to shake, and Tonio took it. "Thank you."

"I'll get you next time. SKYLER!" he yelled across the hall. "I LOST!"

"Got it!" Skyler called back at a much more reasonable volume, and gave a thumbs-up.

The street outside Roll the Ice was as hot as the store was cold, and as empty as the tournament was cramped. Tonio didn't say anything for a long time, which was fine with me. We had plenty of time before round two, and I felt certain Sergeant and Grizzle were around somewhere, trying to spot me breaking the law.

To tell the truth, I was terrified. I'm still terrified. I'm not even three years old, and I might have to spend the rest of my life in exile already! But if you could have seen his face . . . I think you would have felt you were doing the right thing, too. He was staring toward the bell, drifting in and out of a big smile. He was happy. What was my fear, next to that happiness? It felt like I was getting to hold on to his anxiety for a little while, which is all I really wanted to do.

"Thank you, Buster." He leaned over and wrapped his arms around me in a big hug. "You're the best."

If I wasn't already sure I loved the kid, well . . . I was then.

"HEYBUSTERHITONIOCUTEHUGIBROUGHTMIA BUTIDON'TTHINKSHE'SVERYHAPPYABOUTIT!!!!"

(To be clear, that was a dog, so to Tonio it sounded more like "HORFARFARKROARKHRKORKARKIAU!!!!")

We leaned forward on the bench and watched three fuzzy colors zoom by.

"YOU GET BACK HERE *RIGHT NOW*, MOZART!"

(*That* was a human, so to Tonio, it sounded like a very angry Mia in elephant pajamas.)

We leaned back at light speed so we wouldn't get in her way. Tonio looked at me. I blinked.

"?" he asked.

"!" I suggested.

He nodded.

We ran.

Tonio was not much of a runner, but he pushed extra hard to catch up to Mia, and I tugged him along by the leash.

"Hi, Mia," he said.

"I'm busy," she replied.

"Yeah!" Pant. "I see . . ." Double pant. "That! Can we help?"

She watched him from the corner of her eye. "How are *you* going to help?"

Tough, but fair. Tonio was already running out of steam. The steam he needed for running.

"Bus . . . ter . . . ?" he gasped out. Mia looked down at me, running alongside them, and shrugged.

"Sure, if you can get him to."

I couldn't go until he gave me a command. He dropped the leash and pointed.

"GET!" he rasped. That was good enough.

I turned my attention to Mozart and pumped all four of my legs into a faster run. "Coming your way!" I barked. "Let's make this believable!"

"Gotcha!" Mozart yipped back. The crosswalk up ahead was Big Hand, not Human, so we couldn't cross. "I'm turning around!" He whipped around a streetlamp and headed straight for us. "Dodging left!" he called out just before we collided. I snapped right to miss on purpose, letting him zoom past me. He gave Mia a lot of space, then dove easily between Tonio's legs.

"Alley!" I barked. Mozart curved hard and ran between buildings. I left the humans behind and followed him around the corner.

"BOO!" he barked, jumping out from behind a trash can. I scrambled my legs into a sudden break—my ears flattened and I growled reflexively. Mozart yipped a little laugh. "Gotcha. Now hurry up and put me in your mouth before the humans get here."

I gently scooped him up with my jaws and turned to pose proudly as the kids rounded the corner.

"Finally," Mia grunted.

"I'm going to die," Tonio gasped.

Mia collected her anklet from Mozart's mouth and untied a leash from her waist. I dropped Mozart.

"Don't be so dramatic." Mia rolled her eyes.

"No—" Tonio croaked. "I'm serious, I—" He tried to get a whole breath but couldn't make his lungs do it, so the air fluttered unpleasantly at his throat. He tried to fan himself with both hands, but it didn't look very effective. He gave up and clutched at his chest, stretching the green fabric of his shirt. "I think I'm having a heart attack."

"You're not having a heart attack," Mia told him.

"I can't breathe!" he argued.

"You can breathe enough to talk," Mia pointed out.

"That doesn't mean anything!"

She crouched in front of him, elbows resting on her knees. "I think you just *exercised*." I tossed myself over his lap and tried to help him pull out of what was now,

I was sure, a panic attack. Tonio squeezed his eyes shut, clenching and unclenching his hands.

"Ooooh," Mia said. "Is this your psoriasis?"

Tonio shook his head once, fast. *"Anxiety,"* he corrected. "And no!"

But then his heart rate came down a little bit, and he said, "Maybe."

Hands buried in my fur, he laid back on the pavement and kept his eyes closed. He focused on his breathing for a minute, then said, "Yeah, I think so. I'm okay."

Mia stood up and checked her pajamas for dirt. "Thanks for your help."

"You're welcome," Tonio answered, surprised.

"I was talking to Buster."

Tonio didn't know what to say to that. He opened his eyes and stared up at her from the ground.

"I'm gonna go," she said at the same time Tonio told her, "I'm sorry!"

They both stopped to replay what the other one said in their heads, and then said, "Sorry for what?" and "Okay, you can go." At the same time. Mia gave Tonio a look, and he went first this time.

"I didn't mean to surprise you when I said I was moving." He wiped some sweat from his forehead. "I didn't really think you would care. We're not really friends like you and Sloan."

Mia shrugged. "Yeah, well, Sloan and I aren't really friends like me and Sloan, either."

"Don't say—"

She held up a hand to stop him. "I mean, who cares? I barely know you, you're kind of creepily quiet most of the time, and you might throw up on me at, like, any second. We're not really friends. I don't know why I was upset, either."

That was a little bit of progress, even if it came hidden in some insults. She went from *who cares?* to *I was upset*, so at least she wasn't trying to pretend it didn't matter to her.

Tonio pushed himself up to a sitting position. He winced and yanked his hands off the hot pavement and tucked them into his lap. *Try walking around on it all day,* I thought. "I can help you, if you want. To figure it out."

"Huh?"

"Why you're upset. My doctor says that sometimes our brains are like a mystery, even to us, and we have to try to figure out our feelings on purpose." He blushed. "Like a detective."

Mia rolled her eyes. "That's stupid." But then she looked down at him with a softer expression. "Why do you even care, anyway?"

Tonio didn't hesitate. "Because I think you're wrong. I think we *are* friends. And I want to be a good one."

Her face flared into an expression that I thought was

anger at first—it looked a lot like her angry face, but maybe that's just her Strong Emotions face—and then tears started rolling down both cheeks. "That doesn't make sense. I'm not even nice to you."

Tonio was choking up, too; I think mostly because she was crying. "You're always honest with me. I think that's better, sometimes." He wiped at his eyes and laughed a little bit. "Even when you are a little mean, yeah."

Mia sighed. "I was going to leave, too."

Tonio already knew that, thanks to me, but he obviously couldn't explain that right now, so he just said, "Oh?"

"Sloan's parents used to say stuff like 'You're over here so much, you're like another daughter!' or 'Maybe we should just adopt you!' So . . . I thought maybe they would. But that was a stupid idea. I didn't even tell her, but I guess she figured it out, because she called to tell me that it *wasn't* possible, and I had to stay in Bellville. I guess I was just mad about that."

"But *you* asked *me* to be your friend," Tonio argued. "Sort of. And that was before she said anything."

Mia rubbed her elbow uncomfortably. "I just felt like it. I don't know why."

Tonio nodded. "I think we're the same."

She gave him a disbelieving look.

"Not the same in a lot of ways, but . . . it seemed like the only way to really fix what was making you sad was to move, right? But you didn't really want to move. You know everybody here, and you love your family, and you've got all your dogs around. Does that sound right?"

Mia nodded, slowly.

"So maybe you were hoping I would give you a reason to stay?"

The door to Roll the Ice chimed as it opened. "Tonio?" Devon's voice called. "Are you out here?"

Tonio gave Mia an apologetic look and called back, "Yeah, I'm here."

I could hear Devon's nice sneakers jogging along the sidewalk. His head poked around the corner first, and his big smile lit up the alleyway.

"Who's that?" Mozart yipped. I kicked him.

"Mia!" Devon was oblivious to the complicated expressions on everyone else's faces. "You made it!"

Mia looked, confused, between Devon's grin and Tonio's bashful expression. "What do you mean?"

"Tonio's been worried about you all day. He fixed up your deck and even got Skyler to let you join in on the second round." He wagged his finger and did his best grumpy-adult imitation. "You should really try to be on time for things, you know. The second round of the tournament is about to start!"

Tonio stood up. "You don't have to go," he said. "I just thought you might still want to. Three hundred dollars, right?" He unsnapped one of the pockets of his shorts and pulled out a deck box for her. "Just for playing a game."

Mia pulled a deep breath in, then let it out in a big sigh. "Yeah. I'll stay." She took the deck from Tonio. "And you should, too, you know."

Devon laughed. "Of course *he's* staying. He won in the first round! You did, too, technically."

They turned and started walking toward Roll the Ice. Mozart jumped for joy, and my tail wagged its absolute hardest.

We'd done it. We'd made our people happy, at least for a little while.

Isn't that what a Good Dog is supposed to do?

⸺ 22 ⸺

Mia strolled into the game store just like someone who wasn't bringing a puppy in against the rules and wearing only elephant pajamas.

"Where's my sign-up sheet?" she yelled over the crowd. Devon laughed. Tonio's face carried enough embarrassment for all three of them. "I've got some beams to blade!!!"

Skyler handed her a clipboard. Mia dragged the pen across it with a series of lightning-quick scratches and passed it back while a dozen adults watched and tried not to laugh at her energy. Only one spoke up—Phil, the grumpy one from our first visit to the store.

"She should really be disqualified for showing up this late." His eyes glared out from under bushy eyebrows. Skyler returned a stern look.

"Special circumstances, Phil."

Phil harrumphed while she listed off Blademaster names and table numbers.

"Nevod versus StoneSeraph, table six."

"Got it!" Devon winked at the other two kids and dragged his backpack over.

"Malbrain and Combuster versus Five Paninis, table three." Tonio glanced at Mia, who shooed him along.

"And at table four, Cool Name versus . . ." She squinted. "The Inevitable Winner of Tonight's Tournament?" Skyler looked over her clipboard at Mia. "That can't be your Blademaster name."

Mia was already tossing Mozart onto table four. "You said it, not me. You're on, Cool Name!"

All three kids won that round. Tonio went into his match ready to fight back, Mia didn't miss a beat with her power-first fire deck, and Devon's yellow deck kept him dancing quickly around his opponent, then dancing victoriously when he grabbed the last Spirit Battery.

Mia rolled her eyes at him on her way to Tonio's table, where she booted his opponent—a nice woman whose deck was entirely robots—out of her seat so the three of them could talk strategy between rounds.

"You shoulda seen me!" Mia slammed her hands down on the table for emphasis. "I had two meteors in my first hand, and on turn three—Bash, the Twin Barrier! She came in and stunned all the Merborgs, and by turn four, it was over."

Devon turned to Tonio. "How was your match against the sandwiches?"

The corners of his mouth quirked up. "Well, it turns out they weren't just paninis, but were, in fact, a human. And I won." He flinched at Devon's playful arm punch.

"Look at you! That was almost a joke!"

Mia drummed the table with her fingers. "I wasn't done with my story!" she complained.

Devon nodded seriously. "I see. We must have been confused, after the part where you said, 'It was over.'"

"That was *obviously* for dramatic effect!" She raised her hand at him, palm up, and looked at Tonio. "Why are you even hanging out with this guy?"

Tonio saw the chance to plant a seed of friendship. "He's actually—"

"Because I saved some of his throw-up and used it to cast a spell and make him my friend."

"That's *so* gross."

"Can we stop talking about my throw-up, please?"

Round three, Devon lost to Phil, which he took okay even though you could tell he was disappointed. Tonio won, which as a trend was making him increasingly nervous. Mia also won and faced Phil in the semifinals.

When *she* lost she didn't take it well, yelling "This is GARBAGE!" for everyone in the shop to hear. "I bought this at the store, opened it, used it, threw it away, they took it to a landfill." Mia scooped up her cards in a big, angry motion. "A hundred years passed, humans got so advanced they didn't need landfills anymore, but when they came by with their trash-cleaning lasers to convert everything to clean energy"—she let her chair fall back as she stood up—"the new guy tried to shoot it and the other guy stopped him and was like, not that one, new guy." She dumped her cards on Tonio's table. "Not Phil's battle strategy. *That's* just garbage."

"I can't believe he got both of us," Devon commiserated. "I beat him when we were just playing casually before, but I'm using the same deck, so . . . I guess he knew what was coming."

"I'm sorry," Tonio said honestly. "I hoped you guys would win."

"The sparkly dragon is what really got me," Mia said.

"He's got *OM*?!" Tonio was stunned. "How am I supposed to win against that?"

Mia crossed her arms. "I don't know, but you have to. You're our only chance to take this guy down."

I could feel his heartbeat skyrocket. "What? What do you mean?"

"It's the finals! You two are the only ones left."

Tonio shook his head. "Maybe one of you could play for me instead? I don't know if I'm ready to be in the finals."

"Not ready?!" Devon looked confused. "You've won every match! You are, by definition, the most ready out of everybody here."

"Except for Phil," Mia pointed out.

"Right," Devon said. "Except Phil. But this is your first tournament, and he's probably done like a thousand."

Tonio's eyes flared wide.

Mia gawked at Devon. "Do you think before you say *anything*?"

"No!" Devon declared with a smirk. "Unlike you, who obviously plans everything you do *very* carefully."

"I dunno," Tonio interrupted before they could escalate into an argument. He wrung his hands on the edge of his shirt and tried not to let the stress show on his face. "I didn't expect to make it this far, and maybe that's enough."

"No way." Mia leaned her chair back onto its back legs.

Devon said, "We just gotta beat Phil the old-fashioned way: pumping up your confidence and helping you win with the power of friendship!" He pulled a Sharpie out of his backpack. "What if we put our hands together and I drew a smiley face on them?"

"What's that gonna do?" Mia asked.

Tonio shook his head. "I read online that drawing on your skin is bad for you."

"Oh." Devon deflated. "I saw it on a show once, so I thought—"

"We can try it!" Tonio blurted out. "It's probably not that bad!"

"It's okay. It was a bad idea."

"No, it wasn't!"

"Yes," Mia said, "it was." She pointed a card at Tonio. "You made me come all the way in here, and you promised to split the money with me. So you can't quit. You just gotta barrel right in and beat him as fast as you can, before he can get set up."

Tonio said, "That makes sense."

Devon shook his head. "You want my advice? Phil wins when he stays all calm and strategic, and he's got a basically perfect deck. But he falls apart when he loses control—I beat him before because he was so worried about losing to a kid, he freaked out. You want a chance, you gotta throw him off balance."

"Thank you," Tonio answered, with an expression that, to me, showed he hadn't processed any of it. I noticed a strange movement under the table and lifted my head to see around the bottom of the chair. Tonio was tapping his leg—the first signal we'd learned in training. He wanted to go outside.

"Heeeeeeeeeey," I whined. "I gotta go!!!! I really gotta goooooo!" I pawed at his ankle.

"You sound like a puppy." Mozart giggled from the table.

Tonio scooted his chair back and looked down with fake surprise. "Oh," he said, "looks like Buster needs to go to the bathroom. I'll be right back."

"Okay, Tonio," Mia said. Then she turned to Devon. "What if we set Phil's pants on fire during the match?"

Devon thought about it. "I think we'd probably get Tonio disqualified."

"Fair."

As soon as we stepped outside, I smelled something on the wind. Two somethings: one big, one small, both *very* official and important. The officers. I tried not to give away the burst of fear I felt, and casually looked around for any sign of them.

"Thank you, Buster," Tonio said. I very carefully kept my face forward, and my body unresponsive. *Where are they?* He led me across the street, to a bench in the little bell park. "I'm gonna mess it all up. I already have. Mia and Devon are nothing alike, and now they're only talking because they want me to win, and if I don't win, they'll know they shouldn't have bothered." I wanted to help him so bad, but I couldn't do anything. It felt like we were back in the beginning, when I was "just a dog," and he was a boy I couldn't help as much as I wanted to.

Be a Good Dog, I reminded myself. *Don't talk back.*

"What should I do?" he asked me.

A rustle in the bushes. Two pairs of eyes peering at me from a hedge beside the bell. Tonio didn't notice them, and I couldn't do anything to let him know we were being watched.

He talking to you? Officer Sergeant underspoke. I started to pose, but she cut me off. *Don't answer that. I want to see what he does.*

I did, too, but I kept my eyes on the officers. Tonio

was nothing if not observant, so I sent prayers silently up to Laika that he'd realize what was happening.

The pause went on for way too long—me watching the officers watching Tonio.

Finally, Tonio sighed. "I wish you could talk," he lamented. "Maybe you'd give me good advice."

I relaxed. It sounded a little forced to me, but I was pretty sure neither of the officers knew Tonio as well as I did. It was believable enough.

All right, you can underspeak. Carefully. Officer Sergeant relaxed a little, too, but Grizzle's fur stayed on end. *We've received some evidence—*

"INCRIMINATING evidence!" Grizzle barked.

"*Nearly* incriminating evidence, that you have not been as careful as you were instructed to be when you moved to Bellville."

I tried to get ahead of what I was sure they were about to bring up—the video. "Nothing happened with the computer!" I rushed to explain. "And I've been a Good Dog. I've even helped Mozart—"

"Plot to change the course of his human's life?" Grizzle interrupted.

Sergeant explained, "We followed him here. We saw that you worked together. I also saw you underspeaking in front of your human the other day, even if I couldn't confirm communication took place."

"You're in trouble!" Grizzle growled.

"But I didn't do anything!" I protested as convincingly as I could muster.

"I have enough to report you as it is, Buster." Sergeant cut her eyes sideways. "Grizzle wants to. But I don't take my report lightly. I know what it would mean for you." *The Farm*, I thought. *No more Tonio.* "And we're not cruel."

I bowed my head in understanding and tucked my tail in deference, but inside I was boiling. Sergeant was trying to make it sound like they were being nice, but really they were threatening me. How is that *nice*? They held all the power—and really could ruin my life, based on decisions a bunch of dogs made centuries ago. How is that fair?

My fear gave way to anger. So what if I'd broken the law? I was *right*. And they were bullying me into hiding who I was, staying quiet when my friend needed me, and calling it *not cruel*.

"Consider yourself on a very short leash," Sergeant said. "We'll be watching more closely until you prove you can be trusted with humans."

I lowered my body even farther but couldn't resist a sarcastic positioning of my foot. Tonio noticed my bow, and I felt him shift and look ahead to where my nose was pointing. But when I looked up, they were gone.

"I guess we should go back inside," he said.

He looked up toward his bedroom window like it would move itself closer and let him climb in. I hadn't helped his nerves—in fact, I'd probably made them worse, since he could tell I was nervous, too. I stood up straight and rested my chin on his knee; he scratched behind my ears. Like a normal boy and his normal dog.

That was, at least, a little nice.

"I really don't want to ruin everything," he whispered. "I've been trying so hard." I flopped my tongue out of my mouth and licked his knee; not Underspeak, and not anything human, either. Just a weird dog move. He made a grossed-out face, but I think he got it.

Dog smell washed over me, and I followed the wind with my eyes—there was Sergeant, peeking around the corner of the Square, still watching.

— 23 —

Skyler came out of Roll the Ice's front door as we approached it, blocking our way.

"Hey," she said. "I just wanted you to know, before you go inside, that I tried to talk them out of it, but it's what they always do for the finals, so . . ."

"What?" Tonio asked, trying to look around her into the store. "Talk them out of what?"

She kicked her leg back onto the door. "It doesn't matter. What matters is that you can do this. And, just in case, I'm sorry."

Her vagueness was starting to scare me, too. What had they done in there?

Skyler pushed the door open with her foot so she could keep an eye on him. Tonio walked inside past her . . .

. . . and then he turned around and tried to walk back out. I sat on the ground to make that a little harder—his wrist caught on the leash and he didn't even try to pull me, just stopped halfway out the door with his arm outstretched. "No. No way."

I took a look inside.

All the tables had been pushed to the edges of the room, and all the chairs were arranged in a wide circle.

Except for one table.

Except for three chairs.

Phil was already sitting in one of them, shuffling his deck.

"I'm sorry," Skyler repeated. And then Devon and Mia were there, talking over each other.

"Remember what we talked about! You have to take him down quick—"

"But keep in mind what he's doing, and don't use up all your strong cards early—"

"And don't be too predictable, because you need to make him nervous—"

"Just have fun!"

"But also win."

Tonio, standing, was as tall as Phil sitting down.

"We getting started or what, kid?" Phil hollered.

Mia finally seemed to notice how scared Tonio looked. She lowered her voice and stepped in the way of his view of Phil. "What's your problem?"

"What do you think?!" Tonio hissed out with uncharacteristic harshness, and gestured to the room.

Mia grinned, unbothered by his intensity. "I know. I was just messing with you."

"That's not nice!!!"

She shrugged. "Well, earlier, someone told me that I'm better than nice." Tonio didn't answer. She continued, more seriously. "I didn't want to leave my room today. Or, like, ever. But I'm glad I'm here right now. And you'll be glad when you wreck this guy's whole deal with Principia's Mirror Blast!"

"Plus," Devon said, "it's okay if you don't win."

"But there's a prize!" Tonio protested.

"Yeah, but it's just three hundred dollars. Who cares?" The skin could have been melting off his face, judging by the looks Tonio and Mia gave him. "Okay, never mind. But it's a game. Don't stress so much about it."

Mia considered Tonio's expression and shrugged in vague agreement. "Yeah, that's true, I guess. And *I* already lost, so I *guess* it doesn't matter if you do, too."

Phil yelled, "This round was supposed to start three minutes ago! I won't be forced into a tie just because you stalled over time."

Mia stuck her tongue out at Phil as Tonio sat down at the table. All the other adults—about twenty had stuck around to watch—settled into chairs around the room that were too far to really see the cards, as far as I could tell. Mia and Devon sat together, which was a small victory on its own. They scooted their chairs up closer than everyone else's.

I couldn't risk saying anything—there was a clear view from the front windows—but I nudged Tonio and he looked down. I shook my whole body out like I was covered in water. Not Underspeak, not human—just Tonio-Buster speak. He smiled and shook out his hair back at me.

Let's do this.

"*That* chair is for Combuster!" Skyler explained. I hopped up. On the chairs, Tonio and I were about the same height, which was funny. I sniffed at his ear with my wet nose, and he shoved me away with a tickled giggle before he remembered to be nervous.

"AND NOW," Skyler announced, "for the FINAL MATCH! SuperPhil versus Malbrain and Combuster!"

A few adults let out small *woo*s for us.

"Oh, great," Phil grumbled. "So now if I win, I'm the jerk who beat the kid and his dog."

"Lose and it won't matter!" Mia suggested loudly.

Tonio grabbed the box holding his cards and wiggled them out into his other hand. He shuffled systematically, laying cards down neatly across six different stacks and shuffling those gradually together. (Bridge shuffling would be faster, but this was easier for Tonio's smallish hands.)

After three of these moves, the weight of Phil's impatient stare made it clear they were as shuffled as they were going to be. Tonio placed his deck next to Phil's, and their hands crossed over each other's decks to cut them: each placing the top half to the side, then the bottom half back on top. An honorable gesture, that ensured neither was cheating with their shuffle.

Phil flipped a coin. "Call it," he said. Tonio wasn't expecting this, so he stumbled over an answer.

"Tail—or, he— I—" He didn't answer before it clattered to the table. Heads. "Sorry."

Phil sighed, exasperated, and tried again.

"Heads!" Tonio called out.

The coin landed. It was tails. Seven cards for each of them; Phil played first.

And, listen, no one would love to go into the minute details of this match more than me, but I don't want to waste everyone's time. I would love to tell you about the first back-and-forth of this match, because it was *really* important to the next five turns, and basically Tonio and Phil froze each other's first Manabytes with stasis, which would *seem* like it equaled out, but Phil's turn advantage plus two turns of Tonio drawing no new Manabytes meant Phil got ahead pretty fast in terms of resources—but then he *kept* playing Manabytes, so it seemed like maybe he was overcharged, which is what Blademasters say when they draw too many Manabytes and not enough heroes, spells, or tech. I thought this might ruin the game for him, but then he drew a black hole and wiped the board, which—

. . . I guess I did end up telling you about most of it, but for the Court's purposes, the card-by-card details don't really matter. Mia was right; Phil's deck *was* like

Tonio's, but where Tonio's deck stalled, stabilized, and balanced, Phil's deck destroyed. Over and over. Phil removed any cards Tonio placed on the field, even at the expense of his own. Black hole, black hole, black hole. No movement.

He was stalling very effectively, and Tonio was starting to get frustrated. They played in total silence save for brief descriptions of what they were doing and Mia's opinions on the sidelines.

At the moment everything started to go bad, Phil was actually down one Spirit Battery (Tonio'd gotten an early hit in, like Mia suggested) and was sitting on a couple of good backup heroes (like Devon wanted him to).

And then he played Om, the Martian Dragon.

The monster's foil face, which I thought seemed beautiful before, was suddenly a lot more intimidating. Tonio froze when he saw it. Phil just smirked.

"Did you get this from a booster pack?" Tonio asked.

"No," Phil said, "I bought it here."

"At Roll the Ice?"

"Yeah."

"Was it the only one?"

Phil shrugged. "I think so."

Tonio frowned. *Dang.* In all the commotion about Mia and Devon, I forgot that Tonio wanted something, too.

The only card he couldn't draw himself. But Phil had gotten there first.

"His power lets me pull black holes back from the AfterFile once per turn, and—"

"He's got Grav immunity," Tonio realized. "So he won't be affected by them. Or my stasis fields."

"Right."

Tonio tried to play Cordurboy, but he was sucked into a black hole immediately, and then the next turn Om took out one of Tonio's Spirit Batteries like it was nothing.

Devon gave a little wail. "It's not over," Mia assured him. "There's still two more!"

In the time it took her to say that, Tonio had lost another one. His heart was pounding and sweat was trickling from his armpits as he stared, tunnel vision, at the battlefield, racking his brain for anything he could do.

I wasn't in his head, as much as I sometimes wanted to be, and this wasn't his room. He wouldn't feel comfortable talking to me in front of all these people, and I wasn't supposed to talk back to a human, anyway. But I could guess how he was feeling, and that guess told me he was giving up.

I could imagine Tonio thinking there was nothing on the field, nothing useful in his hand, and no plan he could think of to win. If he lost, he couldn't split the money with Mia—and wasn't that why she was still there? When that was gone, one of his only friends would be gone. And then she'd stop talking to Devon, and Tonio would move, and Devon would be alone and bullied. And Devon mostly talked to Tonio about Beamblade, anyway, right? What if Devon didn't want to be friends with a loser like Tonio once he saw that Tonio really *was* a loser?

"Tonio? Are you okay?" Skyler asked.

And it wasn't just those two. Everyone in Roll was watching him, and at least one of the adults was rooting for him. And everyone he'd beaten that day, and even me, Buster. He'd feel he was letting us all down if he didn't do exactly the right thing, in that moment, to win the match. And he didn't know the right thing, so he'd believe he already ruined everything, wouldn't he?

I hope by now you can understand what it must have been like to be in his head.

All the lies he was telling himself.

All the pressure he was putting on himself.

"Do you need to go outside? Tonio?"

Most of those thoughts were nonsense. They were wrong. It was anxiety; that's what it does! You accept one thing that's not *exactly* true, and then that convinces you to believe something that's *mostly* not true, and before you know it, you believe something completely false. But once you let yourself believe the first one, it's frozen. It's a rule—a law—in your brain. And unless you ask questions of those thoughts, search through the mystery for the lies, you keep moving forward believing things—often horrible things—that all try to convince you the only right move is not to play.

Phil spoke up. "Official Beamblade tournament rules say a player cannot go more than two minutes without making a move. He's definitely already past half that."

"Are you serious, Phil?" Skyler asked.

"I'm just trying to play by the rules, unlike *some* people here."

Tonio's breath was staggering, and his eyes were welling up with tears. He stared straight at the table and tried to make his panic attack as small as he could, tried not to make a scene, but the adults were starting to get nervous that he wasn't moving at all.

"Could you just chill out, for one second, Phil?" Skyler said.

"Sure, I can chill out for exactly thirty more seconds."

Tonio needed a break. He needed time to do the work, solve the mystery, and investigate his thoughts.

"Come on, buddy," Skyler said. "You can do it."

I realized, suddenly, what I could do.

We were a team, after all.

"Ten seconds," Phil grunted.

"ARF!" I barked, to grab everyone's attention. I threw my paw up on top of Tonio's deck and pulled a card off it.

"What's that dog doing?" someone called out.

"Buster?" Mia said.

I wedged the card between my nose and paw and flipped it over my paw so Phil couldn't see it. Tonio's eyes moved, finally, to me, with a stressed and confused expression. *Bad brain*, I posed. *Play along.* I licked his forehead quickly and sloppily to add something like *Don't worry* onto that, and grabbed a card from the hand he was holding up. I tossed the card—a Suspended Manabyte—onto the table, and used all his Manabytes to summon the hero I just drew:

Principia, the Galaxy's Reflection, landed on the battlefield, featureless metal skin under a flowing mirror dress. She was an *extremely* lucky draw, especially for this moment. She copied the abilities of another hero on the field, which meant she could borrow Om's Grav immunity. She'd be safe from those annoying black holes.

The rest of the room, and probably everyone here in court, was more concerned with the fact that I had played a card than that a good card was played. Everyone was staring at me, and I tried to ignore them and focus on what mattered: Tonio, and the game.

His breath was the loudest thing in the room—I'd bought him another two minutes, but he wasn't calming down. His knuckles dug into his leg as he finally dragged his eyes up from the table and saw everyone staring at us. With great effort, he lifted his fist onto the table and twisted his knuckles in a paw gesture to me.

Why? he asked. *Trouble*, he added, using his other hand, too. I was relieved—talking was always hard for him when he was having difficulty breathing, but it seemed like he could underspeak, at least a little.

I glanced toward the window but thought better of looking for the officers. *Whatever.* I'd made my choice, and if I'm honest with myself, I know I made the choice back when I first played Beamblade. Tonio was worth it.

Still, I didn't really want to be responsible for changing everyone's view of the world forever just because of a card game. So for the sake of the room, I had to put on a *little bit* of a show. I pretended like Tonio's knuckle movements were training gestures, and I pushed Principia forward, then turned the Manabytes to show they were used. I tapped the table twice with my paw and let out a little bark to try to say *pass*.

The first person to talk was Phil, whose interest in winning overrode his surprise at my decision. "That doesn't count," he protested. "Only the person who signed up can play."

I didn't look, but Mia sounded stunned when she said, "Buster's a service dog. If Tonio trained him to help play, then he's just doing his job." She paused. "But I didn't know he'd trained him this well."

Devon sounded as chill as ever. "And, you know, he kind of *is* signed up. His name's in there and everything."

No one else said anything for a good ten seconds.

Until Phil said, "But—"

"*No buts,*" Skyler cut him off. "He's a dog, Phil. Are you about to really argue he's smart enough to play on his own?"

"Of course not, but—"

"Then shut up about the rules," Keegan pleaded from the audience, "and blade!"

"Against a *dog*?"

"Against Tonio *with a dog's help.*" Mia was sounding like herself again. "And, uh, isn't it your turn? Beep beep beep, my watch says it's been *about two minutes.*"

". . ." Phil glared at me.

I wagged my tail.

"Fine."

Phil couldn't play as quickly now—the black hole wouldn't knock out Principia—and our two heroes had inverted strengths. She had defense where Om had power, and if they fought directly, they'd cancel out and both fall. But now Phil had something he didn't want to lose, so he started playing more carefully.

"Tick, tock!" Mia chimed.

"Quiet!" Phil snapped. His face was flushed—we'd thrown him off balance. He couldn't do anything except resurrect another black hole, so on the next turn, I drew another card and set it in Tonio's hand, grateful that the plastic sleeves protected them from my slobber.

Phil's whole deck was built around black holes, so

there was nothing he could do if they were reflected back at him harmlessly. His cards were reduced to a bunch of big, scary nothings. Still, the holes could eat up weaker cards, so I had to keep passing and drawing until we had something to break the stalemate.

Mia? Tonio asked.

Likes you. Likes Beamblade. I gestured with my nose over to Mia and Devon, who were watching the game and cheering him on when they could. *Maybe likes Devon.*

Tonio took a slow breath. I drew a card and passed the turn.

Devon? Tonio asked.

Likes you. Likes Beamblade, I repeated. *Very . . . calm.* I didn't have a good way to say *chill* in Underspeak.

He nodded and tapped a card to suggest I play it. I drew, did, and passed.

Game . . . bad? I took that to mean he was asking about losing.

Nothing, I answered.

Nothing?! he repeated, alarmed. I wished his vocabulary was better.

Nothing bad, I clarified.

He wiped his eyes with the back of his arm. Phil tested attacking with a smaller hero—Tonio followed with his eyes as I dropped a bubble and slid it forward with my paw, capturing Phil's hero and leaving it too weak to get past Principia.

You! Tonio realized. I gave him a sideways look and dipped my head in a shrug.

Good/Bad, I said, trying to cover everything I felt about the situation in one simple and completely clear thought. *Helping!*

He wasn't totally satisfied with that answer, but he *was* relaxing. I drew another card.

The Gray Beamblade. We both knew as soon as we saw it that it could turn the game around. The Beamblade gained power for every gray card on the field, and since Phil was also playing a gray deck, it could leech gravity from everything on both sides and arm Principia with a hyper-dense, ultra-powerful weapon of pure . . . dark matter, I think? The lore actually isn't totally clear about that.

I looked up at Tonio, and he nodded. "Good boy, Buster," he said out loud. I saw Skyler relax with relief—she'd been tensed and ready to spring forward to bail Tonio out any second. "Have a treat . . . little puppy dog," he added, less convincing. But he did get a treat out of his pouch and toss it up in the air for me to catch.

I wasn't going to *not* eat it.

They're delicious.

Tonio finally lifted his eyes up to Phil. "I'm gonna, uh,

I'm gonna equip Principia with the Gray Beamblade."
He put it down on the table.

Phil stared at it. The crowd leaned forward in their chairs. Did he have something to counter it? A Bug? Some surprise card slipped in from another color?

Ten seconds.

Thirty seconds.

One minute.

Two minutes.

"Whatever," Phil said finally. "I concede." He flipped over his last two Spirit Batteries himself.

Mia and Devon cheered, and then the whole crowd erupted alongside them. Suddenly, everyone was swarming us, petting me and congratulating Tonio. I was surrounded by hands and smiles and laughter.

Mia and Devon hugged Tonio together.

"You did it!!!" Devon said.

"Three hundred big ones!!!!" Mia called out.

"They're normal-sized ones," Devon corrected. "Three hundred big ones would be a *lot* of money."

"How much is a big one, then?!" Mia looked at him incredulously. "I thought that just *meant* money."

"What did you think little ones were??"

"Quarters!!!"

"Excuse me," Tonio said, pushing past Mia and Devon. He ignored the crowd and slipped between them without looking back.

reeeeeeeeeeeeeeeeeeeeeeeeeeeeeeeeeeeeeee

Something, some sound, was nagging in the back of my head. Something buzzy and annoying. I shook it off, dodged the petting hands, and hopped off my chair to follow Tonio.

"Sorry, excuse me." *We should be celebrating*, I thought. *What is Tonio doing?*

reeeeeeeeeeeeeeeeeEEEEEEEEEEEEEEEEEEEEE

And what was that *noise*?

Tonio made it to the bathroom and turned around, searching the ground for—me. He found me and held up a finger. *One second*, he mouthed. Oh. I bobbed my head in understanding but went over to the door just in case and tried to listen in.

REEEEEEEEEEEEEEEEEEEEEEEEEEEEEEEEEEEEEEE EEEEEEEEEEEEE

But that noise was getting really loud now. It was filling up my whole hearing with a high, piercing, horrible shriek.

No one else seemed to notice. The crowd was laughing and joking, teasing Phil and swapping cards, like their ears *weren't* out to get them, except—

"Mozart?" I'd forgotten he was here. *Whoops*, I thought, *he saw everything up close, so I'll have to—*

REEEEEEEEEEEEEEEEEEEEEEEEEEEEEEEEEEE EEEEEEEEEEEEEEEEEEEEEEEEEEEEEEEEE

—*deal with that later.*

"Are you okay?" I could barely hear Mia, mostly picked the words up from the shape of her mouth. Mozart was squirming in her arms, pawing at his ears. Where was it—

REEEEEEEEEEEEEEEEEEEEEEEEEE EEEEEEEEEEEEEEEEEE

—coming from? *Outside*, I was pretty sure, and I had to make it *stop*, but I heard, just barely, the chunky sound of Tonio throwing up in the bathroom.

Oh, buddy, I'm sorry, I thought. *I can't just leave, I have to—*

REEEEEEEEEEEEEEEEEEEEEEEE EEEEEEEEEEEEEE

The assault on my ears was starting to make me feel dizzy, but the sink was running, and Tonio was probably rinsing his mouth out, so in just a second he would

REEEEEEEEEEEEEEEEEEEEEE EEEEEEEEEEE

I staggered to the door

REEEEEEEEEEEEEEEEEEEE EEEEEEEEEEEEEEEEEEEEEE EEEEEEEEEEEEEEEEEEEEEE EEEEE

Tonio washed his hands and

REEEEEEEEEE EEEEEEEEEEEE EEEEEEEEEEEE EEEEEEE

by the time he came out

REEEEEEE EEEEEE

I was gone.

The End

"And that's the end. The officers were using one of those high-grade dog whistles, as you know, and the second I walked outside they muzzled and cuffed me." Buster sat back in his bumper car and tried to calm down—telling the end of the story had raised his hackles. "Which, I'd like to add, was *way* more suspicious than anything I did on my own. Me, the hero dog of the hour, disappearing all of a sudden? Right after I showed off how well trained I was?" Buster couldn't resist a tiny growl of frustration. "It was suspicious the first time, and now it's suspicious again. You get rid of me, there's going to be talk. Somebody will put it together."

The colorful lights of the bumper car arena were still spinning as dawn began to peek up over Juicy Fun Theme Park and Strawberry Orchard. Buster's story had gone on for hours, and many of the dogs attending had fallen asleep curled into balls or splayed out on their backs. Even Lasagna and Pronto looked like they were struggling to stay awake; only the judge showed no signs of drowsiness.

"While the Court appreciates your *excessively detailed*

story, Buster," Pronto said, waving away a yawn with his paw, "nothing you've told us changes your situation. Our first law remains clear: No dog may reveal the truth of our society to a human, and you have done just that." The husky looked up at the judge, who was staring down from atop her bumper car mountain, expressionless. "I'm sure the judge will keep in mind your suggestions for how officers should behave in *future* situations."

Lasagna cut in. "Your Honor, I know we're almost out of time, but I'd like to say a few final things before you make your decision."

Sweetie nodded. "You have the floor, Lasagna."

The corgi lawyer batted his tie straight and coughed once to clear his throat. He shuffled his papers and found the one with his speech written on it. "Your Honor, I come before you today not just as Buster's representative, not just as the best Dog Court lawyer in South Carolina, but as a member of a growing movement in the dog world: those who believe we should, at last, take our rightful place beside humanity. Not as pets, but as equals."

Buster's ears flattened, concerned. Wasn't this supposed to be *his* trial? Shouldn't Lasagna be here just as his representative? *I didn't sign up to be a "growing movement,"* he thought. But he'd told his story. There was nothing more for him to do.

"I, in communication with my fellow dog lawyers

around the world, have discovered something concerning: Incidents like Buster's, where humans have needed a dog and a dog has risen to the challenge, have been happening everywhere. Times are changing! But it would appear that wherever possible, the Court has gone out of its way to hide this from us."

The crowd of dogs was fully awake now—and Buster was surprised back into attention.

But I'm the "Miracle Dog," right? he thought. *I'm the only one.*

Deep down, though, he knew he couldn't be. He remembered how easily Mozart, Jpeg, and Leila were willing to help Mia. Lasagna also seemed to be on his side . . . and that was just in Bellville. If every town had even just a few dogs that agreed with him, then there had to be *thousands*. At least!

"By sending these dogs to The Farm—and then refusing to acknowledge their contributions—you are preventing us from moving forward as a species."

Pronto growled, furious. "This is nonsense, Your Honor. We have seen the horrors humans are capable of. And though I am honestly tired of reminding everyone what this trial is *about*, we are not here to discuss movements, or other dogs, or changes to the law. We are here to decide if Buster has *broken Dog Law, as it stands*, which he absolutely has. I don't understand why we are still talking!"

It was like all the cute and squeaky layers of Lasagna had been peeled away, leaving just a layer of sauce and meat. This was what the corgi really cared about. This was what mattered to him. "If we don't change things now, Your Honor, then when?" he asked. "Dog Law, as Pronto said, has been in place for centuries. It has been *hurting* and *limiting* us for centuries. When do we decide that enough is enough?"

"*We* don't," Pronto argued. "Do you claim to know better than the generations of dogs who came before us? We are happy, and comfortable, and *safe* for a reason. That all changes if we give in to what he's suggesting. It's chaos."

The court was starting to rumble now. Dogs who agreed with Lasagna were arguing with dogs who agreed with Pronto. Buster turned his back to the judge for the first time and watched schnauzers and dachshunds working through the same thing he'd been working through with Tonio. Was it worth it to help a human? Was it worth it to do everything you can with the life you have? Even if it's risky?

Lasagna proclaimed, "The second Dog Law, which I have not heard the representative for the Law mention much this evening, states: 'Dogs must do their best to protect all living things, even food.' Dogs who have chosen to become service dogs have an even greater responsibility to their humans. Buster was acting true to his purpose, and was given an impossible decision to make."

Judge Sweetie shook her head, draping fur swishing with every movement of her long face. Finally, she spoke. "The decision was not impossible, and Buster has admitted himself that he knew he was breaking Dog Law. In my position as judge, I have only one choice: The Farm."

Buster's heart sank with the crowd's volume. So that was it, then. He'd told his story, and it hadn't mattered. He was no closer to seeing Tonio again than he had been before.

"With all due respect, Your Honor, what kind of dogs are we if we let humans suffer just because we're scared?" Lasagna barked clearly and powerfully; he'd practiced this speech. "So many of us believe we need to take responsibility for the world. The *whole* world, and not just dogs."

"I have made my decision," the judge said.

At these words, Pronto relaxed and looked over to them with a faux-sympathetic expression. "I'm *so* sorry, Lasagna. It was a good try, but your little 'movement' ends here."

Lasagna ignored him and underspoke to Buster: *I'm sorry.*

Buster squeezed his eyes tightly closed and imagined what Tonio was doing. He was probably in his room, pacing, worried about Buster and wondering when he was coming home. Or lying on his bed, panicking. Buster tuned out all the carnival music and the crowd of dogs and thought: Had he done enough? Had he helped Tonio enough in their time together to change his life? Maybe he wouldn't ever know. And maybe he should be worried about the rest of *his* life.

His thoughts were interrupted by a bark that pierced through the air, yelled from the back of the bumper car arena.

"Your Honor!" Officer Sergeant called. "Permission to interrupt!"

The judge banged her squeaky gavel to quiet down the crowd, then spoke. "You already have, Officer. Go ahead."

"We caught a human along Juicy Fun's perimeter. He was talking to himself about if he could jump the fence, and wondering, quote, 'whether I would even make a difference if I climbed the fence, anyway, because what am I going to do, ask a bunch of dogs I don't know to give Buster back? It's not like I even really know what's really going on, or whether I'm making things worse. I should probably just go home.'"

Buster's tail wagged on its own. *That sounds like Tonio!*

"We thought he *would* go home after all that, but then he started climbing the fence, anyway, so we went ahead and captured him just in case."

"Well," the judge said with the tiniest bit of humor in her voice, "at least that buys us some time. He can't tell anyone else if he's here."

Buster couldn't contain himself. "Please let me see him! None of this is his fault, and he must be so scared. At least let me talk to him."

The judge drank a few laps of cold coffee from her bowl while she considered his words. "Fine. This case is growing more complicated than I expected, anyway. I need time to discuss today's events with the other judges of the Court. Officer Sergeant, take Buster to his human and keep an eye on them. Lasagna, Pronto, take care of whatever you need to and meet me back in my office. We'll need to finish this privately."

"Thank you!" Buster's tail wagged. He jumped up and down with relief in his bumper car, all thoughts of the crowd, and the Law, and this horrible, horrible day gone for a moment. "Thank you so much, Your Honor!"

Sweetie bobbed her head. "The rest of you go home to your humans, if you've got them. It's early, and you don't want them wondering where you've been. *Up!* Come on, *up, up* . . . Good. Good dogs. Court adjourned."

Reunion

The three pugs formed a tight triangle around Buster and herded him alongside Officer Sergeant, away from the bumper cars. Buster wondered if he should be mad she'd turned him in, and she wondered if she should be angry at him for breaking the Law. Both of them felt bad.

"Dog Court isn't evil," she said to break the silence. "And neither is the judge. We have to worry about a lot more than just one human."

"I know." Buster was going to leave it at that, but he found himself getting more frustrated than he expected. "But if we aren't worrying about any *one* human, then who *are* we worrying about? Because it sounds like we're just worried about us."

"So what if we are?" The officer knew she wasn't supposed to argue with a prisoner, but she outranked the bailiffs, so they weren't going to say anything. "We have to keep our own people safe."

"Safe from what?" Buster huffed. *"Tonio?"*

"You know they aren't all like Tonio. Most humans

aren't." They came to the edge of a huge Ferris wheel at the center of the park, twinkling with colored lights on every box but not moving. Officer Sergeant dismissed the pug bailiffs and stepped through the loop on Buster's leash to make sure he couldn't run away.

"I was a pet before I was an officer of the Court. They weren't— They didn't—" She searched around for the words, then decided it wasn't her job to find them. Buster didn't need to know all the details. "I left because I had to. Not all humans care about us, Buster. You had two chances, with two different sets of humans who loved you, and you threw them both away because you wanted to feel like a hero. That's not anybody's fault but yours."

He didn't know what to say to that, so he didn't say anything. Sergeant stood on her hind legs in the operation booth and pulled a lever. The Ferris wheel rotated slowly around, and Buster caught a whiff of paint, paper, card stock, sweat, and a little bit of his own scent layered under human kid smell. *Tonio!*

Buster patted the ground in relief. He hadn't been away from his human for this long since they'd met, and he was more than ready to see him again. The carts swung around, and around, and around—and then finally Sergeant pulled the lever and stopped the spinning.

Tonio jumped to his feet on the other side of the cart's bars. "Buster!"

Buster barked back and wagged his tail. "Tonio!"

Sergeant pushed a button, unlocking the cart. Tonio took a step out, and she growled. "No chance. Get back in there." Buster translated into simple Underspeak, and Tonio nodded. "Okay. Sorry."

The officer jerked her head toward the Ferris wheel. "Get in, Buster."

"Uh, what? I have to get in that?"

"We don't know how long the judge will be. I can't watch you all day."

Buster's tail tucked between his legs. He shifted uncomfortably from paw to paw. "Okay, but could you—"

"Get in, Buster. Now or never."

He braced himself and ran into the cart before he could change his mind. Sergeant pushed a button and the door swung shut on them while Buster hopped up on his hind legs and licked at Tonio's face. Tonio laughed and pushed him away. "The face? Really? Come o— Ah! Your tongue got in my mouth!! Gross!!!" Buster bumped up against Tonio's legs and let the boy pet him, briefly forgetting where they were.

Then the cart started moving.

"What?!" Buster yelped. "Can't you just leave us on the ground?"

Sergeant posed apologetically. "It's the rules! Sorry, Buster. We'll get you when the judge is back."

Buster whined and pulled himself away from the bars. He laid down in the cart and shut his eyes tight, trying not think about how high up they were going.

"Are you scared, Buster?"

He whined again. *Yes. Aren't you?*

"I'm not really scared of heights, I guess. I am a *little* scared that no one's been around to inspect this in a long time, probably, but—" Buster whined again. Tonio sat down next to him and rubbed his head. He stared out of the gently swinging cart to see Juicy Fun in all its run-down, abandoned glory. "You'll be okay, boy. We're not going to fall."

Buster recognized something in his tone, and in his expression—Tonio was calm, but it wasn't all a good calm. He had a little bit of that face Buster had seen before, after talking to his dad, and when Mia got upset with him. A kind of *nothing*, an absence in his expression. Not sad, not worried . . . just nothing.

He wanted to find out why but couldn't calm his own mind down. No living thing should ever be this high up, especially in a giant machine they weren't even controlling. The Ferris wheel stopped moving when they were all the way at the top—unable to leave, no way to get down even if they could open the door.

After a while of shivering, with Tonio silently petting

him, Buster started to relax. But he felt so *tired*. Head resting in Tonio's lap, fingers running through his fur . . . and he'd been up all night, too. Maybe it wouldn't be so bad if he just . . . took a nap.

"That's better," Tonio whispered. He patted Buster's stomach and watched his breathing relax. Tonio tilted his head back and rested it on the bench along the cart's side. "We'll talk when you wake up."

Buster jolted awake suddenly and set the cart swinging as he frantically tried to remember where he was. The angle of the sun meant it was past noon, and the angle of the *ground* meant they were *way past the height he was comfortable with!!!* Buster barked in surprise and jumped away from the edge. Tonio caught him and pushed him down to a sitting position gently.

"We're okay. It's okay. Look at me." Buster's reddish-brown eyes stared into Tonio's just-brown ones. "Take a deep breath." Buster mimicked Tonio's long breath, held his lungs full for a few moments, then mirrored Tonio's slow release. "Good. Nothing's going to happen to you up here, okay? I've got you."

Buster did start to relax at Tonio's words, and got his bearings enough to underspeak a *thank you*.

"You're welcome." Tonio relaxed, too, when Buster didn't seem to be in crisis mode. "I'm sorry I messed this up so bad, Buster."

You?

"I thought I could save you, or something. I don't know. I thought I'd show up and be a hero. But of course I couldn't do that. I can't do anything that matters."

How did you even get here?

"I asked some dogs!" He threw his arms up. "Because that's a normal thing I can do now, I guess. I knew you were gone immediately, and everybody at the tournament was asking about you. I just said you knew your way home and were tired of the crowd. Like I was. Mozart didn't know where you were, but I went to visit Jpeg. She . . ." He shook his head, not believing what he'd seen. "She printed out *directions for me* from *the internet*. And then I asked Skyler to drive me here. I didn't even have to tell anyone why! Mia didn't really pay attention when I was talking to Mozart, and when I told Skyler where I was going, she just said I was 'the coolest kid ever' for going to a place that was 'so definitely, absolutely haunted' and didn't ask any other questions."

That's amazing! Buster headbutted Tonio's chest. *You got here all on your own!*

"I didn't *do* anything. Oh, and—" He pulled a small plastic bag of dog food and another bag of trail mix out of his cargo pockets. "Devon gave me some snacks to bring. Or he just gave me some snacks for no reason. I'm not sure."

I couldn't resist the snacks but underspoke while I chewed.

You did an adventure! You talked to people. Asked questions. Came all the way out here with no idea what you'd find. That's brave. You wouldn't have done that a month ago.

"Yeah, but it doesn't matter. They caught me, and now we're both just locked up. What is happening? What do they want? I know you're in trouble for telling me you're smart, but—"

They decided I'm a Bad Dog. They're going to send me to The Farm.

"I don't know that thing you did with your paw. Send you where?"

I tried to figure out a way to tell him. *Place . . . like . . . the Lins' shelter.*

"A farm?"

Yes. THE Farm.

"What's that?"

It's supposed to be a place humans have never gone. It's where Bad Dogs go, and where Dog Court is based. I don't know where it is, but I would be there forever. No more humans. You get all the food you need, and it's supposed to be pretty, but there's nothing to do. Just sitting around for the rest of your life.

"Sounds kind of nice," Tonio mumbled.

Buster bared his teeth. *No. I want to be here, with you.*

Tonio's eyes filled with tears almost immediately. "Why? You're only in trouble because of me."

I'm in trouble because I broke the rules. You didn't do that.

"Still. You were trying to help me."

And I would do it again!

Tonio buried his face in Buster's fur. "You're a good friend." His voice came out muffled, but Buster understood.

So are you.

Buster heard someone down at the base of the Ferris wheel. He stepped to the edge—but then thought better of it and stayed in the middle. The cart jerked back into motion suddenly, swinging them toward the ground.

"Am I in trouble, too? What will they do to me?" Tonio asked.

Buster tilted his tail into an unsure pose. *I don't know. I've never heard of what happens when a human finds out.* He didn't want to tell Tonio that he was scared, too. They couldn't do anything terrible to him . . . right? He was a human!

Tonio stared out of the cart and rubbed at Buster's head absentmindedly. "If it wasn't for my anxiety, you wouldn't be here. I wouldn't be here. Mom and Dad wouldn't spend all their time worried about me. Mia and Devon would have a friend who didn't throw up and try to leave all the time. Bellville would have . . . something else. Something better than me."

They were halfway down now.

You don't know that. Buster nipped at his fingers. *Anxiety or not, you are the one people got. And they all like you. We are all glad you are around.*

"But I could be *better.* If I was anyone else—"

Anyone else wouldn't have noticed that I was really smart, even when I was pretending. Buster underspoke energetically, hitting all the poses clearly and deliberately so Tonio would understand. *Anyone else wouldn't care so much about me, or Mia, or Devon, or your parents—you are worried that you aren't doing a good job, but some people wouldn't try at all. You* care, *Tonio, not just worry. That's what matters.*

"I don't know," Tonio mumbled meekly. He wanted to believe it, but there was so much evidence in his head that contradicted it. Buster was just being nice, Tonio wasn't any more caring than the average person, and wouldn't someone who was kind *and* didn't worry be even better than him? "I don't know if you're right."

Buster was about to respond, but the cart rolled to a stop at the base of the Ferris wheel. Officers Sergeant and Grizzle waited for them as the door popped open.

"The judge wants you over at the teacups," Officer Sergeant said, looping a thick rope around Buster's neck. Officer Grizzle guided Tonio's leg into another. Then the officers pulled the ropes taut and led the prisoners off into another part of Juicy Fun.

I'm right. Buster posed as they walked. *I know it.*

Tonio didn't answer.

Tonio's Choice

Before Juicy Fun shut down, the teacup ride had been one if its most famous attractions. The cups were atop a twenty-foot-tall concrete platform decorated in a cheesy mural of palmetto trees under a sparkling night sky, and even the years of being left alone in the weather hadn't worn down the paint. The cups themselves looked like they'd been taken from a grandma giant's dusty cupboard—the patterns were fading, but you could still see the swirls and flowers flowing around the fake-porcelain white.

Officers Sergeant and Grizzle pulled Buster and Tonio up the ramp that wrapped around the platform to the cups themselves. Tonio froze at the end of the ramp, staring at the cup with a blue fleur-de-lis pattern where Judge Sweetie and Lasagna sat awkwardly on the bench meant for humans.

Judge Sweetie barked to the guards, and they unhooked the leashes from both prisoners. Buster stepped forward and noticed a change in Tonio's breath. He turned around to jump up and place his paws on

Tonio's stomach. He barked twice, loudly, and Tonio's head snapped down to look at him.

Buster stood stiff and bumped into Tonio's leg, guiding him to hold on to Buster and lower himself to the ground. When his legs were splayed on the concrete, Buster laid across his legs and took deep breaths in rhythm, trying to guide Tonio's focus back to the physical, the real.

"The judge is waiting!" Grizzle barked. Buster shot him a glare with his lips curled back so far the officer's tail curled under him in a fraction of a second.

"Bad brain!" Buster whined from Tonio's lap while doing the Underspeak for it as best as he could. "Bad brain." Tonio's panic attack had started and it was past the point he would be able to cut it off quickly, but his mind raced as he tried to connect Buster's words into full thoughts in his own head.

I'm anxious, Tonio thought. *These are anxious thoughts. Why? Which ones? It doesn't matter which ones. Even if some of the thoughts are wrong, they're mainly true. No matter what happens here, I've hurt everyone I know. There's nothing I can do.*

Tonio's eyes were squeezed shut, his chest heaving. *It does matter which ones. Start at the beginning. Look at the evidence.*

Tonio caught one deeper breath and felt better knowing

he could still breathe. It always felt like he was never going to start feeling normal again, in the middle of it.

I still don't know very much about dog expressions. I have no idea if any of these dogs hate me.

He looked at Judge Sweetie, who he guessed was the judge because she looked *very* serious.

That sure looks like a frown to me. She seems mad.

There's no way for me to know that! She has a dog face, not a human one! I don't think dogs even smile!!

Plus, they already took off the leashes. They're not tying us to anything. Plus, they're dogs. They're strong. If they wanted to hurt me, they could. But they haven't, and they won't. They have laws, and a court, and a whole world I don't know much about, but they don't seem cruel or evil. I'm not going to die.

His breathing started to slow, and his panic attack started to pass. His heart was still pounding and he was tired, but he was going to feel better. He couldn't handle looking deeper at some of the other thoughts right now: When the cycle got going, when his anxiety spun around itself and created more and more false thoughts, sometimes it hit a place he didn't like to think about afterward. A sadder, darker place that made him feel empty and his brain feel fuzzy.

But he was out of it for now. He scratched Buster's ears and reminded himself he was a real person, in the world, with people waiting to talk to him. Well, dogs. Dogs were also people now, he supposed.

Buster helped his human stand back up, and they walked over to the blue teacup. Tonio mumbled an apology for the wait and slid in first to sit next to the corgi; Buster slid in behind him. When they were all seated, Sweetie waved the officers away and pulled the little door shut. A tablet screen was belted down to the circular wheel in the middle of the teacup, so the dogs could rotate the cup and type with their paws for Tonio to read.

"I wanted to make sure our conversation had privacy," Sweetie explained, both verbally and by typing. Officer Sergeant pulled a lever in the booth and the cup began to rotate around its center, around the center of the ride, and around the other cups. The spin was gentle, but focusing too hard on the movement made Buster dizzy. He kept his eyes on Sweetie once he was sure Tonio had calmed down. "The three of us have reached a compromise—a compromise that Pronto is, perhaps, *less* happy about, which is why he is not here. I'd like to offer—"

"Is everything all right?" Lasagna interrupted, placing a kind paw on Tonio's shoulder and then typing the rest. "I've never seen a panic attack before. That was scary."

"I'm okay," Tonio mumbled. "Thank you." The cup

curled around the edge of the platform, then slingshot its way back toward the center.

Buster glared at the judge. "You made us spend all day in a cage. He's tired, and scared, and you don't even care, do you?"

The judge watched him with a sour expression. "That reminds me." She leaned down below the teacup's center handle and pulled up a basket with her teeth. "I had someone make chicken salad sandwiches. Humans love chicken salad, don't they?"

Tonio took the basket at Buster's signal and opened it up. "Oh, whoa, thank you! I love chicken salad." He also found a little bag of extra meat and fed the pieces to Buster.

"There's a water bottle in there as well," Judge Sweetie added. "And you can take as much time as you'd like."

The teacups kept spinning. Buster's stomach, empty aside from Devon's snacks after a full night of storytelling and a day of curling up in a Ferris wheel, growled loudly at the first smell of chicken. He gobbled up the pieces handed to him, and Tonio ate a sandwich triangle in seconds.

"This is delicious!" Tonio gasped. "Did a dog made this? I—ack—uh—" He reached into his mouth and pulled out a long hair. "Yes. A dog made this. Thank you."

"Of course." Judge Sweetie bowed her head. She waited for their munching to slow down, then started again. "Dogkind has never had a situation quite like this one. We've had scares before, we've had humans learn some of our secrets, but we've never had a human see Dog Court for themselves. We've also never had a human learn any Underspeak, which your human has done remarkably quickly. Still, our typical solution could work here—we would send you to The Farm, Buster, and assign a watchdog to Tonio, who would make sure he never spoke the truth to anyone else." She paused a moment to catch up with the typing.

"But because of your specific situation—and because I'm not heartless—I'd like to offer something different in your case, Tonio. I am willing to send you to The Farm as well, with Buster. The Farm is a beautiful place, truly a paradise—where you would be completely separated from the rest of the world. You would be taken care of, and you would have no responsibilities, but you would also have no further contact with anyone else. You would have no impact on the world, but you would be with Buster. And other Bad Dogs, of course."

"No!" Buster tried to stand but was too wobbly in the spinning cups. He sat back down. "Absolutely not. This is my punishment, not Tonio's."

"I'm not offering this as a punishment." She looked back up to Tonio. "We send dogs there because they can't handle regular society. Based on what I've seen, and what Buster has told me, it seems like you might not be suited to your world, either. So if you want to leave, we can take you. You'll be safe, and no one will find you. I promise."

Tonio wiped chicken salad goop off his fingers, using a napkin from the basket. He pushed his bandanna up and thought about what she was saying. This was what he wanted, wasn't it? Freedom from worry? If he couldn't change anything, if he wasn't around anyone, he couldn't worry about anything. There was nothing he could do differently, nothing he could do wrong.

So many things about the world were scary. What would he do when he got older? What would he do for a job, or for a life? What would happen if he moved to a different city? What if he spent the rest of his life messing up and hurting people? What if he kept having panic attacks, and they never ended as long as he lived? Someplace like The Farm might make that better. And at least that way, Buster wouldn't be alone. Right?

Right?

Buster watched Tonio stare at the sky as they circled the platform. He could guess at what the boy was thinking.

"Tonio," he said, "you can't do this. I messed up, not you. The world needs you to stick around."

Tonio wasn't sure. But he had an idea.

"I think I understand why you do this," he said, addressing the judge. "Why you even have The Farm, and the Law. It's because you don't know what will happen, right? If humans find out that you're smart. The world will change in a big way, and you don't know if that would be good or bad. But since it could be *very* bad, you keep quiet."

The judge bobbed her head yes.

"I get that," Tonio assured her. "I do that, too. When I'm worried, or I'm feeling anxious, I sometimes stop doing anything. I try not to do anything good or anything bad, just in case I might accidentally do something *really* bad. And I could always accidentally do something really bad, so a lot of the time I don't do anything."

He took a drink of water from the bottle and watched the clouds spin in the air. "Buster isn't like that, I don't think. Buster helped me because he wanted to do *something,* even if it might be bad. He wanted to try to do good. Mia is like that, too: She is always doing *something,* and I think that's really cool. And Devon is totally fine with whatever happens and doesn't worry if he's messing up. I want to be that way.

"Dr. Jake says anxiety is a thing that happens in your brain—like something messes up, so you worry too much. But that, sometimes, it's also about what's happening to you. When something is very hard, or I'm very stressed, I can get more anxious. It seems like you are probably anxious, maybe that kind of anxious, right?" Tonio directed this at the judge. She made a pose of confusion. "I mean, you have to worry about all dogs, and about the whole world, and you're still taking time to worry about me and Buster. You must feel pretty anxious, and I bet . . . I bet being a dog can make you feel pretty anxious, too. Keeping secrets all the time."

"Maybe so," the judge agreed. "But what does that have to do with your decision?"

"Why don't you all just go to The Farm? Why don't dogs just leave humans behind, and go do your own thing? Why even live around us if you have to do it like this? It seems so *hard*. It seems like you have to put so much energy into doing so little."

Buster's ears folded back in disappointment. *It sounds like he thinks he should go. That everyone should go.*

Lasagna was eager to answer. "Different dogs will tell you different things. I think, though, that the deepest truth is that we love humans. We want to make a difference in the world where we can, even if it is small. Even if it's slow. Dogs and humans make each other happier, kinder, and safer. We don't have to do those things perfectly for them to be worth it."

Tonio nodded. He'd figured something out. "Yes, exactly! So if that's worth it—making a small sacrifice to do a small good—why not just tell humans the truth? Why not try to do *more* good, even if it's still not perfect?"

"It could be dangerous," the judge explained. "Dogs—and humans—might be hurt."

"Buster helped me. He helped me a little before, and he helps me even more now. I think that was worth it. So . . . no, I don't want to go to The Farm. And I don't want you to send Buster there, either, because I want him around, helping me get better at pushing past my fear." He clenched the handle in the middle of the teacups and bowed his head at the judge. "I promise we won't tell anyone, but I think *you* should."

They spun in silence. Lasagna wagged his tail and turned to the judge. "I *told* you. You see? This is it. This is exactly what I've been talking about. This boy is perfect evidence. He *never* would have said something like this before meeting Buster."

Buster tilted his head at Tonio. That was true, wasn't it? He had made a difference. Tonio was still going to have panic attacks, was still going to worry, but he believed things could change. His time with Dr. Jake made that obvious, but so did his time with Mia, and with Devon. Tonio was different from how he'd been at the beginning of the summer—he was willing to take risks, to push through things even when they were hard.

Was the judge?

She nodded. "You are right, Lasagna. And I'm glad. What about you, Buster? Do you agree with your human?"

Buster wagged his tail. "I do." This was a choice he already made when he chose to reveal himself to Tonio and be a Bad Dog. Doing good, even a little bit of good, was better than doing nothing.

The judge nodded. "Good. Then it's time to tell you the other option."

Tonio watched the tablet screen, startled. "Other option? What does that mean?"

The judge crossed her paws and shook her head. "I hate to be the one to tell you this, but The Farm isn't real."

Buster couldn't tell if he was dizzy from the teacups, or from this news. "What?! But this whole time, you've been—"

"A perfect paradise for dogs?" The judge shrugged. "A place humans have never been? Have you seen the way they've treated this world? They're everywhere. You can't escape them at the bottom of the ocean anymore. No, it doesn't exist." She sighed. "Not yet, at least. And that's because we haven't tried."

Giddy energy was beaming from Lasagna. His tail was wagging, and his ears were up as tall and as high as they could go. "I *knew* it. I knew there was something else going on. Wait until I tell all my lawyer friends, they'll—"

Sweetie placed a paw on his face. "What I'm about to tell you goes against official Court policy, canine tradition, and Dog Law, so we have to be extremely careful. Can you keep a secret?"

"No!" Tonio and Buster both said immediately.

"Well, you have to, for now. Dogs *have* been chang-ing the world. We've just been doing it quietly, behind the scenes, *extremely* carefully. The Farm is a program where we send dogs who need to be removed from society, for one reason or another, and train them into agents for the Court. We would like the two of you to be our first human-and-dog team."

The clips on a briefcase popped. Lasagna pulled out a folder and set it next to the tablet—holding it down so it didn't blow away in the rotating wind.

"This is a contract. If the two of you agree to be ready when I call you—to help the Court when we need it—you can go back home and live your lives like you did before. We'll handle the explanations and the publicity."

"Why us?" Tonio asked. "Why *me?* I'm not cut out to be . . . what, a secret agent? I'm not sneaky, or good at anything like that. I just draw."

"You're who I've got."

It sounded too good to be true to Buster. "How will other dogs feel if we just . . . go back? And what will you ask us to do?"

"The official story will be that I'm putting the two of you under strict surveillance, but realized that pulling you both from Bellville would draw too much attention. I'm afraid it won't make you any more popular, Buster, but it will keep you together." The judge shook her head. "And as for what we might ask of you, that's classified.

I can't say anything more. You'll just have to trust me when I say that we act for the good of Dogkind. And hopefully Humankind, too."

Tonio's eyes fluttered around to the different dogs. He shook his head vigorously. "I can't do this. No way. Why don't you ask Mia and Mozart? Or Jpeg? Or . . . I don't know. Anyone else?"

"Don't tell me you've changed your mind already, Tonio." Sweetie gave him a long look. "You want to do good, right? Even if it's not perfect?"

"I don't know if that's . . ." Tonio's eyebrows pushed together.

"I think your sharp eyes and tendency toward caution will serve us well. But you don't have to agree, of course. I can send Buster away, as planned, and send you back home with an officer on your tail. It's up to you."

Buster read over the contract. It was short, straightforward, and stated that as long as they stayed available to the Court, they'd be free to live the rest of their lives without any interference from Dog Court. He and Tonio would get to just be a kid and a dog. He turned to Lasagna.

"This is real? We can do whatever we want after this?"

"The Court might not even need you. But it's the only way they're going to let you back out into the world." The corgi's tail was wagging again. "And it's some of my finest work, I'd say. Did you see the comma on line thirteen?"

"Uh, yes?"

"*Perfect* comma placement, if I do say so myself. This document is *flawless.*"

"Then I'm in." He looked up at Tonio. *What about you?*

Tonio's hands clenched and unclenched. "What happens if we can't do what you ask? If we're not good enough?"

"As long as you're trying, you're safe." Sweetie pointed to that line of the contract with a claw. "I don't need you to be perfect, Tonio. I just need you to try."

The bandanna was sliding down his forehead. He pushed it back up. "Okay. Then I'll do it."

The judge didn't have any pens, just an ink pad. She, Buster, and Lasagna all put a paw print on the contract. Tonio did each of his fingerprints in a line. Sweetie closed the folder and slid it toward Lasagna, who picked it up in his mouth.

"Well then, you'd better go talk to your parents." Tonio's eyes widened— *Oh, right.* They were going to wonder where he'd been all night, and all day. If Skyler had told his parents where he was, he was *definitely* in trouble. "I need you in Bellville. So your first mission is to *not move.*"

Buster's ears shot up. "That's not fair!"

Tonio gasped. "I forgot that— How am I supposed to . . . ?" He trailed off, lost in thought.

"You'll be fine." Sweetie waved a paw and the teacups

began braking to a stop. "I've arranged for a car to take you back to Bellville. Talk to your parents, get some rest, and keep doing what you've been doing. I'll contact you when I have more information."

Lasagna hopped out of the cup and barked for them to follow, with the folder still in his teeth. Buster looked up at Tonio, who bowed to the judge.

"Thank you. For everything."

"You're welcome." She winked as they turned away. "Show me it was worth it."

Family Dinner

A limousine waited for them outside the park, and Tonio spent the ride staring at the heavily tinted divider, wondering if a dog was driving.

"Hello?" he called to the front, with no answer. "Thank you for driving us!" The car stopped in front of his house. When he got out and looked back, the car windows were too dark to see inside.

He finally thought to ask Buster while they were walking up the stairs to the Pulaskis' home. "Can dogs drive? Do you have special cars or something?"

Underspeak was hard to do while climbing the stairs. Buster bounded up to the top and answered, *Dogs can do anything! I couldn't smell who was driving, though.*

Tonio checked the many pockets of his shorts for keys. "Have you ever driven?"

No, but I would. Cars are amazing!

"Wrong. Cars are scary."

You only say that because you've never chased one. They run away like cowards!

"They don't—that's not—you're joking, right?"

Buster rolled onto his back and kicked his legs up in the air. *Yes!!!*

Tonio laughed and scratched at his tummy. "I hope they're not mad," he whispered.

Buster rolled back over and shook himself off.

Just tell them what I told you to say.

"Your excuse is pretty complicated."

It'll be fine.

Tonio sighed, unlocked the door, and pushed it open. Buster lifted his nose to the air and sniffed the sickly sweet fake-flower smell from Mr. Pulaski's cleaning, the powerful snack food aroma from Mrs. Pulaski's office, and the calming smell of his own fur, where it survived vacuuming.

"Hello, my Tonio!" Mrs. Pulaski waved a knife in greeting from the kitchen. "Just in time for dinner!"

They didn't even notice I was gone. A pang of shame shot through Tonio.

Mr. Pulaski peeked around from behind her, mixing something in a bowl. "Did you have fun at Mia's?"

Tonio blinked. "Uh, what? Where?"

Both his parents laughed. Mrs. Pulaski shook her head. "Did you just wake up? That's perfect, because it's time for . . ." She used the blunt side of her knife and half a stick of butter to drum unevenly on the counter.

"BREAKFAAAAAAAAAST FOR DINNEEEEEEEEER!"

Mr. Pulaski crowed. "I'm making pancakes; your mom is making eggs." He turned to Tonio and knelt on the ground with a serious look in his eyes. With the mixing bowl tucked under one arm, he raised his other hand up to Tonio in a desperate gesture. "Join us, son."

Mrs. Pulaski snorted. *"Join us,"* she repeated in a deep voice, "and together we will make the most *powerful breakfast* this dinner has ever seen!"

"BUT WASH YOUR HANDS FIRST," Mr. Pulaski gasped.

"There is probably dog on them!!!" Mrs. Pulaski agreed. They both cackled with laughter while Tonio stared, stunned. Buster realized he had never seen the two of them awake and relaxed at the same time. Was this what they were normally like? Happy and goofy?

Tonio was more concerned with how their whole bit had started. "You guys knew I was at Mia's?"

"She called us last night. Is everything okay?"

Every part of Tonio's body relaxed. "Yeah. Everything's fine." He hung Buster's leash on the wall and went to wash his hands in the sink while Buster found a place in the dining room to watch without getting in the way.

They put Tonio to work heating sausages in the pan, and Buster's mouth watered at the smell. Mr. Pulaski asked about Beamblade, and Tonio described the tournament in excited detail—leaving out for now the part Buster played, which was probably best.

And then, when they were seated and eating, Mrs. Pulaski reminded them: "I got a call from Dr. Jake yesterday." Tonio's heartbeat immediately spiked. *Oh, right. He said he was going to do that.* "How have your sessions with him been going, Tonio?"

"Do you want me to be honest?" Tonio asked. Buster wagged his tail. *Good start.*

Mrs. Pulaski nodded immediately. "Of course."

"Will you listen to me?" Tonio asked. "All the way until I'm done?"

Now it was Mr. Pulaski who said, "Of course."

They'll hear me, Tonio worried, *but they won't understand.*

Then he corrected himself. *No. I don't know that.*

"I'm not going to—I can't just—" Tonio's confidence faltered. He wasn't sure of himself. He hadn't worked through all his feelings about anxiety, either, and trying to be serious, clear, and confident all at once was too much.

Buster gave a very tiny *ruff* from the floor, to get Tonio's attention. He scratched his ear and circled a paw around his eye. *More questions,* he said. *Follow the mystery.* Right.

"What do you think it means for me to get better?" Tonio asked. "When will you look at me and think, 'He's better now!'? Not *cured*. But *better*."

Mrs. Pulaski said, "We want you to feel happy, Tonio,

and not worried all the time. We want you to have a chance to be a kid."

Tonio remembered what Dr. Jake had said about the difference between feeling and acting. "Not what I feel," he told his parents. "What I *do*. What would convince you I was getting better?"

Buster's tail wagged. He'd done it! He'd found the right questions to ask. The Pulaskis needed to know what they were trying to *do* before anything could get better. They needed real goals.

Mr. Pulaski started. "Well, you spend so much time in your room. I want you to get out and make friends, like other kids."

Tonio nodded. "Wait a second. I'll be right back." Buster listened as Tonio ran upstairs, opened his door, ripped a piece of paper, grabbed a pen from his pen jar, and ran back downstairs. He drew lines to start a list and set *FRIENDS* next to *#1*. "Okay. I have friends. Mia and Devon. I've hung out with Mia a lot, and I think Devon wants to get to know me better." He added them both to the list. "And Buster's my friend, too. What else?"

Mrs. Pulaski continued. "You'd have fewer panic attacks so they'd get in your way less often."

Tonio didn't write this one down. He shook his head. "I don't think that one counts. I also don't want to have them, but they don't always happen for real reasons, or because I'm actually feeling bad. Sometimes they just happen."

He'd never said that to Mrs. Pulaski before—and he'd also never spoken to them like this. She nodded slowly. "Okay. Well, I want you to feel safe going outside. Going to school."

I can't go back to school. Tonio was surprised by the sudden power of that thought. He focused. *Why? Why can't I go back?* Devon had forgiven him. Mia was his friend now, and she was tougher and cooler than anybody else at school. If they didn't care, then why should he?

No! I can't!

Why not?

There was no reason. He couldn't find a reason. He was scared, but he could handle it. He could tell now that his fear was just anxiety.

I can.

Tonio wrote down *#2: SCHOOL*. "I'll go back. But I want to go back *here*, in Bellville. I want to stay here."

"Why?" Mr. Pulaski asked.

Because the judge asked me, Tonio thought. *But also for Mia, and my parents, and myself. I want to be here.*

"I *do* love this town," he told his parents. "I love the fall festival, and Nice Slice Pizza, and Mrs. Morris's gnomes, and everything. I've had a hard time showing it lately, but I do. I want to stay."

Mrs. Pulaski folded her hands on the table. "But none of these things matter if you're unhappy, Tonio. I'm glad you want to keep trying, I'm glad you're talking to us, but I hate seeing you so worried and so sad."

Tonio looked at his mom's expression and realized she was probably anxious, too. And anxiety was trying its best to help. To be something good.

"Everybody's sad sometimes, right?" he told her. "And anxious. Even other kids. I'm never going to be happy all the time, and I think that's okay. Right?"

Buster wanted to jump with joy. Tonio was so smart!

Tonio's parents didn't answer right away, so he continued. "That's what Dr. Jake means when he says I'm not going to be cured. Not that I can't get *better*, but that some people are sad more often, or angry more often, or goofy more often than others. I'm worried more often. And I might always be like that. But it's not all bad."

"That makes sense," Mr. Pulaski admitted. "I'm sure as heck not happy all the time."

"But I want *you* to be," Mrs. Pulaski said, but with a half smile that showed she understood she was saying something kind of silly. "I want my son to be happy every moment of his long, long life! I want nothing to ever go wrong for you, ever!"

Tonio couldn't help but smile back. "Sometimes stuff is bad! Sometimes I *should* be worried."

"I know, but I hate it." Mrs. Pulaski folded her arms and fake pouted.

"I hate it, too." Mr. Pulaski mimicked her pose and pout.

Yeah! Buster said. He did his best to look the same under the table, lolling his tongue out and crossing his legs over each other.

Tonio laughed. "It's not fair!! But it's true, I think."

Mrs. Pulaski took the paper from Tonio and wrote: *#3: TALKING.* "You are wise, Tonio, and I don't know how you got this way. But if you really want to stay, if you think you will be okay, then I need you to keep talking to us like this. Even if it's hard."

Tonio's eyes widened, and Buster's tail wagged. *Yes! We're going to get to stay!*

"Okay. I will."

"My turn!" Mr. Pulaski took the pen and paper and wrote *#4: PLAYING BEAMBLADE WITH YOUR DAD.* "This is a very important part of any anxiety treatment. I read it on the internet. Also, I'm better at talking when I'm playing a game!"

Mrs. Pulaski rolled her eyes. Tonio grinned. "Okay, okay. I'll play Beamblade with you. I should warn you, though, I'm a champion!"

"Good. I love to lose." He winked at Tonio, who laughed. "And if you're sure about this, really sure, I'm glad. I don't think we should leave Bellville, either." Mr.

Pulaski gestured to their plates. "Now . . . finish your breakfast! It's definitely cold by now!"

All three of them were happy to leave the serious conversation behind for a little bit. Tonio dropped sausage for Buster while the family joked, and gossiped, and complained. They finished their food, and the adults collected the dishes to clean in the kitchen. Tonio pushed his chair back and knelt on the floor to give Buster a hug and whisper in his ear.

"Thank you, Buster. Good dog." He froze. "Oh, sorry. That's probably a stupid thing to say, huh? If you're a person?"

Not stupid at all. Buster wagged his tail and licked Tonio's face. *You're welcome, Good Boy.*

●━● Acknowledgments ●━●

There were times when I thought I would never finish this book. It followed me through several new homes, a new state and city, and practically a whole new life. So there are a lot of people to thank. I'm writing this during self-quarantine, so I'm feeling the presence and absence of these folks very deeply, but they keep me going now just like they did when I was trying to complete this story. Buster wouldn't exist without them!

First, of course, Austin Jenkins. Thank you for being behind the scenes of everything I create, supporting and listening and always asking, "How can I help?" Even from states away, you've remained the reason anything I do gets done. The bounds of your patience and kindness are so-far undiscovered, and you make the world a better place both actively and passively, just by living in it. You'll probably keep getting two a.m. texts about every one-sentence idea that pops up while I'm washing dishes.

Also of course, Michael Shillingburg. Even though you "don't really read" (exposed) I am thankful for your ear, your kindness, and the number of times you've talked me through tears. You are a brilliant, talented, and thoughtful person. Thank you for the amazing environment you create in our home, the plants you grow, and the loving way you care for our cats. (And thank you to our cats, Chao and Topaz, for being big babies and keeping us company in the hardest times.)

And finishing the primary trio of this story's support squad is my editor, David Levithan. My life is permanently different because of the chances you've taken on me, and I'll never be able to pay you back for all you've given—I can only hope to make something good out of the tools you've provided. Thank you for believing in me even when I don't, and for being the most generous and thoughtful friend and teammate anyone could wish for.

The whole team at Scholastic has been amazing across all of my projects so far, especially Maya Marlette. You handle more categories of problem than seem possible in a single job, PLUS edit your own books, PLUS are an incredible board game player and comedian. That's my friend!!!

Thanks to Charlie Olsen for keeping the train running, making me look professional, and sharing your love of comics and Mario Kart. You always have all the answers, and you're always the first to say yes to my weirdest and truest ideas.

My therapist during the writing of this book, Patrycja Baska, was an incredible help when I was exhausted and tired from staring frankly and directly at my own anxiety during this process. To my past therapists, and all the therapists and doctors who listen: thank you.

My parents, Kim and Connie and Jason, and my siblings, Jacy and Willow and Jack and Rianna, keep dreaming big right alongside me! Seeing my family support each other and push themselves to new and greater heights inspires me, too. I strive to be as cool as the rest of them. And thank you to the wide web of grandparents, aunts, uncles, and cousins who still care about how I've been, even when we're apart for a while.

Thank you to my other early readers, Dr. Charlie Kamen-Mohn, Nick Splendorr, and Rianna Turner, for their advice and guidance. And thank you to Dr. Paul Baker for his suggestions in the early stages of talking about how to represent Tonio's anxiety honestly and accurately.

It should be no surprise to anyone after reading this that games are close to my heart. I believe one of the greatest and most important things we can do with each other is play, so thank you to all the people who played with me during this process, among all their other kinds of support: Peter Reitz, Andy Carter, Lucy Ralston, Faith Jones, Tony Ransom, Patrick Brick, Ryan Kingdom, Dr. Karl Kamen-Mohn, Erin Lovett, Sean Ireland, Nick Kelly, Sydney Rappis, Leon Barillaro, Kelly White, Noah Salaway, Sofi Pujol, Tyler Lawrence, Andrew Nelson,

Mila Nery, all the kids in the Dalton D&D group, and everyone who even played a single board game with me during this time!

Thank you to my book world families: Avid Bookshop in Athens, Georgia, and its booksellers past and present, WORD Bookstore, and Anyone Comics. (My comic book squad, Nick Eliopulos and John Jennison, finally got me back into X-Men during this, which I am impossibly grateful for.) Thank you to Holley Brown and all the other librarians and bookstores who hosted me during the *Top Elf* tour! Also shout-out to the New York Public Library for being way, way, way cooler than I could have even imagined.

If you are someone who listens, pays attention, and cares about what the people around you are feeling and struggling with: thank you, too. I hope this book reminds you of how important that work is.

Oh, and thank you for a decade of being an extremely good boy, Bogart. I miss you.

⬤━⬤ About the Author ⬤━⬤

Caleb Zane Huett is a tabletop gamemaster, former bookseller, and definitely not a dog with a pen name. He's a graduate of the University of Georgia, and he's really good at trading card games. Eight different dogs have protected him throughout the years, and he currently has two cats who are furious they weren't featured in this book. You can find him at calebzanehuett.com.

Humor and heart come unleashed in
BUSTER UNDERCOVER

BUSTER
UNDERCOVER

BOLD DOG.
NEW TRICKS.

CALEB ZANE HUETT

Prololgue

Tonio had never been in a dog crate before, and if he was being perfectly honest with himself, he didn't love it. Out of habit, he checked to see if his bad feelings were because of anxiety or reality: *I feel trapped.* Well, he was locked in a dog crate, which was really just a nice way to say *cage.* It was a cage designed for a Great Dane, big enough for him to sit down and stretch out. But it was still a cage, so it definitely made sense to feel trapped.

I feel like something bad is going to happen. There was a lot of evidence for that, too. The man who'd just thrown him in this cage certainly hadn't seemed to have Tonio's best interests in mind.

I wish Buster were here. Tonio and his dog, Buster, hadn't been apart this long since they'd met. Missing him made the most sense of all.

"Very cool," Tonio mumbled miserably. "Everything *really is* terrible."

A little whine and the jingle of a collar caught Tonio's attention, and he noticed for the first time he wasn't alone. The room was filled with more than a dozen empty dog crates, but one other was occupied. A few feet from him, a Shiba Inu smirked from behind several layers of metal bars. Tonio jumped in relief and banged his head on the roof of the cage with a clang. He'd been hoping to find her here.

"Jpeg!" he cried, rubbing his head to check for any new bumps.

you think you've had it bad? try going weeks without any internet. The dog bobbed her head and wagged her paws in Underspeak, the physical language of dogs, ending with a gesture Tonio didn't know. Tonio's Underspeak vocabulary had grown a lot in the time since Buster had started teaching him, but every dog's Underspeak was a little bit different. It always took some getting used to. Jpeg did each pose with less enthusiasm than most dogs, giving it a very casual, lowercase vibe.

"I don't know what that word was at the end."

it means lol. i'm spelling it out, see? She repeated the twist of her tail and tap of her paws.

"That's a lot of work to say 'lol.'"

is this what's important right now lol? She huffed air out of her nose. *w/e dude.*

Tonio pressed his forehead against the bars. "I'm sorry. We tried to find you, but instead I got caught, too."

not that I'm keeping score, but that puts you like 0–2 on rescue attempts, my good human.

"Yeah, I know. I'm not cut out for this." Tonio picked at his fingernails. "I never should have talked to him. I knew this would happen. And—" A rhythmic thudding upstairs silenced him. Footsteps. He realized there were no windows here—just cold blue-gray walls and a door without a handle.

you knew you'd be locked up in a dog crate in a basement somewhere, awaiting a shady government organization to finally get serious about interrogating you, lol?

"Nothing about that feels very 'lol' to me, Jpeg."

agree to disagree. Tonio looked around for anything else that might help. He tugged on his crate's padlock, but unfortunately it was doing its job. His backpack was thrown a few feet away, out of reach. He didn't have anything in there that could help him anyway, unless there was a way to pick a lock with fancy markers.

This is why my parents should let me have a phone, he thought. *For when I need a ride home from my job as a secret agent for dogs.* He laughed out loud just a little— Jpeg was pleased—but the joke also made the reality of his situation sink in. He had to squeeze his eyes closed and settle on the rubber floor of the crate when his heart rate spiked.

Now is not a good time for this, some part of him thought, while the rest of him started to feel suffocated. The bars were too close, his clothes were too damp— why was he sweating so much? Why was it so muggy in this room? He didn't know where he was, what he was doing, or what was going to happen to him. He grabbed a bar on either side and pushed out with all his strength but only grew more frustrated and scared when nothing moved. He started to feel dizzy—was he breathing? When was the last time he'd taken a breath?

"ARF!" Jpeg barked. Tonio cracked his eyes open to look at her—her smirk was gone, and she was standing up. *SHUT UP*, she underspoke.

"I didn't—"

SHUT UP. WE'RE GOING TO BE FINE. LOL.

"Nothing—nothing is—what are you *saying*? Everyone thinks I'm at a sleepover. Nobody is coming for us. There's going to—"

LITERALLY WHO CARES. Jpeg's big, exaggerated Underspeak and flippant attitude were surprising enough that Tonio was calming down despite himself.

"How can you say that? How do you know we're—"

EASY. Her right hind leg lifted to scratch around her collar a half dozen loud, jingly times. *i'm gonna break us out of here, lol.*

Buster's Report

On my lawyer's request (hi, Lasagna), I've decided to use my extra time (and nervous energy, since Tonio isn't here) to type up everything that's happened since my Dog Court case over the summer. I'm not *technically* on pawrole, but he thinks having more evidence of our "success" as a human-dog duo will be helpful going forward.

I'm not sure this will be so cut-and-dried, though. Our semester has been complicated, and Tonio and I aren't exactly on great terms right now. So I'm going to be totally honest and let you edit it however you want, Lasagna. Maybe you'll find something useful in here. It'll at least help me gather my thoughts.

My name is Buster Pulaski (formerly Buster Vale, né Buster Stray), and I'm currently licensed as a psychiatric service dog specializing in anxiety and panic disorders. My human is Antonio Pulaski, and he's currently licensed as a sixth grader at Bellville Middle School. Both of us were recently made agents of The Farm, a secret branch of

Dog Court operating outside of Dog Law in order to ensure the safety and protection of dogs in a world where humans don't know that we're . . . well, people. (Am I allowed to say that in this report, Lasagna? I hope so. Again, delete whatever you want.) It feels like every dog on earth seems to know about what happened last summer, when Tonio found out the truth about me and, through me, *all* dogs, but the official story is that we're being closely monitored by Dog Court, and no one else is supposed to know about The Farm.

If you saw the court case, you know there was one teeny-tiny (okay, maybe kinda big) thing that I did in front of humans that got me arrested: I played Beamblade, the popular science fantasy trading card game for people of all ages, at a public tournament in front of a couple dozen humans. Whoops!

The rest of our summer was spent covering for that moment. I recruited a bunch of dogs at the shelter in town to pretend that Tonio could train them to play a card game designed for humans, planning to just show it off once or twice and let it fade away, but Mia Lin (the daughter of the shelter's owners and Tonio's best friend) saw potential for a scheme.

That's where this story really needs to start: At the Lin Family Dog Shelter's First Annual Official Beamblade Dog League Tournament and Adoption Day, featuring "genius dog whisperer" Tonio Pulaski.

The shelter was built into what was left of an old farm, from back when this part of town was all farmland. Mia's dad Jeff inherited it from his grandparents, and her other dad Danny is a huge dog lover. When they realized the nearest dog shelter was over an hour away, they repurposed the land, got all the permits and permissions they needed, and started collecting strays around Bellville. Of course, with just the three of them, they realized keeping all those dogs entertained was difficult—so instead of leaving dogs in cages all day, they opened the space as a dog park for everyone in town.

As I'm sure you know, Bellville changed overnight from a nowhere town to a *huge* hub of dog social life. Suddenly, it was easy for strays, pets, and service dogs to connect without being suspicious. The shelter was always packed with hungry dogs, and—for reasons I'm still not clear on—food costs money. The Lins' budget is always tight. Which brings me back to the tournament.

"Ref! We need a ref over here!" a man yelled across the dirt field. He stood up and waved in our direction. I was lying, belly in the sun, beside the kids working the event— Tonio, Mia (who I've mentioned), and Devon, the newest kid to join their grade and Tonio's other best friend. They wore matching sunflower-yellow shirts with the shelter logo, and Tonio had even cut one to wrap around my harness so I matched.

Tonio squinted in the sun and brought a hand up to his

forehead to shade his eyes as he looked for Skyler, the older teen who had a Beamblade judge's badge.

Devon nudged Tonio and said, "You should go-nio. You're the expert, and Mia's busy." He grinned before Tonio could raise an argument, red-blue-and-black braces (Spider-Man colors) proudly displayed. "Hurry!" he insisted. Tonio stumbled forward, curls flopping on the side of his head that wasn't shaved down. I rolled over and trotted along behind him.

Cardboard Beamblade battlefields were set up in rows down the field, and dogs were dueling against each other while humans monitored their progress and helped with the parts that required opposable thumbs, like shuffling. The battlefields were a perfected version of what Tonio and I had used for our first game together: low shields on either side so dogs could set down their "hands" without their opponent seeing, and a place in the middle for clashing heroes and fragile Spirit Batteries.

The haircut suits you, I underspoke as we walked toward the waving man. Tonio shrugged, but I could tell he was pleased to hear it. He'd drawn up the style himself and handed it to the hairdresser the day before; it was the first time I'd ever seen him show an interest in his "look," and I suspected it was because Devon was always talking about what he would do if he had Tonio's big curls.

"What's the problem, sir?" Tonio asked the man while I underspoke *What's up?* to the dogs. A small-for-her-age German shepherd named Bella was playing opposite a large-for-his-age tricolor collie named Mozart, who'd had a growth spurt over the last couple months. His face stretched out long to emphasize his permanently cocky expression, and the rest of him grew multiple feet longer. It's always disconcerting when you stop watching a puppy for *one second* and suddenly they're bigger than you! He was just as fluffy, though, and maybe even more irritating.

Don't worry about it, old man, Mozart underspoke. I gave a dismissive tail wag at his answer and looked at Bella.

He's cheating! The shepherd posed emphatically. *And he thinks he can get away with it because humans are watching.*

"They started growling at each other all of a sudden," the man explained to Tonio. He looked nervous behind his reflective sunglasses, and his fingers fidgeted with the camera around his neck. "I don't know if it's because of the game or what, but I thought I should get someone."

Tonio nodded. "I'm sorry if they scared you. Let me, uh, see what I can do." He crouched down lower to the ground and looked at me.

She says Mozart's cheating, I explained.

His hands came together in front of him and did a few quick movements in a way we'd practiced—his hands were ears, front paws, back paws, and tail in that order. It was slower than real Underspeak, but less obvious than imitating a dog in front of everybody.

Mozart, are you cheating? I translated for him.

No, Mozart huffed.

Yes, he is!! Bella gave a little bark of affirmation.

You're not? Tonio smiled. *Then what's the problem?*

The collie shrugged. *She's just mad that she's losing.*

I'm not even losing! With a smooth movement, Tonio held up a card and gave a treat to Bella, to fake like he was doing a training trick. He turned the card and showed it to Mozart.

The Phishing Rod needs energy from four Manabytes, though, and you've still only got three. So how'd this get on the field?

A flash interrupted us, and all four of our heads jerked up to see the man in sunglasses snapping a picture of us talking.

"Sorry!" He dropped the camera back down to his chest and held his hands up when he saw the expression on Tonio's face. "Seeing you training them is just so fascinating—I thought my daughter might want to see! But I can delete it."

Tonio's heart was beating fast, and I could see him thinking through it—what had he been doing? What would his hands look like in the picture? Could we all be in trouble because of this random man? I placed a paw on his foot, and Tonio rested a hand on my head, nodding. "No, it's fine. I was just . . . surprised. Thank you." The man apologized again, and Tonio looked back to the dogs.

Mozart clamped his teeth down around the Phishing Rod card and pulled it away from Tonio, dropping it haphazardly back with the other cards in his hand. *I must have made a mistake.*

Uh-huh, I added. Mozart glared at me, and Bella wagged her tail triumphantly. Tonio scratched Mozart behind the ears and gave him a treat, too.

"It should be fine now." Tonio gave one short nod to the man with the camera and started walking back to the other kids, but he'd barely turned around before the man was in front of him again.

"Actually, I have a question. What's the process if I'd like to adopt one of these dogs?"

Tonio was still avoiding eye contact—he was a lot more comfortable talking to dogs than adults. "You can talk to one of the Lins. But just so you know, Mozart isn't for adoption. He's—"

"Oh, no, I saw on his tag. I'm interested in that dog over there." Tonio followed the man's pointed finger to a Shiba Inu who looked like she was furiously digging a hole at the edge of the field.

"Jpeg?" Tonio blinked, surprised. "Oh no. You don't want Jpeg."

The man was taken aback. "Why not?"

"She's . . ." He looked down at me, and I gave him a sympathetic but unhelpful look in return. There was no way they'd let this guy take Jpeg. "High-energy? And she can't be separated from Leila." Tonio held his hand out to gesture toward the muddy part of the field, where the biggest dog in the whole park was wrestling loudly with a whole group of other dogs and winning.

"Oh, okay." The man looked disappointed but stopped following Tonio and held his hand up in a good-natured wave. "Thank you!"

Tonio dipped his head goodbye again and made a few subtle gestures toward me. *There's something weird about that guy.*

Really? I glanced back at the man, who was snapping a picture of another one of the Beamblade games—which tons of people were doing, including taking videos with their phones. *He seems normal to me.* I figured it was just Tonio's anxiety talking.

After a moment, he shrugged. *Just a feeling,* he told me. I let it drop—probably anxiety, right?

I should have trusted that feeling.

— 2 —

"SURPRISE!" Devon and Mia had cleared the judge's table of adoption papers and Beamblade cards while Tonio was gone and replaced them with a tray of cupcakes. Tonio froze and looked between their smiling faces like a rabbit watching wolves.

"Is it somebody's birthday?" he asked. "Did I forget to bring a present? I didn't—I'm sorry, I must have—"

Mia shoved a cupcake into his hands, chocolate with vanilla frosting. She'd cut her T-shirt into a loose crop and placed it on top of a tank top for a layered effect—Mia was always like that. Nothing was quite good enough unless she'd had a chance to put her own stamp on it. "They're for you. Devon made them."

"I made the card, too." Devon held out an envelope marked *TO: Tonio Pulaski FROM: Your Best Friends.*

"Yeah," Mia admitted, "but it was my idea."

"My birthday's in February!" Tonio protested, carefully holding both like trophies he hadn't earned.

But Devon shook his head and said, "Read it!"

Tonio had to set the cupcake back down to open the envelope. Mia pulled a big bone off the table—one of those fancy real ones, not the fake chewy kind—with a bow around it and threw it down to me. I snatched it out of the air and chewed gratefully around the wrapping.

Saying he "made it" was generous—Devon had clearly bought a card and scribbled over it. *Originally* the card said *Happy One Year Anniversary,* but thick permanent marker edited it to say *Happy* ~~One Year~~ *Two Month Anniversary (Of Going To School)*. After reading it, Tonio dropped his arm down casually so I could look inside— neither Mia nor Devon knew the truth about dogs, so we had to be careful. Taped to the card was a terribly drawn, fake Beamblade card of Malbrain and Combuster, the Blademaster names for Tonio and me. Power: 999999; Health: 999999; Special Abilities: Being a Great Friend, Making Things Come to Life by Drawing Them, Eyebrow Expressions, Dog Whispering.

"We know you almost didn't come back—" Devon started.

"And it's extra hard for you to stay, on account of your brain problems—" Mia continued.

"So it's worth celebrating!" Devon held up a cupcake to make a toast. "Two months!"

"Two months!" Mia cheered, raising her own cupcake to his. I threw in a short bark for good measure. Tonio's whole face and neck had blushed red, and I could tell his eyes were welling up with tears—but he blinked them away and smiled.

"Thanks, y'all." He sniffed. "It hasn't really been *that* hard."

Cupcake crumbles blew in the wind as Mia shook her head. "Maybe *I* should get a card, then, because I wish it was summer already."

"Tonio's right!" Devon argued, mouth full. "It hasn't been bad at all!"

"Oh, really?" Mia wagged a frosting-covered finger in Devon's face. "Is that how your locker feels, too?"

Both Tonio and I tilted our heads at the same time. "Your locker?" Tonio asked.

Devon waved his hand dismissively and grinned. "It's nothing. Don't worry about it." I saw Tonio's jaw set in a way that made it very clear he *would* worry about it, but there wasn't any time to argue—Jeff, Mia's shorter dad, jogged up to interrupt.

"Mia, could you and your friends get another adoption package together? We've got another one. Our tenth adoption today!"

"YES!" Mia cheered, and she high-fived her dad. "Who's getting adopted?"

"Jpeg! She's going home with a nice man visiting all the way from Myrtle Beach."

"YES!" Devon cheered, and raised his hand for a high five. No one gave him one. The rest of us were thinking the same thing: They couldn't take *Jpeg*. I thought of a hundred arguments, and Mia, thankfully, started voicing them.

"Myrtle Beach?" she said. "That's like three hours away!"

"Not even."

"It's practically Colorado," she mumbled. I nudged against her hand to show support. Her best friend, Sloan, had moved to Colorado the year before. Mia still missed her.

Jeff gave her a sympathetic look. "Not nearly as far. And he's really excited—apparently his daughter grew up with a Shiba who died last year. She'll do more good there than here."

Mia's heels dug into the dirt. "We can't just give Jpeg to some random guy who showed up today out of nowhere!"

Jeff lifted his hat to run a hand through his hair. "He didn't just show up today, Mia. He emailed us a few weeks ago, and we've done a video tour of his house. We even talked to his daughter—who I think you'd like. She was a lot like Sloan!" I felt my heart sinking down into my belly. Before I'd met Tonio, Jpeg was one of the only dogs who was willing to be my friend, when everyone else was spitting "Miracle Dog" and accusing me of breaking Dog Law. She was still my best friend, maybe, other than Tonio. And all it took was one video call for the humans to send her away!

I hate being a dog sometimes.

"Jpeg is *ours*. She's been here forever. Why would you—"

Jeff crossed his arms in a parent kind of way, the kind that means you're dangerously close to hearing someone say *And that's final*. "I know. I even asked for a much higher adoption fee, because he was so specific about needing Jpeg, but he didn't bat an eye. There will be more dogs, Mia. This whole event was your idea, and it's *working*. This is good news. Don't let it ruin your day." It had ruined *my* day. Jeff thought better of his crossed arms and opened them, pulling her in for a hug.

Mia glared off to the side and didn't return it. "What color collar?" she mumbled. "For the package."

"Green." Jeff kissed her on the top of her head. "Thank you." Devon caught on to the mood and didn't try to talk over Mia's sour expression. Tonio looked down to me, concerned, because I wasn't following behind.

You can go talk to Jpeg, he underspoke with his hands. *It's okay.*

Thank you, I answered, and left to say goodbye to my friend.

Jpeg mastered the art of secret typing a long time ago. From afar, she looked like a perfectly normal dog digging a hole, but up close she was typing on a tablet buried a few inches under the surface. (It never mattered that she was always digging the same hole, or that she never moved any deeper, because humans' assumptions do a lot of the work for us.) The soft clicking of her nails on the screen was disguised by the noise of the tournament, which was loud enough that she'd foregone Underspeak in favor of actual barking.

"Don't worry about breaking anything—the program's mine and it sets the odds automatically, so they're perfect." She tapped a few more times and gestured for Leila to look over her shoulder. Leila was somewhere between a mastiff, a Saint Bernard, and a bale of hay—and the undisputed wrestling champion of South Carolina. She loved Jpeg more than anything, and Jpeg loved her, too—though she wasn't quite as good at showing it.

"I'm not worried about the program, Jpeg." Leila nudged the Shiba with her nose. "I'm worried about you!"

"Worried about me?" She didn't look up from her tablet. *Click click click click click.* "Why?"

I stepped up closer to get their attention. "Because you're leaving, right?" Leila posed a hello to me, and I posed back. "Today."

"Ugh." Jpeg tilted her head and narrowed her eyes in frustration. "Not you, too. *This isn't a big deal.*"

Leila whined and turned to me. "She knew about this. She saw the video days ago and didn't think to warn me about it. This man lives *hours* away! I just found out she's leaving—basically immediately—and somehow that's 'not a big deal'?"

I felt a prickly, embarrassed feeling in my neck, and that sinking feeling in my stomach got worse. "Why didn't you tell us?" I asked Jpeg.

"Because, like I keep trying to say, it's not a problem. I have a plan!"

That didn't make me feel any better. "What is it?"

"I'm a terrible pet, and if he even has a *flip phone*, dog forbid, or *something* that can connect to the internet, I can ruin his life bad enough he'll be sure I'm cursed in less than a month."

"That's not much of a plan," I argued.

"It doesn't need to be! I'm a genius! I'll turn his smart fridge into a karaoke machine or whatever—I just have to see what the setup is like."

"But what if you like them?" Leila asked, a sad look in her eyes. "What if you meet his family, and you see the beach, and you see how easy it is to play pranks on tourists, and you love all of it?" Her voice dropped low, almost too quiet to hear. "What if you don't come back?"

Jpeg stepped back from the tablet and pushed her face to Leila's, forehead-to-forehead and nose-to-nose. "I wouldn't leave you. Trust me. You'll see me again in no time, you big jock."

I made Jpeg promise to message me on Doghouse chat as soon as she could, then left them alone. I felt helpless in a way that's hard to avoid sometimes when you're a dog. But what could I do? I didn't think Jpeg should have to go anywhere she didn't want to, but it felt like the whole world disagreed with me.

Not the *whole* world, I reminded myself as I walked back through the Beamblade tournament. Lots of dogs agreed with me. Judge Sweetie agreed with me—at least enough to take a chance on me and Tonio. Dog Court might not be ready to tell all humans the truth yet, but we were fighting a future where they would be. I decided right then: I would do anything The Farm asked us to do. My human and I would be the best team we could be, and we'd pave the way for a future where dogs could live however they wanted.

All we needed was a mission.